THE
QUAIL
WHO
WEARS
THE
SHIRT

Jeremy T. Wilson

THE
QUAIL
WHO
WEARS
THE
SHIRT

Jeremy T. Wilson

Tortoise Books
Chicago

Now who's, I say who's responsible for this unwarranted attack
on my person?

— Foghorn Leghorn

Ramblin' Man

It was Tuesday night. Trivia night. Me and Marty were trying to defend our reign as champions, but Valentine was making it difficult to concentrate with all his squawking and clacking at the pinball machine. Other than trivia night, the bar wasn't much for games, so the pinball machine mostly sat idle, crammed in a corner between two old bourbon barrels until Valentine brought it to life. He was over there singing along to the steady riff of "Ramblin' Man" grooving from the machine's ancient, dust-plugged speakers.

Some quails could sing. Valentine could not.

"Try to ignore him," I said.

"How about we kill him?" Marty said.

It might not have bothered us had we been winning. It was one of those nights where we got nothing right, where I questioned every answer Marty gave and he questioned every answer I gave, then one of us got all pissed at the other for insulting his intelligence.

I ordered Valentine a shot of Old Crow—the whiskey special on trivia night—and went to talk to him. The pinball machine was a tribute to the Allman Brothers Band and their heyday, the band's logo immortalized on the psychedelic backglass amidst a bevy of magic mushrooms. Around here, everybody loves the Allman Brothers, taking pride in their middle-Georgia heritage, and capitalizing on their legacy by naming themed chicken wing sauce after Gregg and Duane and designing overpriced bus tours to their alleged Macon haunts. I never cared for their music, ten-minute guitar grooves best suited to torture terrorists. The Brothers always seemed like hippie imposters to me, inheritors of a pain they never knew. White dudes, high on mushrooms, crying about being tied to the whipping post. Even as a white dude myself, I prefer Otis Redding as a local musical hero. There has never been or will ever be a voice more soaked with soul than Otis's. Otis could pine for a peanut butter sandwich, and your eyes would fill with tears believing his life depended on him nabbing the creamy treat, worried it was perpetually beyond his reach.

I watched Valentine flip flippers and grind his groin into the pinball machine while he kept that silver ball screaming through chutes and orbits, nailing targets at will, the ball constantly in play with little to no fear of the out hole. The red digits on the scoreboard ticked off at a dizzying clip, his points adding up so fast I couldn't settle on his total. Valentine had six empty shot glasses on the bourbon barrel beside the machine, and I set the full one down beside them.

"Could you knock it off?" I said.

He waited until the silver ball was swallowed between the legs of some fringe-vested groupie, when he had just enough time to shoot his left hand out, swipe the shot off the barrel, and knock it back in one gulp before the ball rocketed out of her crotch.

"Gotta beat my high score," he said.

At the top of the machine, a window reserved for the high score displayed an astronomical sum of digits, so high I didn't know how to compute it. What comes after a trillion? Three letters glowed in the window like red matchsticks: VAL.

I slapped a fifty on top of the machine. Valentine never took his eyes off the playfield, swiped the fifty as fast as he'd grabbed the shot, stuffed it in the front pocket of his jeans, and let the silver ball clatter anticlimactically down the out hole.

"You can take over if you want."

"I don't," I said, and went back to my stool.

Sister Rose liked to call out the questions through a bullhorn, a totally unnecessary affectation as all the teams were crowded around the bar, well within earshot of her Camel-scorched voice. Sister Rose was the bartender we loved best. She hadn't been a sister for God or anyone else's sister, but somebody in her past had started calling her Sister Rose and so it stuck. Maybe it was her benevolence to all the downtrodden drunks of Charity, her solemn vow to listen to them moan and groan and not judge, at least not to their faces. She was somewhere in her sixties, overweight in that way that made her seem tough instead of lazy, unafraid to wear T-shirts with the arm holes cut out and jean shorts that squeezed her thighs like marshmallows in a denim s'more. Her hair hadn't changed since she'd served me my first legal drink almost twenty years ago. It was like someone had hollowed out a football and wedged it on her head.

Her bullhorn whistled and buzzed. "Who provided the voice for such classic cartoon characters as Bugs Bunny, Yosemite Sam, Speedy Gonzalez, and Elmer Fudd?"

Marty clapped his hands and elbowed me in the arm, assuming I knew the answer due to my healthy knowledge of cartoons—mostly Looney Tunes, some Hanna-Barbera, a little Disney from my kids. And he was right. I did know. Mel Blanc. I scribbled his name down on our notepad.

Valentine came to the bar and looked at the answer I'd written. "That ain't right," he said.

"It sure as hell is."

"No, no. Mel Blanc voiced the first three, but somebody else did Elmer Fudd. Blanc did Barney Rubble, too. Did you know that?"

I didn't, but I told him of course I did.

I tore the answer off the notepad and handed it to Sister Rose, who tallied all the right answers on a chalkboard and put her mouth to the bullhorn. "The voice of these characters was provided by the multi-talented Mel Blanc."

Valentine shrugged. "It ain't right just cause she says it is."

He watched us play a few more rounds, snapping his finger like he was close to the answer but couldn't conjure it, but he never disagreed with any more of my responses. He asked me to give him a ride home, but the game wasn't over and I'd already given him fifty bucks, so I said no.

Valentine left sometime before I asked Sister Rose for my weekly cigarette and went outside to smoke. It was just before Jodi pulled up in her daddy's old Mercedes (right on time like always), just before I tossed my cigarette aside and told her to scoot over, just before we started down a dark Highway 41 thinking it was just another Tuesday night.

Love is the Alpha and Omega

Valentine was a total mystery who'd flown into town a while back on a yellow bicycle, a girl's bicycle outfitted with a wire basket and wide U-shaped handlebars trailing rainbow-dyed feathers. He was tall and skinny for a quail, could've been any age from 40 to 60, with a wispy, chocolate-colored plume and a beak you could hang a hat on. He'd strutted into Hubbs Fresh Produce and asked me if I had any work. I told him, no thanks, and gave him a peach, figuring like most quails he didn't want to work as much as he wanted a handout. He came again the next day, so I gave him a quarter slice of watermelon. Day after that he cruised up on that bike and said, "Mr. Hubbs, I appreciate your kindness, but I can't take any more handouts. I'd like to work and earn my compensation with dignity."

"What's your name?" I asked.

"Valentine."

"First or last?"

"Love is the Alpha and Omega," he said.

At that point I figured I really should do more to help. God didn't talk through burning bushes anymore, at least not to me. You had to pay close attention if you wanted to hear him. A quail using red-letter New Testament words was a pretty clear indication that God was encouraging me to help those less fortunate. So I walked him down to Dawn's.

"This guy's looking for work," I said.

Dawn was fingering money on top of her counter display of watches. She wore so much jewelry it was like somebody'd dipped her in honey and rolled her in gold. She was also fond of oversized men's button down shirts with white cuffs and tight, tapered jeans stuffed into pricey high top sneakers. She didn't look up. "You got a car?"

Valentine shook his head, his plume swaying like a weed in a breeze. "Got a bike."

"Yeah? Harley?"

"Schwinn."

Dawn stopped counting her money. She smiled then rolled a toothpick from one corner of her mouth to the other. "You're not a California quail are you?" she asked. "Just being cautious. I've known some slack-ass California quails."

Dawn's Classic Pawn had a reputation for being a refuge for the afflicted, those whose cheeks had rounded and mottled and whose eyes had developed those telltale rings and whose noses had grown sharp and whose chests had puffed up and from whose heads had grown teardrop-shaped plumes of varying color, beauty, and freakishness. Dawn thought her benevolence gave her the right to speak ill of quails. She was of the belief that quails were created by aliens, that they'd secretly come down and implanted spores in humans and were conquering the planet by turning its people into docile human-avian hybrids that they could then farm as an endless food source. Dawn wanted to be live and in-person when the aliens returned for their buffet. Of course, scientists had other explanations, something to do with blood type or environmental factors or lifestyle choices or pre-existing inflammatory conditions, or a latent manifestation of historical trauma. But nobody put much stock in science anymore. Like a lot of the paranoid masses, Dawn had bought into the quack theory that daily supplements of zinc and an expensive herbal tea composed of betel leaves, cacao, and CBD could prevent you from turning quail. I didn't much worry about it. Adult white men went largely unaffected.

"I'm whatever you want me to be," Valentine said.

"Are you fast? How about fast?" Dawn licked her finger and peeled off a twenty from her pile of cash. "Tell you what. Go load me up at China Garden," she said. "Stop at Squire Package and get me a bottle of Clamato, picante, and when you get back, we'll talk about work."

Valentine snatched the twenty and was almost out the door before Dawn whistled through her teeth. Valentine turned around and she tossed him a pink Care Bear backpack that she'd grabbed from a pile of boxes stacked with junk. "Don't gyp me on the sweet and sour sauce, hombre."

Despite being 100% white American with a royal redneck pedigree, Dawn liked to pepper her speech with Español.

Valentine shot her a thumbs-up and lit out.

"How much you want to bet we never see that dude again?" she asked.

I didn't care one way or the other, but I liked taking money from Dawn. "Fifty?"

We shook on it and waited.

"What do you think about a Snuggle-thon?" she asked.

"Pardon?"

"A Snuggle-thon. Or a Snug-a-thon. I'm still toying with the nomenclature."

"Where you headed with this?"

"We're a country divided, Lee. I think we could all benefit from getting together and loving on one another. Human contact."

"Does this take place at a gym? A park?"

"Yeah, yeah, some place big. We can film it with a drone."

"I don't think people really want human contact from strangers. Hell, I can't get my own wife to snuggle with me."

Dawn laughed. "You know what'd fix that?" She pulled a pair of diamond earrings out from under the counter. "Treat her right, she'll treat you right."

"I treat her right."

"I just got a shitload of really nice sheets. Egyptian cotton. Like eight hundred thread count. Fit for a queen."

"Nah. We've got a king-sized bed."

"No. No. Katherine's the queen. Treat her like a queen. Why do you always have to be so difficult?"

Dawn continued to extol the virtues of snuggling while she tried to sell me a hunting rifle, a Tag Hauer watch, a Blu-ray player, and an elliptical machine before finally giving up and relaying all the local gossip she'd managed to accumulate since I'd seen her last. Somebody had a miscarriage. Somebody came out as a "homo," but didn't mean to. Somebody had cancer. Somebody turned quail. Somebody died. The gossip in Charity was always the same.

Valentine returned pretty swiftly with lunch from China Garden, extra sweet and sour sauce, the Clamato, and change. I took a fifty off Dawn's pile of cash to settle her debt.

That afternoon she put Valentine to work running errands and holding up a sign for the pawn shop out by the boulevard that said *Casa de Empeño*. An odd marketing strategy, in my estimation.

Daddy Issues

Jodi and I met every Tuesday night at 10:00. She picked me up from the bar in her daddy's old Mercedes with the bench front seats, and I got behind the wheel, and at some point in our aimless wandering, she would unbuckle my belt and unzip my pants and do things to me my wife wouldn't do. But this Tuesday that's not what happened.

Jodi gave me her two weeks' notice. Said she was going to the Amazon to live with the Bulo, some indigenous tribe whose primitive way of life was threatened by oil drilling and deforestation. I told her good luck, and that her job would be waiting for her when she got back.

"I might not come back," she said.

Jodi wanted to be a writer, went around collecting experiences like some people collect souvenir caps. She was twenty five years old and still lived with her widowed mother, her daddy having died at the cement plant explosion when she was twelve, and she and her mother had overcome much adversity to be in their respective positions, meaning relatively successful adults, and some might say that the reason she was doing what she was doing with me involved some deep-seated "Daddy Issues," but that'd probably be oversimplifying things. But here's the thing about oversimplifying: once you start to run through all the other reasons a person does the dumb shit they do, the shit that's bad for them, the stuff they know will not benefit them in the long run, once you account for all the possible reasons, you usually return full circle to the most simple one.

We drove for a little while longer, and when she didn't make a move, I figured we were going to have a talk. She told me how she really wanted her mind and spirit free of any moral entanglements so she could devote herself wholeheartedly to her mission, and what that meant was, she'd told my wife about our liaisons.

"You did what?" I said, trying to remain as calm as possible, hoping she was joking, or lying, or setting me up for a potential blackmail situation.

"I told her. About us."

The road ahead was dark. Trees pressed closer to the shoulder and squeezed us between faded white lines. The dim headlights gulped bugs. "What did you tell her exactly?"

"The truth. What we've been doing."

I beat my fist on the steering wheel, pressed the accelerator. "What the hell is wrong with you, Jodi? Jesus Christ!"

"Don't yell at me!"

"You'd rather me hit you?"

"You're a douchebag, Lee. You know? A real fucking douchebag. It was giving me an ulcer. An *ulcer*. Who gets an ulcer?"

"You couldn't drink warm milk? Take some Alka Seltzer? Did you not think what this might do to my life?"

"*Your* life?" she said. "*Your* life?"

I will admit that my concern for our immediate safety was compromised during this argument. And so, yes, I may have taken my eyes off the road for a brief second in the heat of anger, but the victim was not totally innocent here. There's some recklessness in quails, everybody knows that, something about the plume affecting their frontal lobe. And I wasn't the only one who'd seen him knocking back shots one after another. So I stand by him being partially responsible for his own demise.

A thump on the hood. A screek. Metal on metal. Like a twenty-five pound bag of onions had fallen on us from the sky.

I slammed the brakes. My head plunked the steering wheel. Jodi and I looked at each other with wide eyes, our breaths spastic. "It's going to be okay," I said, more to myself than to her.

I killed the lights and the engine, got out of the car thinking a deer had probably leapt from the woods and landed on top of the hood. But, no, deer don't ride bicycles.

It was Valentine. The fool was all pretzled up in a heap next to that yellow bike he was always riding, the whole mess bathed in red from the taillights. What a night! I knew I shouldn't move him, but he and the bike couldn't stay there in the middle of the road. That stretch of Highway 41 would still have cars at that hour. We couldn't have passersby pulling to the shoulder to see what's up, asking if we needed any help. People in Charity would do that sort of thing. We had to move fast.

I hooked Valentine under his armpits. He smelled like whiskey and iron. He was heavy for such a skinny dude made of bird bones, but I managed to drag him to the other side of the car, down an embankment and close to the tree line where the woods started. I wanted him to roll over, groan, bring himself to a knee, shake out the cobwebs and say something funny to lighten the mood. But he wasn't talking.

Jodi climbed from the car. "Is he dead?" she asked. "Please tell me he's not dead."

"It's possible."

"You have *got* to be kidding me!" Jodi fell to her knees at the side of her car, clasped her hands together in prayer. "Oh God, please don't let him be dead. Please, please, please, God."

Jodi was so dadgum hot, bent over and blubbering in those tight white jeans that made her ass glow in the dark like the flesh of an apple, all that wavy dark hair convulsing in a mess. Why'd she have to go and ruin a good thing? This is the problem with anybody under thirty. They think every little thing's a big deal, every decision carries the weight of the world, can't buy a pair of jeans without feeling guilty, every wrong must be righted, every word must be polite, and everybody deserves a life of happiness and fulfillment. Her idealism had her blinded to reality. What did anyone gain from her telling my wife? Nothing. Everybody lost.

I had no interest in playing games without a winner.

I wanted to leave her there. See how she dealt with this problem on her own. But I couldn't do that to her.

I helped her to her feet, smoothed her hair behind her ears, tilted her chin up to look at me, thumbed an invisible tear from her cheek. "We're going to make this fine, all right? Now listen. You need to hide. I'm going to act like you were never here, okay?"

"What? Like you were just out driving my car? Why were you driving my car? Did you steal it?"

She had a point there. Smart girl. The Bulo would be lucky to have her, probably make her chief. "Yeah, okay. That's right. You're right. We got to get rid of the evidence."

I picked Valentine's yellow bike up by the frame and searched for a place to hide it, somewhere far away from its former rider. The back wheel was bent, folded over like a taco shell, and the front wheel was completely missing. I didn't see it anywhere. Shit.

I dropped the bike. "There's a wheel missing. Look for his wheel."

Jodi didn't move, suddenly in some kind of shock.

I searched for anything glittering in the road, a spoke, a reflector. Nothing. No sign of the wheel.

I held Jodi by the shoulders. "Call Marty. He's at the bar. He'll be here in two seconds. You know Marty, right?"

She stared at me without blinking, her eyes starched stiff and white.

I shook her. "Officer Bishop. Marty. You know him."

She nodded.

"Remind him you work for me. And how I tell all my employees to give him a call if they ever get into trouble. He'll appreciate that. He likes to feel important. I'll hide in the woods, and Marty'll show up, and you'll tell him this fool was drunk as piss riding his bike the wrong way down the highway in the black of night and you hit him."

Jodi snapped out of her daze. "*I* hit him?"

"That's your car."

"Uh-uh. You did this. I didn't do this."

"I'm not even supposed to be here!"

"But you are *here*! And I am *here*! And a man is right *there*!" She jabbed a finger toward Valentine's body.

"Damnit, Jodi." I took a deep breath. "Fine. Help me get him in your trunk."

I bent down next to Valentine, and I knew then, without a doubt, unlike my previous speculation, that he was dead. It was like every element that conspired to bring him to life had vanished and he'd become another dead quail on the side of the road.

Jodi was wrong. Valentine was no more man than his bicycle.

Given the circumstances I figured he wouldn't be needing that fifty dollars anymore, so I squeezed my fingers into the curve of his front pocket. I had to dig deeper than I wanted. Found money will bury deep in a poor man's jeans. Finally I felt the crease and pinched it out and put the money in my billfold where it'd come from. Something about this did not feel exactly right, but the dead do not need money wherever they're going, so really it would've been a waste to send him off to the afterlife packing an extra fifty bucks that a perfectly healthy man could put to good use in this life. I made a mental note to stick it in the offering plate at church.

The car door slammed and I turned to see Jodi tearing out of there, the wheels kicking up a tantrum of dirt and gravel.

Nobody Notices an Icemaker

It took some persuasion and an explanation of the urgency of my situation to get Marty to help fix the mess. He said I wouldn't get away with it. Said my luck had finally run out. Said that I showed a level of disregard that, frankly, scared him and made him wonder about our lifelong friendship. "I was joking when I said we ought to kill him," he said, standing over Valentine's body.

"Don't you cover shit up like this all the time?" I said.

"That don't make it right."

"You're a cop. Since when do you care about what's right?"

"I've got morals. You ever heard me curse?"

I'd had way too much of people talking about morals. Like it's so easy to confess a sin or to stop cursing or to teetotal your way to some moral high ground. Morality as self-help. Bullshit. "That's all it takes?"

"Part and parcel."

There was no time to argue. I told him he could have whatever he wanted from my store, gratis, forever and ever amen, if he'd just do me this simple fix. Report a hit-and-run while I hid in the woods.

"Even the gift baskets?"

"Up to a certain price. I can't give you a hundred-dollar gift basket every day."

"You don't think a life is worth a hundred-dollar gift basket?"

My head was starting to hurt. "Whatever you want. Just shut up and help me."

Marty sighed and hiked up his belt. "Take his bike with you. Can't have some superhero detective come out here and check the bike for traces of paint, run the paint into a database, match it to the make and model. Then boom, he's got truth and all you got is trouble."

"There's a wheel missing."

"Well let's hope nobody finds it."

I grabbed the bike by its frame and dragged it and myself deep into the woods. I don't know the exact details of what Marty said or did, but an ambulance came quickly, along with the flashing blue lights of at least one other police car. But there were no flashlights shining in the trees, no detectives sniffing out clues and gathering forensics, and pretty soon all that was left was Marty, whistling around the edge of the woods.

"You can come on out now," he said. "He's dead." He lingered for a moment to let the gravity of the words sink in, then asked me if I wanted to pray with him.

I poked my head out from behind a pine tree. "Let's just go."

"I hope for your sake he ain't got friends in high places. Or low places for that matter. A covey that might start poking around and get you in deep doo-doo."

I came fully out of my hiding spot, dragging the bicycle behind me. "I doubt it."

"Get rid of the bike," he said.

"You got any ideas?"

"I'm not the one that ran him over, friend."

I threw the bike in Marty's cruiser and shut the trunk, an easy fit without the front wheel. He drove me home while I kept an eye out for that missing wheel in some foolish belief that it might still be out there rolling down the highway searching for the rest of itself, or being drawn to its owner like a lost puppy.

"You ever heard of *The Secret*?" Marty asked.

"No." I had no idea what the secret was, and didn't care to know.

"It's a book Cora gave me," he said. "Came out a while ago, all about the laws of attraction. Got some good stuff in it. Practical wisdom. Says that we get back what we put out. So if you're full of hurt thoughts and feelings, you're going to attract hurt. If you're chock full of crazy, crazy is what you'll get. Like a magnet. People are like magnets, Lee."

"What are you trying to say?" I asked.

"Nothing. Making conversation is all."

"Don't."

Some may not see my initial reaction as being properly shaken or saddened or shocked, or whatever it is that most people think their own reaction would be. But let me tell you something, until you're driving a car that's not your own and having a fight with a girl who's not your wife when a drunk quail lands on your hood, then you have no idea how you would react. Self-preservation. When I saw what had happened and that we were a part of it, I put a plan in motion to save the lives that were left to live, mine and Jodi's, and by consequence, my family's.

When we got to the house I barely had time to lift the bike out of Marty's trunk before he pulled out of my driveway, his arm extended from his window in a farewell wave, like he'd dropped me off after a round of golf.

I locked the bike in the toolshed behind my house where it would be safe, at least until I figured out how to make it disappear. Not a permanent solution, but I didn't have time to come up with anything else.

I still live in the house I grew up in, although I'd made considerable upgrades: a new pool area complete with hardscaping and manicured flower beds, a gazebo, and snotty Southern furniture surrounding a stacked stone fireplace, a new sun room off the rear of the house, no more wallpaper, new hardwood floors, a bigger garage, new kitchen with an under-the-counter ice maker, the kind that makes those perfect cylinders of ice with the divots in the middle so you might balance each cube on the tip of a pencil if so inclined. The house was filled with more of our remodeling efforts, but most people wouldn't even notice half the ones that cost the most money or gave us the most pride. Nobody notices an ice maker.

The house was quiet, everybody asleep like they should be. I filled up a glass with ice from my ice maker and cold filtered water from the fridge before I crept upstairs to bed.

Kat rolled over when she heard me come in. "Where you been?" she said, not bothering to open her eyes. All soft, sleepy, and warm, a slice of white bread at picnic. She did not immediately leap from the bed and yell at me for my philandering, so there was no need to bring it up.

"My phone died. Sorry, sugar." I kissed her on the forehead.

"You stink," she said.

Typically I wouldn't shower after trivia night at the bar. Showers after a night out reek of deceit. But she was right. The smell of dead quail was on me.

I took a cold one, a practice I thought was reserved for psychopaths. I let the cold water flow and stood directly below the shower head so that the arc from the spray cast out beyond my body, the cold drops merely misting my shoulders until I got used to the temperature. I managed to stand fully under the spray for a ten count. In fact, by the time I got to eight I was already able to stand it, and I saw how people did this, and why they would keep doing it, and maybe I would too.

I dried off and examined the spot on my forehead where I'd hit the wheel. A small cut and a bump at my hairline, barely noticeable. I applied some generous dabs of Neosporin. My beard itched, so I grabbed a comb and scratched deep into the thick patch of hair, still mostly black without the aid of old-man grooming products. I had no use for Viagra either.

I turned on the TV and got in the bed, needing some time to decompress from the events of the evening. The Braves were still on, playing the Dodgers out west. I've always wanted to go to L.A. Seemed like the type of place where you could slip on some sunglasses and everybody would think you were rich and famous and invite you to pool parties and celebrity galas. Always seventy degrees and sunny, Pacific time, so slow and chronically late you couldn't help but lose your cares over coastal breezes and all-day mimosas. Of course, they've got wildfires and earthquakes and liberals, so I guess we've all got our regional shit to deal with.

I watched the eighth and the ninth, the sound muted, listening to Kat breathe slow and easy while I traced my thumb over the veins in the top of her hand, wondering what I might tell her in the morning.

The Braves lost, couldn't mount a two run rally despite getting the leadoff man on and in scoring position with less than two outs. Then the broadcast started over again from the first inning, like this time the outcome might be different.

Man Up

Lisa sat in her high chair, blueberries smashed all over the tray and a sippy cup of milk rolled on its side. Leo colored with markers, or rather one marker, everything on the paper blood red. Kat cooked eggs and bacon. In front of my empty seat at the table was a steaming cup of black coffee and a bowl of yogurt with cut up peaches and granola. My head hurt.

I took a seat, sipped my coffee, scrolled through the news. Nothing about an accident.

Lisa kept trying to grab the phone from me, so every now and then I'd flick a blueberry across her highchair tray to distract her. She was into everything, able to take a couple of steps now and cruise all over a room holding on to coffee tables and armrests and people's legs before plopping on her diapered butt. She'd already gotten two black eyes from falling face-first into the hearth. She'd be walking full on any day now, and once she started walking she'd be trouble.

"Did you win last night, Daddy?" Leo asked. He was scribbling a giraffe all red from neck to foot.

"Did we win?"

"Your trivia game. Did you win?"

Nobody wants to hear their daddy's a loser. "Yeah," I said. "We won. We always win."

Kat moved Leo's red giraffe to the corner of the table where it joined a stack of pages with other monochromatic animals, a blue hippo, a purple zebra, an orange peacock.

Sometimes I feared for my boy's future. He had not been like his sister. Leo was scared all the time, a crier, a cuddler, a thumb-sucker, and I was ready for him to grow out of it and start to get himself dirty, scrape some knees and elbows. Man up.

Kat sat a plate of eggs and bacon in front of him, and a much smaller plate with much smaller bites of eggs and bacon already cut up for Lisa. "How come you never take me to trivia night?"

"We've already got a team," I said. "Me and Marty are a team."

"What if I got my own team? I bet me and Cora could beat you and Marty."

"Not a chance."

"Do y'all cheat?"

Here we go. The subtext to her question was obvious, but I had no intention of confessing anything or begging forgiveness until she came right out and said what she knew. I planned to deny everything and tell her that Jodi was high on women's empowerment after some course at the community college, and was looking to sabotage a prominent male figure of the establishment as part of her feminist agenda. Generally, Kat avoided conflict, and sometimes had to work herself up to a confrontation through a series of small, passive-aggressive steps, if she got there at all. More often she bottled it all up and expelled any issues with intense bouts of cardio.

My mouth was full of yogurt and granola, so it was easy to stay silent.

Kat pulled up her seat next to Lisa in the high chair and forked up a piece of egg for her, which Lisa clearly did not want, registering her distaste with a tight grimace. "It's got to be real tempting to peek down at your phone when you need the answer. Ask it what you need to know. We all succumb to temptation."

I swallowed.

Lisa swatted the fork out of her mama's hand. Kat picked up a piece of egg with her fingers and tried to shove it in Lisa's mouth.

"Don't cheat," Leo said.

"We don't cheat!" I said.

"Fine," Kat said, and stopped trying to force-feed our daughter.

I scarfed down the rest of my yogurt and went upstairs to get dressed for work. A Hubbs Fresh Produce golf shirt, a light blue one with a small peach logo where the horse or gator would normally be, and a pair of khakis. I always wore khakis, even though they got dirtier than jeans. Khakis told everyone who ran the show.

As I brushed my teeth I inspected my forehead. The sore was still there, but I'd have to pull my hair back and point it out if I wanted you to see it. I was lucky it didn't elevate to the status of a knot, more like a bite, red and raised and circular and glossy, like it might need popping, and when I touched it it sent vibrations all the way down to my left shin. I dosed it with some more Neosporin and left it alone.

We all went to the garage and Kat strapped the kids in their car seats.

After Lisa was born, Kat said she was tired of driving her old Honda Accord and was concerned for the safety and comfort of her growing family, so she made me buy a crossover.

I hate crossovers: vehicles that can't make up their mind. I preferred my twenty-year-old Ford F-150 because I liked its workhorse nature and could continue to beat the crap out of it without worrying about its appearance, the scrapes and dings and dents that should be the natural result of truck ownership. Badges of honor. At the end of every year, my father-in-law encouraged me to buy a new truck as a business expense, but I never wanted a new truck when nothing was wrong with my old truck. I wanted no part of the luxury truck set, with their leather and woodgrain and extra seats and built-in coolers and satellite radios and name-brand cross-promotions. A truck's a work vehicle. Get a boat if you want to play. An added bonus of my old truck was that, unlike most modern trucks, it didn't have an extended cab, which meant it was unsuitable for the transport of children.

Leo wore a blue swimsuit patterned with anchors and a white swim shirt with a big goofy-eyed whale and several smaller goofy-eyed sea creatures swimming around. He was meant to look cute, but to me he looked like some tiny, helpless old man beaten down by a life he had not expected, trying to keep his spirits up with ridiculous apparel and slow breast strokes in a lap pool.

"Today's the day, sport."

"For what?"

"Let's put that head under water, okay?"

Leo shook his head and bit his lip like he was about to cry.

"You want a stick cheese for the road?" Kat asked, immediately improving Leo's spirits by offering him dairy products as a distraction from his daddy's challenges.

You can't learn to swim unless you put your head under the water, and this was something Leo could not do. I'd been told to stay out of it, but sometimes I couldn't, especially since

I was the one paying for swim lessons when there was a perfectly good pool in our backyard. I bet if I tossed him in he'd figure it out right quick.

I asked Kat to bring the kids by the store later for ice cream. She muttered under her breath and slammed the car door without offering a kiss or a hug. Leo wagged his cheese stick at me as they pulled away.

Welcome to Hubbs

In the 1930s, a man named Mose Coleman discovered down in Vidalia that his onions were less pungent and more sweet than your traditional onion. My grandfather, Leo Hubbs, had already been growing sweet onions, his own variety, *Allium caritas*, but thought it was a gimmick or a fluke. He loved a sweet onion, but he couldn't imagine anyone else would. It never occurred to him he had a gold mine, but it did occur to Mose. The town of Vidalia had more traveled highways, and the favor of an onion-loving Governor Talmadge (the first one), and proximity to a major port in Savannah (before the interstate highway system), so the Vidalia onion's path to world fame was smooth and easy. Later, my grandfather tried to get Eechacohee County legalized as a Vidalia-growing county and couldn't do it, so he kept trying to market his *Allium caritas* as a different kind of onion: sweeter, juicier, milder, tastier, hardier, and less delicate—all true. But Georgia wasn't big enough for two sweet onions. In the end, the Vidalia Mafia prevailed, and the Charity Sweet Onion became nothing more than a knockoff and wannabe.

My father kept up the farm, kept on growing onions, kept on selling them by the side of the road using all kinds of evasive flourishes to fool the Yankee travelers.

"Are these Vidalias?"

"These are sweeter."

"So they're not Vidalias?"

"Here, have a taste."

"Am I tasting a Vidalia?"

"You are tasting the sweetest onion in Georgia, if not the world."

The farm's largest revenue stream became bulk sales to cut-rate grocery stores and restaurants who didn't give a shit one way or the other what sweet onion they had, but the Hubbs family name and their version of sweet onions remained a joke in agricultural circles.

I grew to regret my father once I understood his many failures. He was a man who was always looking back with fond nostalgia to a falsely idealized past, or looking forward to a future some asshole had promised him would be better. Men like him never paid attention to the here and now, believing it to be of little value, and so they drank themselves into their dreams. Our garage was filled with half-finished projects and crap my father had ordered with the intention of devoting himself to hobbies other than drinking and daydreaming. An archery set, coffee roasting equipment, scrap wood for birdhouse and picture frames, a DIY taxidermy kit with this evil-looking fake squirrel, model rockets, watercolors, but he never did any of it because, like a kid or a plant or anything else trying to live, these things all took too much time, a commodity he wasn't willing to share. I held firm to the belief that my father deliberately tried to put the family out of business so he could run away from everything, move to Florida and play fast-pitch softball while smoking cigarettes and living off his inheritance.

But then we all got lucky when the old man up and died, a massive heart attack while he was reeling in a bass, fell right out of his fishing boat and drowned. My brother, Pierce, thought we should sell all the land and assets, cash out and move to the coast to work on our tans and save sea turtles. Thankfully, nobody in the family ever listened to Pierce, so we kept on farming and modestly getting by. Until three straight winters of a relentless and recurring yellow bud disease had the Hubbs family on the ropes and our onion yields in the toilet. But then, as if by divine intervention, I ran into Katherine Freeman buying cans of San Marzano tomatoes at the grocery store. She'd just graduated from UGA and was putting her comparative literature degree to good use by being wealthy. I hardly recognized her. When she was younger she wore boy's clothes and kept her hair cut like a boy's and played softball and refused makeup, a practice nobody quite understood. But that day her hair had grown long enough to pull into a casual ponytail, and even though she still wasn't wearing makeup, it seemed to be because she was trying to show off her natural beauty instead of trying to claim she was misunderstood. She said, "Hey, Lee," and I said, "Hey, you," and much to my surprise, by the time we'd small-talked enough for me to remember her name, she'd invited me for spaghetti and told me to bring a baguette and some brie. I didn't like brie, so I took her some homemade pimento cheese.

Kat was the youngest daughter of one of the largest peach-and-pecan-farming families in the state. I didn't think about her much when we were growing up because she was a good seven years younger and a lot weirder, but her sister Susan was in my class and we made out once on a trampoline in her backyard. Her older sisters were quick to marry off and start families and spend money, and the rumors were that Katherine was a lesbian, a drug addict, a basket case, a sociopath, a ball buster, a Jesus freak, a folk singer. But she wasn't exclusively any of these things, she was simply waiting for the right man. Well, here he was. They say that money doesn't grow on trees, but it might as well when it comes to Georgia peaches and pecans, so the union of these two middle-Georgia farming families saved the sweet Charity Onion by subsuming it under a more prosperous and reputable umbrella, that of peaches and pecans.

I floated the idea of opening a retail outlet for all our bounty, and because the Freemans didn't want to spoil their good name by having it associated with low-rent onions, and because they were certain the enterprise would fail, they were more than happy to have the store bear my name: Hubbs Fresh Produce. No apostrophe. (I'm familiar with the laws of grammar, but I find the apostrophe pretentious.)

The store was on Richard Downer Boulevard, Exit 173 off I-75. Richard "Dick" Downer was a racist senator, finally driven from office by a stroke at the tender age of ninety-three, whose legacy included personally making sure Eisenhower's Interstate system ran through Charity's backyard. Jokes about "Dick Boulevard" never got old. Most of the businesses on Dick Boulevard were major fast food chains, hotels, and filling stations, anything that catered to the interstate traveler. Hubbs Fresh Produce was close to the exit, a BP Station and a McDonald's away from the on/off ramps, which made it super-convenient for all the tourists making pit stops on their way to and from Florida. The interstate was the only reason Charity didn't get sucked down the vortex of the dying small town. Hubbs Fresh Produce billboards stood on either side of I-75, North and South, advertising sweet onions, fresh peaches and pecans, ice cream and cobbler, dry goods and sundries, fried onion rings, only thirty more miles, only fifteen more minutes, exit now!

The store resembled an old Cracker Barrel, because that's what it had been before we converted it to Hubbs. Inside the store we sold a bunch of Kat's cellophane-covered goody baskets, and branded clothes, and pictures she'd painted, and all that high-Southern pastel crap that tourists, online shoppers, and subscribers to *Southern Living* go ape-shit for, along with ice cream and cobbler and onion rings. Outside the store was an open-air produce market shielded from the elements by an extended tin roof. There were two shifts, eight to two and two to eight, shorter hours in the off-season. The store opened at noon on Sunday so everybody could go to church. The boy employees wore overalls, and the girls dressed more or less like Daisy Duke. A.J. was the unnamed head of the exterior, and Jodi was the unnamed head of the interior, and although I didn't like it if that's what they called me, I was the boss.

I parked my truck in my usual spot, a dirt patch next to the dumpster, saving the prime front parking for the customers. One of these customers was smoking a cigarette in the makeshift smoking section, stacks of hay bales arranged like living room furniture, smoker's poles poking everywhere to help keep morons from shoving their cigarette butts in the bales.

I nodded to him, "Mornin'."

"Unfortunately," he said.

Welcome to Hubbs.

Inside, Jodi pulled two cones of peach ice cream from the dispenser for a couple dressed in matching plaid shirts. I was surprised she'd come to work, but more surprised she'd cut all her hair off overnight, all her wild and wavy hair gone, hacked to pieces like somebody'd taken a weed eater to her head. Likely some condition of her spiritual cleansing. At least she hadn't shaved her eyebrows. Sometimes when I closed my eyes all I could see were her beautiful eyebrows, bushy critters hurtling through space and time to undo my belt. They had a language all their own. Her eyebrows moved independently from her expressions and revealed her truest thoughts. She had a pink butterfly barrette pulling the clumps of longer hair away from her face. All it did was make her look young, too young, like a dadgum thirteen-year-old boy at a psych ward with a history of self-mutilation.

"I like your hair," I said, and went to work.

Nobody had started the kettle of boiled peanuts for the day, and instead of yelling at everybody, I did it myself. The boiler was an overkill, the MK-80, an eighty-quart stainless steel outdoor cooking behemoth fueled from a tank of propane, but tourists loved to see the novelty of boiling peanuts, a delicacy they'd usually never seen before, and boiling them in plain sight made the smell enticing and difficult to resist. After a few hours they were ready to be fished out of the kettle, drained, poured into double paper sacks and served hot. If anybody wanted peanuts to suck on for their drive this morning, they'd have to take them cold from yesterday's leftovers.

When I finished with the boiler, I nosed through flats of tomatoes and baskets of peaches for spoilage, filling the slop buckets with all the lost soldiers that had rotted overnight. Mr. Ferris came by every afternoon and picked up the rotten buckets as well as whatever onion ring grease we had left over to fatten up his hogs, claimed he'd repay the favor with free bacon or thick cut pork chops, but I'd yet to put any of the man's pork on my table. Tomatoes, when they turned, infected all the other tomatoes around them so that they'd all start to juice and develop white moldy sheens that stunk so bad you could smell it in your sleep. There were always a lot of bad tomatoes. A busted watermelon at the bottom of the watermelon pyramid leaked sticky juice from the corner of the crate, so I had to take each watermelon off the pyramid to get all the way to the bottom, then stack them up again. For some reason, this morning was filled with bad onions, flattened and festering black in sacks, so I had to cull those and then make sure all the sacks were the correct weight. Everything smelled like death, and I had to take frequent breaks to wash my hands.

While I worked quality control A.J. worked inventory, starting with the peaches, bringing fresh ones out from the cold room. His given name was Andrew Junior, but he was not actually a junior. His daddy's name was Claude. He was the best employee at Hubbs and the only black one, which along with Ben as the only quail, qualified as a diverse workforce. When A.J. was a freshman, a group of boosters, myself included, helped pay his tuition to Charity Christian Academy so he could play basketball. He was 6'3" then but hadn't grown or filled out much in three years, still stick-thin with a mop of short dreads that made him look like a palm tree. This past year, as a junior, he averaged nine points and five boards per game. Not bad, but not exactly worth private school tuition either.

But A.J. was an artist at arranging all the peaches so their bright red bottoms beckoned all the people. He put the fresh ones in the basket first, not as a cheat, but to mix up ripe and not so ripe, so customers didn't have to wait two days before they could enjoy their peaches, or come to find out they'd all rotted by the time they'd reached Valdosta. At Hubbs Fresh Produce you could buy a small basket of peaches for nine dollars, a large basket for nineteen, or a half bushel for thirty-nine. The odd pricing encouraged dollar tips. Every morning A.J. also restocked and reset all the summer fruits and vegetables we bought from other local farms or from farmers driving up and down the interstate selling their wares exit to exit: tomatoes, cukes, zucchini, Silver Queen sweet corn, field peas, summer squash, okra, blueberries, scuppernongs, watermelon, honey-dew, cantaloupe, you name it. Summer was golden.

Lately I'd been giving A.J. more responsibility: gave him a key so he could open and close the store, let him work double shifts to earn more money, allowed him the leeway to negotiate some purchases from farmers hauling their harvest up and down the highway. As long as he didn't buy watermelons from Jolly Hayes.

I hesitate to admit this because it may sound racist, or at least would appear that way, but I could never buy watermelons from black farmers, because my father claimed they tasted different. When pressed, he wouldn't be able to describe any particular agricultural influence black hands would lend to the watermelon; nevertheless, he refused. "We all have different tastes. And it's all right to keep 'em different." A bitter segregationist. He told me a story about how his father, my grandfather, had brought a watermelon home one day in peak summer, a gift from a black man he'd sold land to. On this land the man grew watermelons, and the watermelon they cut into was yellow and not red. It might've tasted good, my father never said; he just sat there assuming for the rest of his life—and infecting his children's life with the same belief—that black folks grew the wrong-colored watermelons.

But A.J. was sympathetic to Jolly, and since I'd expressly requested he not buy the man's watermelons, A.J. had gone ahead and bought figs from him instead.

As far as I knew, we had yet to sell a fig.

After we got everything running smooth, I poured myself some coffee and went into my office. I didn't stay in the office much, preferring to be outside keeping an eye on things and talking to customers. There weren't any windows, nothing but a tight cinderblock room with a desk and a computer and a filing cabinet and an old leather chair and oriental rug that Kat threw down to brighten up the place and make it feel more cozy when I had to fire people. I had pictures of the kids on the desk and some art that Leo had drawn taped to the walls and one of Kat's paintings, a big one of a rusted silo against a threatening sky, the silo poking up from an overgrown field like a middle finger. Truth be told, I didn't care all that much for Kat's paintings: sloppy oils of decrepit landscapes, kudzu-covered pickup trucks, poor folks fishing off bridges into dry creek beds, dilapidated porches with peeling tin roofs. Southern ruin porn.

A.J. knocked on the office door and poked his head in. "Can I show you something, boss?"

"C'mon in."

"Try this," he said. He held a baking sheet with eight individual tiny pies topped with slices of bright, puckered fruit. I took a bite. Still warm. Sweet, creamy, and delicious. I took another bite.

"Roasted fig tartlets," A.J. announced with pride.

"I see you found something to do with the figs."

"Me and Ben made them."

Ben. Another one of my best employees. Respectful. Still said "yes sir" and "no sir" to everybody. Could unload a truck bed of melons faster than you could say the word. Only trouble with Ben was he was shy to a fault, asked permission to take a piss or to get a drink of water, couldn't make a decision on his own, always kept his plume hidden underneath a Hubbs Fresh Produce cap turned backwards. Who knew he was also some kind of gourmet chef?

"That's not all," A.J. said. He set the baking sheet on the desk and left the office. I ate another one.

He came back with a white plate full of rolled-up meat skewered with frilly toothpicks. I popped one into my mouth and slid the toothpick out. Savory and sweet, with a crunchy and nutty middle. Was there cheese?

"Prosciutto-wrapped figs," A.J. said. "Pecans and goat cheese. You can also use melon. Pretty standard."

Standard for who? Sure, the treats were tasty, but there was no real need for Hubbs Fresh Produce to turn into a gourmet appetizer store where people sat around drinking tea and eating tartlets, as good as they were. Kat sold enough of that froufrou crap. But these days you had to be gentle to your employees, so I could at least let A.J. and Ben hold on to their restaurant fantasies for a bit. No harm. There were figs, and they weren't doing anybody any good sitting in the cold room.

"You and Ben aren't fooling with this while you should be working?"

"This *is* working."

"Tell you what, why don't you give me a list of some other ideas y'all got. Maybe we'll sell them."

"Seriously?"

"Maybe we won't."

Ben poked his head in and interrupted our meeting. "Your friend's out there stealing product," he said.

"What friend?" I asked. "I've got lots of friends."

"The cop," he said. "Loaded his cruiser with about fifty dollars' worth of stuff he ain't paid for."

"I'll take care of it."

"Remember that time he stopped us?" A.J. asked.

"Profiling," Ben said.

"I'm sure there was more to it than that," I said.

"Whatever. Keep your camera rolling." A.J. took his phone out of his pocket and held it up. "Power to the people."

Marty stood next to his police cruiser parked out front, while his trainee Todd sat in the passenger side practicing a series of strange facial expressions into the camera of his phone, like an actor scrolling through a range of stock emotions. Todd was buttoned-up and green, straight as a lamppost and just about as quiet. Marty was good for him. Marty liked to do all the talking.

Marty leaned on his cruiser and chomped on a bright red peach.

My forehead itched, so I gave it a scratch. "What'd you get today, buddy?"

"Nothing much. Some peaches, watermelon, 'maters, two cukes, couple slices of cobbler, but I already ate mine."

"Next time maybe be a little more discreet about it."

Marty took another bite of his peach, glanced inside the car at Todd. "We need to talk," he said. "Why don't we take a ride?"

"Why can't we talk right here? I've got work to do."

"They won't miss you," he said, and opened the back door of his cruiser. "Get in."

I got in, like me and all the product he had pillaged were under arrest.

"Hey, Todd," I said.

Todd put his phone away and slipped on his mirrored shades to match Marty's. "Your bathrooms are very clean," he said.

The Wheel

Marty's desk was in a wide-open room with lots of other
desks. The whole station smelled of burnt coffee and wet paper
and resembled every small town police station ever put on
television. Fake wood-paneled walls. A water cooler next to a
vast corkboard pinned with bills and wanted posters and mug
shots of serial murderers and thieves. An old poster of McGruff
urged me to take a bite out of crime. Two other cops, Daryl and
Colby, chatted each other up. Some old plainclothes fart typed
slowly on a computer in the hunt-and-peck method. A lady cop
talked on a rotary phone.

Todd went to his desk with a slice of cobbler and a bag
full of tomatoes. He sat down and started picking at the cobbler
with a plastic fork, glaring at the two of us like we were the cool
kids at the lunch table and he hadn't been invited. I sat across
from Marty in a vinyl chair with shredded orange padding. He
ripped his sunglasses off and flipped them on his desk,
squeaked back in his office chair and laced his fingers together
over his gut. "Hey, Todd," Marty called. "How 'bout you run get
some froyo? Be real good on that cobbler. My treat."

"I don't really want any froyo," I said.

Todd came over and Marty handed him some money.
"Put some Reese's on mine."

"The cups or the pieces?" Todd asked.

"The pieces."

Todd looked at me.

"I'm not hungry," I said.

"Are you lactose intolerant? They've got some that's lactose free."

"No, thank you."

"Todd loves froyo," Marty said. "Turned me on to it. Now I've got another bad habit I can't lick."

"No, sir. This is one you *can* lick," Todd said, and laughed at his joke all the way out the room and down the hallway.

Marty joined him with a fake laugh until Todd was out of earshot. "Listen," he said. "That dumb-dumb thinks he's gonna leap right over me for that promotion. He's hoping if he makes a big bust he'll get to play detective. But that ain't happening."

The Charity Police Department had two divisions: the patrol division, made up of uniformed community college graduates with acne scars; and the detective division, who, according to Marty, got paid more to sit around and eat takeout Chinese. The two town detectives had been a constant source of bitching for Marty, who felt they were incompetent, egotistical pricks. He was largely proven right when they were both fired— along with a few sheriff's deputies—for being part of a county-wide meth ring. Since then, Marty'd been angling for a promotion to fill the vacancy, but hadn't gotten much traction. Now Todd threatened to take what Marty thought was his.

"You carried me down here to bitch about Todd?" I asked.

Marty laughed. "Says he wants to open up a QCI."

"Is that a froyo shop?"

"I really thought you'd be taking this more seriously," Marty said. "A Quail Crime Investigation. Get the GBI involved. Says he thinks it a little odd that I happened upon a hit-and-run with no evidence and no suspects. He's got nothing to go on, though. Just be aware...he might be asking questions."

Marty opened a manila folder from the pile on his desk and handed me a piece of paper. An incident report from the night before. When Officer Bishop noticed a man lying on the shoulder of Highway 41 at approximately 10:37 PM, he investigated the scene and found Clarence Hart unresponsive and reeking of booze. The victim showed signs of trauma, a meeting with a motorized vehicle.

"Who's Clarence Hart?" I asked.

Marty handed me another piece of paper, this one folded in half down the middle. I opened it up. "Meet Valentine," he said. "A magnet for misfortune."

I'd never seen a criminal record before, but that's what this was, a rap sheet, the collected crimes of someone whose name I'd never known. He'd been arrested once for armed robbery, twice for assault, once for unlawful discharge of a firearm, once for public intoxication, a charge for indecent exposure, and too many drunk driving offenses to tally. I was halfway down the sheet, still reading, when Marty snatched the paper from me. "One more quail who won't be missed."

This seemed callous for Marty, and even if it was true, it felt wrong to celebrate the fact. Something happened when I read Valentine's real name and saw all those offences. He became a man with a past, and this made me feel sorry for him in a way I couldn't explain. "So there's no family or anything?" I asked. "Next of kin?"

"Not any that would testify to grief."

My left hand trembled and my body flashed with heat, like I was breaking out in a rash. "So that's it?"

"Unless you grew a conscience overnight."

My stomach flipped. I thought I might throw up all over his desk and ruin his police work. "Can I get some water?"

"Be my guest."

I went over to the cooler and gurgled out some water into a paper cone cup. The water tasted like metal and was warm as an armpit. A bill on the bulletin board held the pencil-sketched portrait of an older quail couple, both of them smiling. They were wanted for a series of robberies at restaurants and fast food joints, stealing people's used grease. I could've sworn I'd seen them at the store buying up peach ice cream and boiled peanuts. Then again, a lot of quails looked the same to me.

I squeezed out another cup full of water, turned around and surveyed the rest of the room. Daryl and Colby laughed like they were telling dirty jokes. Marty was picking something out of his ear while he flipped pages of a dog-eared paperback. I was lucky to have him as my friend, somebody willing to save my ass and sabotage his trainee's advancement, and in return all he expected was to be well-compensated with *gratis* peaches and gift baskets.

So why did I feel sick?

I reached for another drink of water but stopped short of the cooler. In the corner, propped against the wall, was the wheel, Valentine's missing bicycle wheel. The yellow trim around its rim gave no doubt it was his. Here was some evidence that could potentially blow this whole thing up, but Marty hadn't mentioned it. Was he messing with me?

I walked unsteadily to Marty's desk, lowered my voice. "You weren't going to tell me about the wheel?"

Marty whispered, "What wheel?"

"The wheel missing from his bike, remember?"

"Sure."

"Well, it's right there." I pointed to the corner.

"I don't see a wheel," Marty said.

He was right. The bicycle wheel had vanished. Nobody'd come and taken it, but it was gone. I rubbed my eyes and looked again.

No wheel.

I was no man of visions, like that blind folk artist Kat liked who etched his prophesies into fence posts, but I swear to God I saw that wheel.

"Relax," Marty said. "People can't find what they aren't looking for."

Corn on the Cob

Marty dropped me at the store after he stopped at Subway to grab some lunch. He offered to buy me a sandwich but I wasn't hungry. I poured a cup of coffee and went into the cold room and sat on a five-gallon bucket of soft serve mix. Sometimes I liked to sit in there and think, especially when confronted with the multiple dilemmas of being a boss. I liked the way the chill goosebumped my skin after I'd been sweating. Helped calm me down, ease my inflammation. I always thought more clearly in the cold.

But my breaks in the cold room were often interrupted, and today was no exception. It wasn't long before Jodi came in with her jacked up hair. The heavy metal door shut behind her like somebody pumping a shotgun.

She folded her arms across her chest, concealing any effect the chill might have on her nipples. "Lucky for you my daddy's car's not messed up," she said.

I sipped my coffee. Steam rose from the white Styrofoam cup, so thick and clear as it curled out it could almost form letters, spell stuff out for me to read in the frigid air, little messages. Today the steam unfurled in a feathery plume.

"Lucky for *us*," I said.

Jodi grabbed an ear of Silver Queen corn and shucked it, let the silk and husk fall to the floor, sunk her teeth into the cold, raw kernels. The girl loved raw corn. "We should find his family," she said. "Send his mama some flowers, tell her we knew him and he was a good man."

Jodi must've hacked off a chunk of her brain with that haircut. Her suggestion served as a reminder that intelligence is temporary, fluctuating like the weather. One day you can be brilliant, and the next you can be raining a shitstorm of stupid from the sky. We all operate on this continuum. Even Einstein had an off day. We were not sending anybody flowers, much less his mother. What would the note say? *We ran over your son. Oops!* I didn't want to think about him having a mother, because to think about her meant there was someone out there who was obligated to love Valentine unconditionally, and that was not a person I could deal with. To face his mother, the woman who gave him life, would be like facing God. And I had a pretty good idea of what God might say.

"Don't you think you've done enough talking?" I said.

"We should at least pay for his funeral. Raise money. *Something.*"

"Let me explain something to you. Guys like that don't get funerals."

"Why? Because he was a quail?"

"No, because he was an asshole," I said. "I just got back from talking to Marty at the station. Valentine was a criminal. We ought to thank the Lord he was the kind of dude who won't be missed."

Jodi ate the corn like a typewriter carriage eats paper, moving her teeth all the way down the cob before returning where she started, rotating the corn to a fresh row of kernels and gnawing again. "What if I said that about you? What if I said I wouldn't miss you?"

"Aren't you going to miss me?"

"Don't count on it."

This hurt. Jodi'd been good for me and I'd been good for her. Offered her some stability at the very least. After two years at college learning she didn't like college, she took some time off, or got sent away, depending on who you ask. Traveled across Mexico helping orphans learn to read and write fairy tales in English. Came back and still wasn't ready for higher ed. Her mom's breast cancer didn't help the situation. She stuck around Charity taking false pride in her personal sacrifice for family and working on what she called a cancer "anti-memoir." Then she came to Hubbs looking for work, and for the past couple of years that's where she'd been, my generous unlimited unpaid time-off policy allowing her the opportunity to pursue a number of experiences worth writing about: selling handmade soap in Costa Rica, hiking a piece of the Appalachian trail with a mattress on her back, saving the endangered woodpeckers of the Okefenokee. With her mom in remission, Jodi was now open to more adventure, this time in the Amazon.

It never occurred to me until that moment that I might've been just another experience for her to write about.

"*I'll* miss *you*," I said.

"You'll miss getting your dick sucked."

Well, true. A man has needs, and if those needs go unfulfilled by his wife, he might find himself succumbing to the advances of a woman who eagerly fulfills those needs. But there was more to our relationship than that. We had excellent conversations. I could say things to Jodi I'd never say to Kat, stuff about the kids, worries I had that I didn't want to trouble my wife with for fear she'd think I was weak. "I thought I meant more to you than that," I said.

"What about what other people mean?"

"What do you mean?"

Jodi nibbled the last bites of corn off the cob and talked as she chewed. "You can't go on living like this forever," she said.

"Like what?"

"Like you've won something, some game everybody else has lost."

"You'd like me to stop being successful?"

"I'd like you to stop treating everybody like they owe you something, and start thinking about what *you* may owe *them*."

I stood and took a step closer to her. I was done being lectured. I didn't owe her anything. In fact, she owed me. "You can't fix Valentine," I said. "But you can fix my marriage. So why don't you go tell—"

"You may not care," she said. "But I care."

"Enough to risk your big chance to live with the natives?" I asked. "Your once-in-a-lifetime opportunity, as I think you put it. Leave it alone, Jodi."

She pointed the corn cob at my nose. Her eyebrows narrowed. I could tell she wanted to say something clever and biting, a sharp piece of wit that involved the corncob as a prop, one last word to really stick it to the man. It took her a second.

"Take this cob and shove it," she said, and dropped it on the floor, where it rolled toward the drain.

The door made a different sound this time when she left.

I followed her out. Kat stood there holding Lisa on her hip with Leo at her side. No doubt she was thinking me and Jodi'd been in the cold room squeezing each other's fruits.

"I put my head under!" Leo said, beaming like he'd split the atom.

I tousled my boy's hair, still smelling of chlorine. I had to stop myself from telling him it was about time. "All right," I said, and gave him a high five. Lisa held her hand up too, and so I doled one out to her for doing nothing.

"What'd Jodi do to her hair?" Kat said.

"Whatever she did it happened in the dark."

"She's cute. Don't you think?"

She was fishing. I wasn't biting. "I haven't really thought about it."

"Mama said I could have an ice cream," Leo said.

"Let's do it."

So I went in my store and sat with my family around one of our circular marble parlor tables and we all ate peach ice cream together.

Blessed Assurance

That evening, Kat wanted all of us to go to church, typically not part of our Wednesday night ritual. Said she was feeling like she needed some spirit in her tank, which I took to mean she intended to pray for her family, and for guidance as to how to proceed with her adulterous husband.

Wednesday night church was a lackluster affair, filled with blue-hairs and zealots, lonely folks and those who fueled their need to feel superior to their friends who didn't attend Wednesday night church. They could see them later in the week and say, "Oh, hey, I missed you at church Wednesday. Were you there?" Knowing full well the answer to that question.

The Hubbs family took their seats toward the back of the right side of the congregation. Kat gave Lisa her phone to play with—a baby-rattle app—and Leo immediately went for the bulletin and a pew pencil to start drawing. Twenty or so other parishioners dotted the pews. Their every move echoed through the church: every cough, every crossed leg over slacks, every unwrapped Werther's Original. We sang an opening hymn. "How Great Thou Art." Not really one of my favorites. Why was God always needing to know how great He was? I could hear Kat singing beside me, her sweet lilt hovering over everyone else's drone. She had a pretty singing voice—no reason to ring up Nashville, but a voice you'd like to hear if you were in need of uplift, which was every single soul attending Wednesday night services at Charity United Methodist Church, including myself.

We sang the hymn together and then sat down and let the choir—consisting of a mere six members this evening—perform one on their own, a song I didn't recognize. Pastor Phil stood behind the pulpit and thanked everyone for coming, and then asked them to join together in prayer. Pastor Phil always prayed for very specific public works programs or concerns personal to individual church members. I worried he was going to say my name, out me to the congregation, but he prayed for swift replacement of the water mains along his street.

Leo showed off his gray scribbles. I had no idea what it was supposed to be, but told him it was great. He drew a grid for a game of tic-tac-toe. We played and I won. I believe the only way to get good at a thing is to keep practicing that thing, and there's no incentive to keep practicing that thing if you think you can win every time.

The offering plate came around while we were playing, and I passed it along.

Pastor Phil's sermon was on pets, or how people should be more like pets. He brought a puppy up there with him to illustrate how people often treat their pets better than their fellow man. Everybody said, "Awwww," instead of "Amen." Pastor Phil liked to get whimsical on Wednesday nights thinking it would pack the pews. It didn't. He urged us to broaden our compassion, to see all of God's creatures as puppies. I'm not sure that would help, because when you get right down to it, puppies can be real assholes.

Pastor Phil kept the sermon short and sweet because he knew nobody really wanted to be there on Wednesdays any longer than necessary. The window for self-righteousness shuts as the length of time spent in church increases and you realize all the other things you could be doing. When he was done and we were about to start singing the closing hymn, Kat raised her hand like she was feeling the Holy Spirit. I didn't know what she was going to say, but I wanted no part of it. I did not need her airing our private matters in front of God and everybody, so I gently tugged on her arm.

She shook loose and stood up.

When Pastor Phil didn't acknowledge her, she called him out. "Pastor Phil," she shouted, and the murmurings of the congregation came to a halt.

This wasn't typical behavior at CUMC, where congregants sat in their pews and digested their worship dished up family style. I prepared myself to prove the rumors of her madness and to drag her out with a hand clasped over her mouth. Nothing to see here folks! Amen.

"Yes, Katherine," Pastor Phil said.

I tried to hold her hand, pull her down, but she jerked away.

"Can we sing 'Blessed Assurance'? I'd really like to hear that one right now."

Pastor Phil cleared his throat and smiled. He liked what she was doing. Here was a member of his flock so moved by his words about treating people like pets that she was compelled by the Holy Spirit to hear some divine music. Praise Jesus. "We don't usually take requests, but if you feel called to sing we should sing."

And so we did. Even me. I couldn't help it. I was moved.

Jump In

I yanked a towel from the dryer and poured myself a Diet Mountain Dew and vodka in a Styrofoam cup filled to the top with ice from my ice maker. Outside, the morning was bliss: big blue skies, wispy clouds, birds chiming noisily in the trees. I grabbed a long net and skimmed the top of the pool free of pine needles and magnolia leaves before I shoved off in my padded float, a blue-striped lounger complete with cushioned armrests and cupholders. The current eased me lazily around the pool while I soaked up the sun and sipped my drink. My phone rang on the glass top table, still smeared with a yellow sheen of pollen, but the risk of trouble wasn't worth getting out of the pool. Leaving everybody on their own at the store in the morning invited a potential for all hell to break loose, but given all that had happened the past couple of days, I had to take it easy, slip into the day casually like a pair of old shoes you don't have to bother untying. I ran my own business for a reason.

After a half hour or so, Kat came outside. She had on a suit, gray slacks and blazer over a white blouse unbuttoned strategically to show off her clavicles, sexiest bones on a woman's body. Her hair was in a bun, like she was about to testify before Congress. Except she was barefoot.

She dipped a toe in the water.

"Feels good," I said. "Jump in."

She took a deep breath and exhaled. "It's taking a lot of courage for me to stand here right now. I would like you to acknowledge my courage."

I took a sip of my Dew. "You look real good in that suit," I said.

"I thought I could ignore it and it would go away," she said, "but it's not going away."

"I'm not sure what you're talking about, sugar."

"Shut up and let me talk. You're always talking. Talk. Talk. Talk. Well now I've got something to say."

This was it. Proceed with caution. "I'm listening."

"I'm leaving," she said. "I'm going to get a job."

I rolled off the lounger and into the pool, frog-stroking my way under water, holding my breath long enough to think of what to say next, the right words that would calm her down and help her realize she was where everyone needed her to be: at home. No doubt this whole job thing was a result of what she knew about me and Jodi, but if I appealed to her mothering instincts, lauded the legacy of motherhood as the most noble of pursuits, she'd feel guilty about abandoning her family.

I surfaced, slicked my hair down and folded my arms on the edge of the pool, looking up at her, a vision backlit from the sun. "You have a job. You take care of our kids."

"That job sucks. Why don't you try it for a while."

"You paint. You're a good painter."

"You can't make a living painting pictures."

"Why do you need to make a living? You're parents are richer than Texas."

"Because my husband's a sorry sack of shit who fucks his employees."

Well-played. She'd hooked me and reeled me right in.

Technically, I agreed with the 42nd president of the United States with regard to the definition of fucking, strictly relegating it to intercourse, so there was no reason for me to say anything other than, "What the hell are you talking about?"

Kat kicked her foot in the water and splashed me in the face. She stormed up to the house, leaving a solo wet footprint across the poolside concrete.

I pushed out of the pool, grabbed my towel, and was drying off when my truck pulled out of the garage. It wasn't enough she was leaving me, she had to steal my truck, too. I hustled after her but I was too late.

Inside the house, Leo was mesmerized in front of a cartoon with his thumb in his mouth, and Lisa was crying in her playpen trying to hoist a fat little leg over her prison. I lifted Lisa out of her playpen and put her on the floor to keep her from turning the whole damn thing over.

"Watch your sister," I told Leo.

Leo registered his acceptance with a loud suck on his thumb.

I hurried upstairs and got dressed, khakis and a dark gray Hubbs Fresh Produce golf shirt. Kat would be back. She couldn't stay gone. Her life was too good here, and when she did come back I'd need to have answers. Was there a lesser crime I could admit to? Back rubs in my office? The whole thing a misunderstanding? Or should I blame it all on Jodi, take advantage of her reputation for insatiable horniness? Say it was a one-time thing in a moment of weakness and beg for forgiveness? No. Whatever Kat thought was happening was over anyway. Jodi'd be eating bats and licking toads in a couple of weeks, so calling her a liar was still my best option.

When I came downstairs I found Leo in the same spot but Lisa was gone. "Where's Leese?"

Leo shrugged.

I checked in the kitchen, the playroom, the patio. I'd left the back door open. I raced outside, afraid she'd fallen in the pool, that she'd somehow crawled down the steps and rolled herself right into the deep end. Maybe she'd be a better swimmer than her brother.

I hurdled the steps and scanned the pool. The lounger floated on the eddies created by the pool jets, teasing me, a memory of relaxation. I heard a laugh.

A chair was pulled over on its side, and Lisa sat under the glass top table jamming her pudgy fingers into the screen of my phone. Had she come all the way down here just to get my phone? Had she seen it shimmering from the house and had to peck after it like a curious crow? I picked her up, told her no, told her that she shouldn't leave the house like that, that she scared me, that she could've really hurt herself, could've even been killed. I slowed down and raised my voice so she could understand. She must've gotten parts of it, because she started crying right before she tossed my phone in the pool.

A Tom is a Tom

After I skimmed my phone out of the water, I stuck it in a bag of rice, something I'd heard you were supposed to do with waterlogged phones. I figured I'd be getting a new one. Knowing what Lisa was capable of getting into, I thought better of locking the kids in the house and leaving them alone, so I piled them in Kat's crossover to take to work.

I pulled out of the garage to a loud crash and scrape of metal, like I'd backed over some of the kids' toys. Leo started crying and Lisa started laughing.

I got out and found the muffler sitting there like roadkill. This piece-of-trash Ford product was less than two years old. I could drive without a muffler, but it's loud as hell, and if you're not careful you can cloud the interior with invisible noxious fumes, making breathing difficult. My passengers were too precious to be sucking carbon monoxide this morning. I killed the ignition.

"What happened, Daddy?" Leo wanted to know.

"The muffler fell off."

"Did you hurt Mommy's car?"

"It kind of just happened."

"How?"

"I'm not sure. Sometimes stuff just breaks."

"Like an arm? Can my arm just break?"

"No, your arm can't just break. You've got to fall out a tree or something like that. It won't just break in the night while you're sleeping."

"I'm never going to climb a tree."

"That's no way to go through life, sport."

I took them both inside, dropped Lisa in her playpen and Leo on the floor, and turned on the TV. I called A.J. on the house phone. It was yellow and hooked to the wall and had about an eighty-foot cord on it because my mother used to like to roam free through the kitchen and living room before the days of cells and cordless phones. We hardly used it now, but never found a reason to get rid of it. I'd coiled the cord and tied it with a rubber band to keep Lisa from strangling herself. I told A.J. to come pick me up, then sat down with the kids to watch some TV while we waited for our ride. I took the controller from Leo and navigated away from the Kat-approved kid's show they'd been set up with earlier in the morning to an old cartoon I recognized and enjoyed a helluva lot more: *Tom and Jerry*.

I love cartoons because anything can happen. A frog can sing and dance. A coyote can order terrorist equipment by mail. A duck can get shot in the face and never stop being daffy. The rules of logic and life do not apply, yet they have so much to say about logic and life. Cartoons are not beholden to physics and gravity and flesh and bone and all the countless stresses of reality that are sometimes, to be honest, too much to handle.

In this one Tom gets smashed by a piano, and his soul takes a long escalator ride up to the sky. Once there, a train conductor reviews his case, judging who gets to board the Heavenly Express. All these poor, disheveled, hurt cats and kittens get to climb aboard, but Tom, apparently because he's spent his life torturing Jerry, can't board the train. The conductor tells him he's got to get Jerry to sign a letter of forgiveness if old Tom wants to get to heaven. The conductor gives him an hour, and if he's not successful it's eternal damnation at the hands of a devilish bulldog wearing green shoes and stirring a scalding pot.

At the sight of the devil-dog, Leo got up off the floor and joined me on the couch, his thumb-sucking going a mile a minute. I put my arm around him and let him nestle close. The bulldog *was* pretty scary. Lisa didn't seem to mind. She was tossing all her toys out of the playpen and on to the floor, one after the other.

So Tom makes Jerry a cake, gives him some cheese, begs and pleads, does all he can do, everything he knows to do to get Jerry to sign, but the clock keeps ticking and Jerry refuses. When he finally gets Jerry to sign, it's too late. Instead of the golden escalator to heaven, Tom falls in the devil's boiling pot.

Leo hid his eyes. But I'd seen this one before and knew the truth.

"Watch, sport," I said.

Leo peeked through his fingers to see Tom getting sparked by hot ashes ejecting from a fireplace.

It had all been a dream.

This episode couldn't help but be speaking directly to me and my recent experience. Sometimes the world is too damn obvious to be of random invention. But more than being of divine providence, what struck me about this episode in the context of the *Tom and Jerry* canon was that, even after Tom's lesson from the dream world, he kept right on chasing Jerry. Which goes to show that you can't change nature. A Tom is a Tom.

Leo didn't want to watch any more *Tom and Jerry*, but couldn't decide what cartoon he did want to watch, so I scrolled through a thousand options until a horn honked from the front driveway, saving us all from contagious indecision.

A.J. drove a vintage Cadillac DeVille he'd inherited from his grandfather, steel blue with a faux-convertible top he kept waxed and shined with Armor-All. The car had small portholes behind the rear windows, and they were covered with some vertical shades or blinds that made the car look like it had gills, a big fish swimming down the highway.

"What's the matter with your truck, boss?" A.J. asked, striding out of the car, a sight to behold.

Since I'd last seen him, he'd finagled some of his dreads into a plume that sprouted from the front of his head. It was dyed bright green and looked like a bundle of string beans. He was also wearing makeup around his eyes and on his cheeks designed to make him look like a quail. This would not do.

"What's the matter with your face?"

"Are you going to tell me I can't wear makeup at work?"

"Did you open the store this morning looking like that?"

"I feel like myself."

"Feel like yourself without the makeup."

I went around to the garage and fetched the car seats. A.J.'s Cadillac was not equipped with the latch devices of modern cars that allow for their easy insertion and removal, so it took us a good fifteen minutes to get the seatbelts locked in, and even then the seats were wobbly. "Drive slow," I said.

A.J. had his phone plugged in to the tape deck playing some talk show or game show, something where a crowd found lots of things hilarious.

"You let Jodi change *her* hair," he said.

"I didn't *let* Jodi do anything. She's a big girl."

"So why can't I wear makeup?"

"Because you'll scare all the customers."

"A boy in my swim class wears makeup," Leo said. "Maybe he's a girl. He has earrings."

"Don't you want all your employees to be comfortable?" A.J. asked.

"Not if it makes all my customers uncomfortable."

"I'm tired of Ben feeling all alone. Like he's the only quail."

"He is the only quail."

"But what if I want to be one, too?"

"You can dress up at Halloween."

"Being a quail ain't a costume."

"It is if you're not a quail."

"But what if I *feel* like a quail?"

"I feel like fucking Frankenstein sometimes but you don't see me walking around with dadgum bolts in my neck."

"A dollar in the swear jar, Daddy."

The crowd on the radio laughed. "What's this we're listening to?" I asked.

"Wait, Wait, Don't Tell Me: The NPR News Quiz."

"You listen to NPR?"

"What? Quails can't listen to NPR?"

The crowd laughed again.

Why anyone would pretend to be a quail was beyond me. Even the real quails only looked like birds, with none of the advantages. The first ones it happened to believed they were turning into superheroes and could fly, so there was a rash of quail deaths caused by these fresh idiots leaping from buildings and balconies and water towers only to realize their arms were still arms, their legs were still legs, and their bones were now more brittle than ever. Then came the claims of mental illness, that the plume crept down into the victim's brains and bore holes in their lobes rendering all of them dumb or insane or violent or incapable of common human sense and decency.

After all, who in their right mind would jump from a building believing they could fly just because the hair on their arms had started to turn downy? Supposedly it was not at all contagious or transferable, but there were entire corners of the internet where people made a living challenging the official story. Quails were said to be ruinously lazy, slept so much they refused to be roused by the likes of earthquake tremors, sonic booms, or sizzling bacon. They were also rumored to be sexual deviants, doing things with that plume that had many churchgoers apoplectic. Marty had dropped hints about the truth of that claim. When Cora turned quail he'd said it'd allowed her to explore aspects of her identity she had thus far left dormant. "Kinky stuff," he'd said. These rumors resulted in a pseudo-medical market for quail plumes said to cure everything from erectile dysfunction to anxiety and depression and infertility. Of course, quails insisted there was nothing at all different about them other than the way they looked, and most believed they shouldn't cut their plumes or pull them out or have them surgically removed because nobody knew exactly what that would do, and so they should wear them loud and proud and be thankful for their new selves, for the opportunity to be different in a world where so many people were the same. Most of them did have wonderful singing voices, and the Atlanta All-Quail Choir put out an excellent Christmas album every year, but there was nothing to prove whether or not their voices were a direct result of their turning quail.

But one thing was certain here: dyeing your hair and wearing makeup did not make you a quail. "When we get to work you're washing your damn face off," I said.

"That's another dollar, Daddy."

Pat-a-cake, Pat-a-cake

I was wrong about all hell breaking loose in my absence. The store was getting along fine, employees all upright and trustworthy, customers licking ice cream cones and cuddling bags of onions, peaches pyramided high, their ripe red asses teasing Yankee travelers. Maybe I should've taken pride in the fact I'd established a self-sustaining business, but nobody wants to see how easy it is for the world to keep spinning without them.

I took Leo and Lisa into my office. Set Leo up at my desk with a stack of copy paper and some highlighters and put Lisa on the rug with a peach, hoping it might occupy her for a spell. She picked it up and bit right into it, no hesitation. The fuzz gave her a shiver, then she giggled.

There was a knock on the door at the same time my in-laws clambered in like a comedy duo, G-Pop and Memu, both of them dressed in matching peach-colored Hubbs Fresh Produce shirts, khaki shorts, and Mickey Mouse ears.

Why the simultaneous knock and enter? Wasn't a closed door supposed to keep people from coming in? Wasn't a *knock-knock* intended to be met with a *who's there?* Either you knock or you come right in. To do both is to register your ineffectual personality.

I wondered what they knew, if Kat had already confided in them and here they were ready to avenge their daughter's honor, but it was pretty clear they had other things on their mind.

"What in God's name happened to your colored boy?" G-Pop asked.

"His name is A.J. And that's not really appro—"

"Well he looks like Dennis Rodman. Wish he played like him. He's out there scaring the customers away."

Kat's father, Mr. Riley Freeman, G-Pop to all his grandkids, hadn't worked a day in his life, the proud beneficiary of the Freeman family's fortune. Neither had his wife, Mary, Memu. But they both liked to act like the retail establishment had been their idea, and were always coming in monitoring what was going on and pilfering product and making suggestions as to how I might make things better. For many reasons I was forced to tolerate their behavior.

"I told him to wash his face," I said.

Memu picked Lisa up off the floor and bounced her in her arms. Peach juice ran down her chin.

"What're you drawing, Leo?" Memu asked.

Leo wasn't drawing anything. He was never drawing anything that resembled so much as a creature alive or dead, or a house, hut, rocket, or spaceman: always random colors in orderly patterns. This morning he was making a gay pride barbershop pole.

"It's a fish," he said.

"It sure is!" Memu exclaimed.

"You're low on peaches out front," G-Pop said. "And something stinks to high heaven out there so you'd better find it before it spreads. And the boiled peanuts are under-salted. Are you okay? You feeling all right?"

This was his way of talking to everybody, listing out your always considerable faults and then asking how you were doing, if you had everything you needed, if he could do anything to help you. It annoyed the hell out of me.

"It's been a stressful few days," I said.

G-Pop smiled, bent down close to my ear and whispered. "Does your pussy hurt?"

"Something like that," I said. "Can y'all look after the kids today? Kat's out job hunting."

"A job?" Memu asked. "Why would she want to do that?"

"Beats me," I said.

Memu gave Lisa a nose kiss and Lisa gurgled and laughed. "You can't give her a whole peach. You need to peel it and cut it up for her."

Lisa'd seemed to be getting along fine gnawing on the peach without help. Where did it end? Change their diapers, rock them to sleep, put on their clothes, pick them up when they fall down, wipe their asses, assure them there's nothing to be afraid of, tell them everything they touch is gold, that their colorful scribbles—which bear no likeness to any actual fish— are really the best representation of a damn fish anyone has ever seen. And why? So much harm done from so little. They'll grow up with the singular belief they're special, which is dangerous, especially once they find out they are not special, and when they do they're bound to end up with, at best, a mild case of depression and an addiction to Xanax. It's no wonder there's a generation of kids whose mothers accompany them on job interviews.

"We can't keep the kids today," G-Pop said. "We're packing for our cruise." He raised the mouse ears off his head with a flourish. "We came down here to get some peaches to take with us."

They were going on a Disney cruise. They'd been talking about it for months. Probably the only people on the whole damn boat who'd be without kids. I'd been excited for them to get out of my hair, secretly hoping they'd be so thrilled to meet Mickey they'd lose their shit and fall overboard.

"You can't take peaches with you on a cruise ship."

"I'm going to hide some in my suitcase," Memu said, and raised a shushing finger to her lips.

They'd get bruised and they'd probably split and stain all her clothes, but I didn't feel the need to tell them something they'd already decided to ignore. "How long is it going to take you to pack?"

"We've got some errands to run," G-Pop said. "We'll be in and out."

"I'm kind of in a bind here."

"Why can't we stay here with you, Daddy?" Leo asked.

"I've got a busy day, sport."

Memu handed Lisa to me. "They'll be fine here," she said. "You baby them too much."

"How many peaches fit in a Louis Vuitton?" G-Pop asked Memu on their way out the door.

"Should we take some ice cream?" she asked.

We begin and end our lives in similar states of helplessness.

A.J. squeezed past them into the office. He wasn't wearing makeup anymore, which was good, but his hair was still up in his makeshift plume. Had he pulled the stunt with the makeup to make me care less about his hair? Give up something you never really want in the first place in favor of something you definitely want and it makes you look reasonable. Shrewd negotiating tactic. I was glad I'd given him the leeway to barter with farmers hauling their harvest up and down the highway.

"Low on peaches out front," he said.

"How'd that happen?"

"Nobody brought us peaches," A.J. said. "Mr. Riley took the last half bushel from the cold room."

The man saw that we were low on peaches and still proceeded to take the last half bushel so he could bring them with him on a cruise that wouldn't even let him bring them. This was the sorry-ness I had to deal with every day. But part of this was entirely my fault. Nobody'd brought peaches because it was my job to run to the farm and bring the peaches, and yesterday I'd forgotten to do my job. One thing you do not want to do if you're selling Georgia peaches in the middle of summer is run out of peaches.

"I'll run get some," I said.

"You're gonna need a truck," A.J. said.

"Shit."

"A dollar, Daddy."

Lisa poked me in the eye so I set her down on the floor. She picked up the peach she'd left there and squeezed before licking her hand and laughing.

I asked A.J. to watch the kids for a second.

"Do I look like their nanny?"

"You really want me to answer that?"

"Jodi can do it," A.J. said. "Jodi!" he shouted into the store.

Jodi came into the office with her whacked up haircut, now adorned with two pink barrettes instead of one.

"Watch the kids," A.J. said. "Boss's gotta run to the farm for some peaches."

One of her eyebrows almost leapt off her face. "No more favors," she said, and left.

I told A.J. he could keep his plume and color it whatever color he liked if he'd sit in the office for a few minutes and watch the kids while I ran down to Dawn's to see if I could borrow her truck.

A.J. fondled his fake plume in admiration. "I'm gonna keep it anyway," he said. "But go on."

So I left and walked down to Dawn's, past the Kentucky Fried Chicken and the Subway and into what used to be a Shoney's before it closed and Dawn took it over for her budding pawn empire. She was behind the counter, glasses on the end of her nose, phone wedged between her ear and shoulder, stacks of cash divided into denominations on top of the counter. Somebody I didn't recognize, a quail with a bright pink plume, asked me if I needed help. I told her I was here to see Dawn. She pointed at Dawn before throwing a nylon drawstring sack over both her shoulders and strutting out the door, bouncing as she walked, like she was getting ready to fly. I'd met every quail that worked for Dawn, but this one was new. I hadn't seen Dawn since the accident. Must've already replaced Valentine.

Dawn waved and held up a finger. Her phone conversation was hushed and unanimated, unusual for Dawn. She nodded a lot, said yes, no, laughed a chuckle that sounded like a hiccup, then hung up.

"Guess you heard about Valentine," she said.

My eye twitched and watered. I dug a knuckle in it and rubbed. "Damn shame," I said.

Dawn laughed, which was surprising. Maybe it was one of those hysterical woman laughs, where they are so overwhelmed with a situation that they default to laughing when what they really want to do is cry. Maybe she and Valentine had developed a deep and abiding friendship over the few weeks he'd been her employee. Maybe Dawn knew all his secrets, how tough his life had been, and she was there to help give him a break, a second chance, and she felt good about herself for that, and they felt good being around each other. Maybe they even shared a snuggle.

"Oh, well," she said. "Next time bring me a Mexican quail. They're hard to kill." She took her glasses off and inspected me. "*Que pasa, compa*? You look like shit."

"Just a little stressed is all. Can I borrow your truck?"

"Yours finally give up the ghost?"

"Kat's got it. I need to run to the farm right quick."

Dawn checked her watch and thunked her rings on top of the glass counter. "Everybody wants something from Dawn. Do I look like the damn government?"

"I'll bring you some lunch."

Dawn tossed a jangle of keys on the countertop. "Fill 'er up."

"No problem."

I was almost out the door when Dawn whistled for my attention. "Hey, Lee," she said. "I saw those boys of yours sneaking out your store late last night. After hours. If you know what I mean."

"What boys?"

"You know who I'm talking about."

Ben and A.J. must've stayed late working on their gourmet experimentations. No big deal, but Dawn thought everybody's business was her business. "What're you worried about exactly?"

Dawn raised her hands in a defensive position, like she was being held up at gunpoint. "Never mind then. Get the truck back pronto. I'm due in Macon by two."

"Will do," I said. "Thanks."

Dawn's truck was a behemoth. I needed some help from the foot rail to launch myself into the driver's seat. The back seat was vast, big enough for car seats, and the whole interior smelled like Dawn, spicy perfume, and crisp bills. The clean was obnoxious, the dash and seats and display all freshly Windexed. I cranked the AC and cracked the window for some fresh air.

At the store, A.J. was still in the office with the kids, but he'd moved to the floor to play with Lisa. They were rolling a baseball across the rug, a baseball I'd snagged years ago at an Atlanta Braves game, a foul ball that I told everybody who asked had been a homerun.

"Can I stay here?" Leo asked, still plugging away on his drawings at the desk. He'd be fine. Probably wouldn't move from that spot, too scared to venture into the unknown wilderness of a produce market.

"Sure, sport." I turned to A.J. "Check on him every now and then all right?"

"Will do, boss."

"And can you stop calling me 'boss'?"

"But you're the boss."

"True. But when you say it, it sounds like you don't really mean it. Like you're making fun of me."

"I guess I can try."

"Thank you."

"Thank you for sharing your feelings."

I scooped up Lisa, got her a Ziploc bag of blueberries for the ride, and sat her in the front of the truck while I wrestled her car seat out of A.J.'s Cadillac. The latches on Dawn's truck made the seat installation a snap.

Kat always talked to the kids in the back seat. Said it improved their verbal skills and prepared them for the social norms of conversation. Sounded to me like it prepared them for getting used to people never shutting up. But I figured I ought to give Lisa what she was used to, so on the way I told her the story about the giving tree, because it was one of the only stories I could remember. This boy climbs this apple tree, and he loves the tree, and as he gets older he keeps asking the tree for more stuff. He wants to eat, so the tree gives apples. He wants a house, so the tree gives branches. The tree keeps on giving and giving to the boy, and as the boy gets older he keeps on asking the tree for more and more until the tree is nothing but a stump and the boy is old and needs a place to rest and so he sits on the stump. We'd read it a thousand times between Leo and Lisa, but telling it for the first time on my own made me realize that this boy was a real shithead.

At Freeman Farms, I left Lisa in the truck with the air running while Gabby helped me load the truckbed with boxes of peaches. Gabby ran all of Freeman Farms, and without her all of Freeman Farms would fail. Over the years, she'd taken on physical attributes akin to her job, as some people do, shrinking ever so slightly into the shape of a peach tree: short trunk, long arms. She always bragged about her family's thriving soda business in Guanajuato, but she never seemed to go down there for a visit and I suspected she might've been inflating its worth.

"You sick?" Gabby asked.

I hadn't really taken a long look at myself today, but given everyone's assessment, I must not have been looking so sharp.

"I'm okay," I said.

"What's that noise?" she asked, hoisting a box of peaches into the bed.

I stopped. I didn't hear a noise. "What noise?"

"Sounds like crying," she said, and picked up two boxes this time, shoving them in with the others.

I peeked in the window to check on Lisa, whose mouth was open in a wail, her face covered in wet tears. Dawn must've sprung for the sound-proofing option on her truck. I opened the door and unhooked her from the car seat. The AC had been running. The truck was cool and comfortable. No reason to cry. Maybe since her daddy was busy loading peaches, she didn't know where he'd gone, thought he'd driven out to the farm and left her for good. She missed me.

I held her and bounced her and wiped away her snot with a hand that I then wiped on the side of Dawn's truck, but she was inconsolable, couldn't stop crying.

Gabby finished loading the truck bed. She pulled a lollipop from the front pocket of her overalls, unwrapped it, and handed it to Lisa without asking if I considered it a good idea for my baby girl to have a lollipop. But she went after it like an answer to her prayers.

The lollipop was turd-colored and smelled awful. I took it from her to taste for myself to make sure it was okay. She immediately started wailing again. The lollipop was spicy, with a texture like sandpaper, not anything a typical baby might enjoy. Nothing in the memory of my taste buds recalled such a flavor, rotten citrus rind covered in chili powder. I gave it back to her so she'd stop crying.

"Where do you get lollipops that taste like crap?" I asked.

"Taste is subjective," she said. "Mexican grocery store down the street from the store."

"There's a Mexican grocery store on Dick?"

"Yep. I bet a lot happens on Dick that you don't notice."

I strapped Lisa in the car seat and thanked Gabby for the help.

"You need to go to Mexico," she said.

I couldn't tell if this was a question or a statement. "Pardon?"

"My family would take good care of you," she said. "You could learn Spanish. Expand your flavor profile. Eat some food that doesn't taste like mashed potatoes. Everything here tastes like mashed potatoes."

"Thanks," I said. "What makes you think I need to go to Mexico?"

She frowned and patted me on the shoulder. "Bad taste," she said, and handed me another lollipop from her overalls.

I got in Dawn's truck and left.

On my way back from the farm, I saw that Sister Rose's car was out front at the bar. The day had been trying, and it was only one beer, and if Lisa could have a lollipop then couldn't I have a treat, too? The bar wasn't open yet, but Sister Rose wouldn't turn me away.

I knocked on the door and she unlocked it with a smile.

She served me a cold beer in a bottle and went about restocking the coolers.

"Thought you were trying to cut back," she said.

"Not today," I said. "I brought my designated driver." I sat Lisa on top of the bar, not wanting her to crawl around on a barroom floor, even one that smelled like it'd been bleached within the hour. She slobbered all over her lollipop while I held her in place.

Afternoon bars can be depressing when they're empty, especially if you're the only one drinking. The smell of cleaning products can't cover up the years of spilled booze and piss and cigarette smoke and blood; all that history cuts right through the bleach. Picture a man sitting alone on a barstool in the middle of a summer day, his daughter held steady on the bar top sucking on a Mexican lollipop, the chairs still upturned on the tables, his head hung low and his spine curled, the whole room dark except for the golden glow of the beer, like a beacon of hope, his only fleeting hope. It's almost sad enough to make a man stop drinking. Almost.

The Allman Brothers pinball machine was unplugged, silent. The TVs were dark too. No music. Just the sound of Sister Rose clinking bottles and stocking fridges. Sister Rose had a son who died in the last war. Or the one before that. I couldn't remember. The flag that draped his coffin was folded into a triangle and held in a frame behind the bar. I guess it gave her a bit of comfort to see it, like a piece of him was there with her while she worked. Or maybe it'd been so long by now she'd started to see it like we all did, like just another flag.

"Shame about Valentine," she said.

He was the talk of the town. My eye watered again. I wiped it on my sleeve. "Yes, it is," I said.

"Todd came by here."

"Todd?" I had my arrangement with Marty. But Todd wasn't party to that.

"He told me it was a hit-and-run." She popped the top off a bottle and took a long pull.

I swallowed hard. "What else did Todd have to say?"

"He was wondering why Valentine was walking. 'Cuz, I mean, he was always riding his bicycle. Always. Wanted to know if I'd seen him ride off on his bike the other night. Nobody can find it. Asked me who was here and what all I remembered."

"What'd you tell him?"

"I told him it was likely one drunk quail hitting another," she said. "And that this was nothing unusual for Valentine."

I sipped my beer, but it tasted awful, metallic and skunky. Lisa tried to grab the bottle so I moved it out of her reach, grabbed both her fat little hands and rolled them in a circle for pat-a-cake. *"Pat-a-cake, pat-a-cake baker's man, bake me a cake as fast as you can..."*

"I'd run him home sometimes when he got like that," Sister Rose said. "I'd put his bike in my trunk, but it wouldn't fit all the way without the trunk flying open, so you know what he'd do?"

"...Roll it out, pat it out, mark it with a B, and put it in the oven for baby and me." I lifted Lisa's arms to the sky in triumph. The white lollipop stick held between her lips looked like a cigarette, and I briefly caught a flash of her future, bellied up to this very bar having gone nowhere, stuck in her hometown like her daddy.

I wanted to do everything I could to give my baby girl better choices.

Sister Rose drank her beer then kept on. "He'd fold my backseats down, and he'd lay his skinny ass back there and hold the trunk closed from the inside while I drove him home. Sometimes he'd sing. He had a nice voice. You ever hear him sing?"

"A time or two," I said.

"I'd drop him outside the quail park. He'd take his bike out, thank me for the ride, and I'd watch him weave his way into the dark, that goofy feather on his head bouncing all around like a cat toy. He'd usually fall on his ass before he got too far. Those quails don't know when to quit. They think different, you know? Makes sense. If you start to turn into a bird you start thinking like a bird."

"How's a bird think?"

She tossed her empty bottle in the trash. "Like something's always about to catch 'em."

This wasn't the relaxing stop I'd been looking for, and the peaches needed to get to the store, and I needed to return Dawn's truck, so I asked Sister Rose how much I owed her for the beer. She told me it was her treat.

"Be good," she called as I walked out the door.

If I'd been driving my own truck, I would've used my gas card to fill up at the BP, my preferred filling station, because they have the best snacks and the cleanest gasoline: BP with Invigorate. Too many people don't know how dirty gasoline ruins the longevity of their vehicles. But Dawn's truck wasn't my own, so I found the cheapest option. I bought Lisa a single-serving bowl of Cheerios. She managed to get a few in her mouth before she dumped the bowl in her lap and the crying started up again, so I unwrapped the extra lollipop Gabby had given me and handed it to her. Maybe it was actually some kind of special Mexican teething lollipop, a method dating back centuries to the Aztecs who paused in their games of kick-the-skull to stuff chili-powdered candy in their crying babies' faces. Who knows? But it did the job and I was grateful.

When I finally got back to the store, Leo was sitting in my office chair where I'd left him, but his face was red like he'd been crying. He held a bag of ice on the palm of his right hand. A.J. was there making sure he kept the ice on whatever injury had befallen him.

"You're a helluva babysitter," I said.

"He said he wasn't going to leave the office, and he left the office."

"I had to pee."

"What happened?"

I set Lisa on the floor. She had a yellowish drool all over her chin and lips, like some kind of rabid hound. Leo took the bag off his hand. It didn't look like much. His hand was pink and wet.

"He burned it on the peanut boiler," A.J. said.

"Why'd you touch the peanut boiler?"

"I didn't know it was hot."

"The steam rising from it like a dadgum dragon didn't give you some indication? Think, son."

Leo started to cry. It would take a shit-ton of magic Aztec lollipops to get my family through this day.

I told A.J. to go unload the truck.

I spun Leo round-and-round in the office chair until he started laughing. "It's all right, sport. Live and learn."

"What the fuck did you do to my truck?" Dawn came through the office door yelling.

"I've got my hands full here."

"Smashed blueberries?! Cheerios?! Footprints all over the seats?!"

"Kids are messy."

"You think I don't know that, *compa*? I've got kids. And they don't treat other people's things like shit."

"She's a baby."

"And I guess that's too young to learn respect."

"Calm down. I filled up your tank."

"Give me the keys."

"In the truck."

I scooped up Lisa and held my boy's non-burned hand and we all went outside to watch the last of the peaches get unloaded from the truck into the cold room. A.J. took several boxes out front to start making up baskets. We were down to half a dozen baskets, so he and Ben would have something to do the rest of the morning. Lisa was done with her second lollipop and fussy again, so I bounced her around trying to get her to hush. She was probably still hungry, but I had to put her down to get the car seat out of the truck, and Leo couldn't hold her because of his hand. I handed her to Dawn and she went for her gold chain.

"No, no. You don't have the money, honey."

The car seat dumped a fresh load of blueberries and cheerios and snack crumbs inside Dawn's truck.

"You want me to clean this up?" I asked.

"Fuck you."

"She needs a swear jar, Daddy."

"I'd appreciate it if you'd watch your language in front of my children."

"*Chinga tu madre.*"

"Daddy, my hand hurts."

I took Leo to the dishwashing sink where he pulled up a milk crate and turned on the cold water, surprising me with his ability to do it all himself, to drag a crate over to stand on, to not turn on the hot water instead of the cold. He was growing up.

Out front, A.J. blistered through the baskets, mixing up beautiful pyramids for display. Fine and good, but none of them were ripe, so everybody who bought peaches today was going to have to wait at least until the weekend to eat them.

"Clean up Dawn's truck for me," I said.

"I'm busy."

"I got this."

I took over filling baskets with fresh peaches, me and Ben, working at a steady pace, turning the fruit so the green ones rested on bottom and the bright red ones beckoned the travelers. It felt good to have a steady kind of work to turn my mind to, or rather to take my mind off the way my week was going. Grab an empty basket. Fill the basket. Put the basket on display. Sell the basket. A cycle that made sense, routine worth sinking into. But as I kept going, the peach fuzz crawled up my forearms and embedded itself in my skin like fiberglass. Itched like crazy. Ben did not appear to be having a similar reaction, stocking baskets with speed and grace. The bump on my forehead itched and I went after it with my nails, digging at the hairline until I drew blood and my fingertips were smeared pink. I tried to keep up the work, but the sharp fuzz crawled all over my body like a pornographic thought, spreading out to my chest and in my beard and all down my leg hairs and into my toes until my whole body prickled and I had to run inside.

Leo was still at the dishwashing sink holding his hand under the faucet.

"It feels better, Daddy."

"Good," I said. "Move." I rotated the spray head away from my boy's hands and onto my own and scrubbed. This was not the handwashing sink, so the only soap was dish soap, and even though it would rough up my hands—I encouraged all my employees to wear rubber gloves when they washed dishes—I went after it anyway, soaping all the way up to my elbows. But that wasn't cutting it, so I let the cool water pool in my hands and I splashed my face and neck and after a while the itching calmed down.

This wasn't my typical reaction to peaches. I'd been around them most of my adult life, and sure, if you worked the rows you needed to wear long sleeves to stem the fuzz and the heat, but these peaches had been washed and waxed, run through quality assurance, and held cold, the fuzz all but eliminated before shipping. This was not a bucket full of peaches plucked fresh off the limb.

When the itching was finally under control, I turned off the water.

Leo smiled.

Lisa wailed.

A.J. came in the back door carrying her in his arms. She held a string of something long, gold and shimmering in her fist, clutching it like the last spaghetti noodle.

"Dawn says you owe her for the chain," A.J. said. "And never ask to borrow her truck again."

Ring of Fire

The way the day was headed, the safest place for my family was home, so I had A.J. run us there, but not before a stop at Walmart for some burn medicine, the kind that comes in a spray and feels cool all over. Leo liked it and said he felt better already. We stopped at the Mexican grocery store, too. I was surprised I'd never seen it before, stuck right next to the Mexican restaurant where me and Kat would eat fajitas on Friday nights while her parents watched the kids. Unsurprisingly, all the products were labeled in Spanish, almost like I'd died and gone to Guanajuato. I went through a series of hand gestures and raised my voice at the woman at the front to try and tell her exactly what I was looking for. But she spoke English. I left with a 40-pack of Vero Mango Paleta Con Chile lollipops.

The rice hadn't worked on my phone. It still wouldn't turn on, so I stuck it in the bag and shook it around like I was flouring a piece of chicken for frying.

If Kat had sent any texts hoping to meet somewhere and work it out, they'd gone unanswered. I called her from the house phone, but she didn't pick up. She hated when I left a voicemail but I left one anyway. "Hey, Leo burned himself today on the peanut boiler. I took care of it. But you may want to come home."

The rest of the afternoon we watched movies and tried to keep Lisa intermittently corralled in her playpen, sated with something other than lollipops. For one particularly fun stretch, we turned her playpen over on her and pretended she was a tiger in a cage. She played along. The day dragged on, and Leo worried his mama may not be coming home for supper or to put him to bed. I needed to tell him something to keep him from freaking out.

"Mama might be home late tonight, sport. She had to run to Atlanta to pick up something for the store."

"But what if she doesn't come home?"

"She will."

"What if she doesn't?"

I gave him a dose of Benadryl to calm him down. "She'll come home. Here. Take this medicine for your burn."

I found the adult capsules and took two myself, fearing the itch that had plagued me at the store might return in the night. I put another two capsules in my pocket for later.

I fed Leo a hot dog cut up into tiny pieces because he constantly worried about choking on his food, and Lisa had a big bowl of yogurt and blueberries and a bottle of milk. She cried some more for a lollipop, but I had to put my foot down at some point, so I gave them both popsicles, and when she finished hers, I gave her a pacifier dipped in Benadryl.

I called Kat several more times and still didn't get an answer. She'd probably been trying to text and was now more pissed off at me for not responding. But then, why wouldn't she answer the phone when she could clearly see it was me calling?

The kids night-night ritual was sacred and proven. Kat would start with Lisa and get her to sleep before moving on to Leo, who could keep himself occupied in the bathtub or in his room. No bath tonight though, because I didn't feel like running it, so Leo pitched a fit on the bathmat, rolling in front of the tub and crying about how filthy he was. "I'm filthy!" he kept saying. "Filthy!"

I left him there to wallow in his filth while I rocked Lisa and sang her a song. "Ring of Fire." The only song I knew all the words to. It's not much of a lullaby, but at least it's about love, and she always seemed to like my exaggerated Cash-esque baritone and the pantomiming I'd do on the *down, down, down* part, pretending I might drop her in that fiery ring.

Leo got a hold of himself, brushed his teeth, changed into pajamas, wiped his face with a baby wipe, and went to his room to flip through the pages of his picture books. Eventually Lisa's eyes fluttered shut and her fat little jaw relaxed its work on the pacifier, only bobbing up and down every now and then, a Mexican lollipop in her dreams. I set her down in her crib and turned on her turtle nightlight that projected fake constellations on her ceiling.

I went to finish up with Leo. He wanted three stories— he always wanted three stories—and tonight he had them arranged on his rocket ship sheets in the order he wanted them. *Are You My Mother?*, *When Mommy Comes Home Tonight*, and *Grandmas Make the Best Babysitters*.

"Mama's fine, sport. She'll come and kiss you goodnight when she gets home." After I said it I knew I'd messed up. Leo might force himself to stay awake for that goodnight kiss, no matter how long it took. And I was starting to worry it might not be true.

A ladybug landed on his blistered hand. "Look, Daddy! It's Jill!"

"Who?"

"The ladybug. I named her. It's Jill. She's here every night."

I do not care for ladybugs. They're not cute or precious. Kat couldn't so much as buy Lisa a onesie with a grinning ladybug on it without freaking me out. My brother had dumped ladybugs in my bed when I was seven or eight. Gathered them in mason jars for weeks just to torture me. Why not spiders or lizards or something regularly feared by kids? Who knows? They were tough to exterminate. I felt them crawling in my bed even after they'd supposedly gotten rid of them all. My mother washed my sheets three times. Still, ladybugs weaved between my toes and feathered up my arms. Every night. Until finally they all died. My brother received no punishment, as he denied having done it.

It was all I could do to keep from smashing the ladybug on Leo's hand. "Jill will keep you company," I said. But she flew away just as I was reassuring him.

After Jill left it took a while to get him settled. I read all three books, but Leo asked me to stay and rub his back till he fell asleep, whispering to himself some story about ladybugs. I almost fell asleep too, but once the boy's breathing steadied, I went downstairs and poured myself a tall glass of bourbon over that perfect ice from my ice maker.

I called Kat again. Nothing. I was now officially worried, and started to speculate what the future might look like if she really left me. How would I raise our kids? I'd probably have to remarry right quick, but what available women were out there? Charity was a desert for the middle-aged and single, and a veritable wasteland if your criteria had to include attractive and childless. I wanted to call Jodi, but I didn't know her number, all my contacts trapped in my rice-encrusted phone. She wouldn't answer anyway. Caller ID and cell phones had ruined the spontaneous call. Nobody had to talk to anybody they didn't want to anymore, but maybe society had lost something because of that. There was some value in surprise, being forced to converse with a person you might not necessarily want to talk to, somebody trying to sell you knives over the phone or your aunt drunk-dialing every single soul in her address book looking to be less alone. But nobody wanted to talk to Lee tonight. So I rolled up some deli meat and cheese slices, speared them with frilly toothpicks to feel fancy, and plopped in front of the TV for a night of cartoons, Benadryl, and the bottom of a bottle of bourbon.

The Quail Who Wears the Shirt

Valentine and I sat on the tailgate of my truck in a Walmart parking lot. He looked good, healthy, wearing his favorite shirt, a black western shirt, shiny, with white pearlescent snaps that he claimed were made of ivory. Decorative red piping curled in arabesques all over the front and down the arms. On the back was a picture of an eagle with a giant snake in its talons, a snake three times the size of the eagle. He'd worn the shirt to the bar a couple of times, liked to tell people about it.

"I don't believe in tattoos," Valentine said. "But if I was to get one, it'd be this."

"Why's that?"

"Because. Even if you're a bad motherfucker, there's always something badder."

"So what's badder than the eagle?"

"The quail who wears the shirt," he said. He gulped from a silver travel mug a seemingly endless stream of whatever quenched his thirst. "Now. Tell me of your greatest heartbreak," he said.

"Do what now?"

"These are the rules of the afterlife. I don't make them. Tell me of your greatest heartbreak and you shall be set free."

"Are we dead?"

"Maybe a little."

"I don't get it."

"In the afterlife," he said, "we all get one story to tell. And once you've told it right, you'll be on your way to your eternal fate."

"Who decides if I've told it right?"

"It's different for everybody. And so is the story."

"So you're my judge?"

Valentine nodded. "Tell me of your greatest heartbreak."

The first story I told was about a girl named Stephanie Lamb, the most popular girl in 8th grade, who decided I could be her boyfriend for a whole two weeks. I thought I had it made, convinced of our golden future, the two of us dating all through high school, homecomings and proms, her in low-cut dresses with high leg slits and me in tuxedos with comical cummerbunds, a huge wedding at the Methodist church, a big, white house with shutters, a bunch of beautiful kids, girls growing up to be cheerleaders with bows in their hair, the boys football stars, all of them ruling the known universe.

When I was done telling this story, Valentine reached up and tore off my right ear. Threw it away like a Frisbee. It didn't hurt exactly, not in a physical sense, but I did hurt for the loss of my ear, the pang of losing something I once possessed, forgetting who I'd once been, a man with two ears.

My father walked out of the Walmart, peeled a tangerine for me, and went inside.

"Tell me of your greatest heartbreak," said Valentine.

This one was about the time my brother broke my new fishing rod on the very day I'd gotten it as a gift for my birthday, and how my parents wouldn't replace it because they said I needed to learn to take care of my things. And when I got done with that story Valentine said, "Give me your right hand." I held it out to him and he removed my index finger, propped it on his knee, and flicked it away like a paper football.

My father came out of the Walmart, peeled a peach for me, and left.

"Tell me of your greatest heartbreak."

This kept happening, over and over again, and each time I was done with a story, I'd lose a little bit of myself. Valentine pulled out my right eye and squeezed it in his hand until it turned into a golf ball. My father brought me a slice of yellow watermelon, took out a pitching wedge and smacked the golf ball that had been my eye. I started to believe I was in hell, and unlike what Valentine had explained, there was no way out. I was doomed to tell the wrong story for eternity while I lost all my parts and my father tried to nourish me with fruit.

I stopped talking and laid down in the truck bed wishing I still had eyes to stare up at the sky. It would be blue and there would be birds. Valentine put a finger in my chest and bore a hole through me.

"Tell me of your greatest heartbreak."

I told some other stories, or the same stories in different ways, until I finally gave up and whispered, "I give up."

Valentine transformed into a giant bird. I couldn't see him without my eyes, but I imagined him no longer as a quail, but as an eagle, his white feathers shimmering in the sun, his yellow beak the color of his bicycle wheel, his whole body a majestic emblem of bad mother-fuckery.

"Only love can break your heart," he said.

His huge wings blew warm air on my cheeks and I woke up.

Get Your Act Together!

When I realized I hadn't died and gone to hell, I discovered that Leo and Lisa were missing. Neither was in their room upstairs. Normally this wouldn't be much of a concern, as it would simply mean that Leo had gotten out of bed on his own and had gone downstairs to turn on some pre-approved cartoons. But I'd come from downstairs, and the TV was only on because I'd passed out in front of it. While Lisa had been known to hurl her leg over the side of her crib and climb out on mornings when we were late to get her, she'd usually find her way into bed with Leo. But today their rooms were empty, except for their sleepy smell.

"Leese...Leo," I called.

Lisa's ceiling fan morphed into a bicycle wheel.

I ran downstairs and outside and yelled their names.

Nothing but birdsong.

I scratched my forehead until I drew blood.

In the kitchen I found a note written in ALL CAPS on the envelope of a credit card bill.

LEE

WE DOCUMENT WHAT WE SEE SO THAT OTHERS MAY SEE

1. *DAD PASSED OUT IN A BOTTLE*
2. *BOY WITH A BLISTERED HAND*
3. *BABY SUCKING ON A LOLLIPOP*
   FOR BREAKFAST

THEY'RE WITH US NOW. GET YOUR ACT
TOGETHER!

At first I imagined it was a note from God enumerating my recent lapses in judgment, and for a second after that I thought it might be from somebody who knew Valentine, the type of psycho-quail who would resort to kidnapping children in order to settle a score. But it wasn't God or a psycho-quail. I recognized the maniacal ALL CAPS script to be that of my father-in-law.

How did they sneak into my house and steal my children right from under me?

My phone still wouldn't turn on, the rice totally inadequate at being anything other than rice. This rice business was one more lie the internet made up to get everyone to do stupid shit like pour buckets of ice on their heads and stick their cats in tight quarters. I picked up the house phone to call G-pop, but I had no idea what his number was, or Memu's number. Without my phone and its readily available voice commands and list of alphabetized last names all I had left was email.

I sat down at the computer and explained my position.

Dear Memu and G-Pop,

> *You can't just come in here and steal*
> *my family. My phone is ruined, so I've lost all*

*my phone numbers. Please send me your
digits.*

*God bless,
Lee*

The "God bless" was part of the email signature that Kat
had created for me and was not indicative of any desire on my
part to have God bestow blessings on kidnappers. Was this all
part of Kat's plan, the reason why she'd waited to confront me?
She needed time to prepare her parents to take the kids. Holy
shit! Were they all going on a Disney cruise without me? Was
she that diabolical? Or had I somehow forgotten that this had
been part of their summer plans all along? Leo wouldn't have
forgotten, would've spent last night delicately packing his
things in his Buzz Lightyear suitcase, asking his daddy all sorts
of physics questions about how boats stay afloat.

I called Kat. No answer.

My whole body radiated with the same prickly itch as
yesterday in the peaches, my forehead the main source of the
flame. I couldn't keep from scratching. I ran upstairs and
slathered the sore with Neosporin. All the scratching had
opened the cut, so I tried to cover it up with a Band-Aid, but the
wound was so close to my hair that it wouldn't stick. I'd have to
show some tremendous willpower to keep from making it
worse. But that wasn't my only itch. My beard felt like it was
crawling with fleas, so I went after it with clippers and watched
patches of thick black hair dump in the sink bowl as I carved
paths up and down my neck and cheeks. I splashed my face
with hot water and lathered up and found one of Kat's razors
and shaved until my face was smooth and naked. I hated it, but
I wasn't itching anymore. I'd had a full beard since I was thirty

because I wanted the respect that came with owning my own business and being a grown man, and grown men had beards, and so I grew one, but now that I'd shaved it all off I looked like a baby. Who would listen to me now? Babies have no gravitas. But what was done was done. Beards grow back. I'd made a decision and now I had to live with it, which is also part of what it means to be a grown man.

I take my responsibilities as a man very seriously, and a man has to take care of his family. It's in the Bible. Somewhere in those missives that come after the Gospels. Nothing red-letter, but still pretty important. The red letters always seemed like the letters to heed. You know, the words of Jesus and all. The rest of the New Testament was written by an old horse-faced celibate named Saul, who couldn't get laid and made up all kinds of rules to justify his homeliness and general insecurities. But one thing ugly, old Saul did get right was that a man has to have a family to be a man, and that man has to lead that family, and being a leader means making decisions and living with those decisions, and sometimes that means you will mess up, and you've got to learn that that's okay and to say you're sorry and to not dwell on it and to move on.

I would remember to say this to Kat next time I saw her.

I threw on some khakis and a navy blue Hubbs Fresh Produce golf shirt, but I couldn't help but stare in the mirror at the spot and start to itch it every time, and I knew everybody'd be asking me, *Hey, Lee, what's that on your head, how'd you get that thing?* so I put on one of our very nice Hubbs-branded baseball caps, a big fat peach emblazoned on the face, which would serve the dual purpose of keeping me from scratching and keeping others from asking questions.

I got in Kat's crossover and started it up. Figured I could roll the windows down to avoid the fumes building up from the lack of a muffler. The noise was loud, a rumbling like some kind of prehistoric creature thawed out and come to life, pissed off at having missed so much. I grabbed the shifter knob, but it was like an invisible power held on to my arm, gripping it tight, squeezing to keep me from popping the vehicle in gear. I was dizzy and nauseous, like my insides had all been scraped out with a melon baller. I put my hands on the wheel and tried to take a deep breath but couldn't catch it. My hands were shaking. I opened the door and walked outside the garage into the open air. Put my hands on my thighs and bent over, sucked in and exhaled slowly and deeply until I got my breathing under control. Surely I wasn't having a panic attack. I hardly ever panicked, how could I? I stood straight up, got behind the wheel again, and immediately my chest seized up and I hyperventilated. What the hell?

I went inside and called A.J.

"This ain't *Driving Miss Daisy*," he said.

"I'm having trouble."

"And I guess you expect me to always be there to help with your trouble?"

"Just come get me, please."

"Thank you for saying please."

I hung up and checked email. Nothing from the in-laws, nothing from Kat. So I sent her one.

Dear Kat,

> *Where are you? We need to talk. Lisa dropped my phone in the pool. I've been trying to call you. Did you go on a Disney cruise with your folks? I'm kind of lost and*

would appreciate you answer one of my calls.
I love you.

God bless,
Lee

As much as I didn't want to talk to him, I had to call my brother. He might have my in-law's numbers. Pierce was in Savannah for the summer living with the yoga instructor/law school student for whom he'd left his wife, even though the latter had stood by him while he was in prison. But Pierce was never one to honor past commitments when in the presence of immediate joy. Kat once said I hated my brother because I was exactly like him and it masked my own self-loathing.

"I think rather highly of myself," I'd said.

"That just proves you're not thinking very hard," she'd said.

Pierce had gone to prison for three years for being the godfather of a fake ID empire, selling top-notch counterfeits to rich teenagers, immigrants, and criminals. It happens. Prison was the best thing for him, but afterwards our parents felt the shame of small town judgment and pretended he didn't exist. He'd sent letters to me from prison and I'd responded in a timely manner. Me and Pierce's wife at the time were the only people who went to see him. Now he'd created a totally new life for himself, free of his family name and legacy. What he always wanted. Free of the Hubbs's, free of the onions, free to be somebody new. Not everybody got that chance, or took it when it presented itself.

I could always remember my brother's number because Pierce had picked it himself; the last 4 digits spelled C-O-O-L.

"Why are you calling from the home phone, bro? I thought it was Dad from the great beyond."

"Do you have G-Pop or Memu's numbers?"

"Who?"

"My in-laws. Kat's parents. Do you happen to have their phone numbers?"

He laughed, sucked a deep draw of whatever it was he was smoking and exhaled a loud crackly exhale into the phone. "Has your devotion to immersive mendacity finally caught up to you?"

"Lisa threw my phone in the pool. I lost all my contacts."

"This is serious. A very grave matter, indeed. How is a man supposed to carry on without his contacts?"

"I take it you don't have their numbers."

"Bro, I don't even know what these people look like."

"Thanks, fucktard."

"Use the phone book."

Great advice. Who had a damn phone book anymore?

I looked up Wayne Salley Ford on the internet. A woman answered the phone. "Wayne Salley Ford. Ten minutes from anywhere!" I never understood Wayne's slogan, but couldn't ask him about it for fear it might ruin our business relationship. How the hell can one place be ten minutes from anywhere? And why is this an advantage in the world of car dealerships? I told the woman my muffler had fallen off and asked her to please send a tow truck out to the house to pick it up. Told her it should only take about ten minutes to get here.

"Tough way to start your morning," she said.

"I'm equal to the task," I said.

She laughed. "Clearly you're not."

"Pardon?"

"If you were equal to the task you wouldn't be calling. I'll send somebody out right away."

She hung up before I could thank her.

Next I called Marty at the station. "Can you file a missing person report for me?"

"Who's missing?"

"My wife."

"I don't think so. Saw her driving your truck early this morning. Thought it was you. Why's she driving your truck?"

"Where was she going?"

"She didn't bother to roll down her window and tell me."

"How'd she look? Was she dressed up? Was she smiling? Were the kids with her?"

"I don't really know. She was wearing sunglasses, I think."

"Can you try to find her?"

"Seeing as she's not missing, I don't believe that would count as official police business."

"Listen, if you report her missing, then you find her, you'll be a hero. Probably get that promotion."

"I don't understand what's got you all worked up. She was probably going to get donuts or groceries, or doing something she doesn't want you to know about. Maybe she's got secrets like the rest of us."

"If you run into her again, can you pull her over? Act like she's violated some arcane traffic law or something?"

"U-turns are illegal within the city limits of Charity, did you know that?"

"I did not."

"Not many people do."

"Thank you for your help."

"Anytime, friend."

A.J. finally showed up. I got in the front seat.

"You shaved," he said.

"I did."

"You don't look any better."

"Neither do you."

A.J. wasn't wearing makeup, but he still sported his green plume of solidarity. His phone was plugged in the tape deck and offered business advice from a monotone man with a soporific voice, like he was reading the newspaper out loud to an audience of toddlers who needed a nap. I asked him to drive to my in-laws' house.

"Don't you think one of us should be at the store?"

"It won't take long."

"How long you plan to be without a car?"

"Not sure. But you work for me, so if I need you to chauffeur me around, you chauffeur me around."

"You take liberties."

"You can take the liberty of not coming back to work."

"You wouldn't be able to live without me."

Kat's parents lived on a forty-eight acre non-working farm, unless you call cutting massive fields of Bermuda grass working, which I guess on second thought it is, although neither one of them was ever out there driving the mowers. The whole property was bounded with a black split-rail fence, a sign out front hanging from a pole to prove their dominion over the land: Freeman's.

"We didn't drive out here to steal something did we?" asked A.J.

"Maybe. Stay in the car in case we need to make a quick getaway."

I got out and ran up the front porch steps, rang the doorbell. Nobody came. I tried to peek in the windows but everything was dark, like they'd been gone a long time. There was something ancient about the house, like it had aged considerably since the last time I visited. The paint was peeling around the windows and door frames and a gutter was broken. The hydrangeas wilted, sickly and yellow and thirsty. The garage doors were closed. I went around the back of the house and followed the path down the hill to the pond and to the dock. The water level was lower than normal, the surface still as glass, the mud along the bank dried up in veiny cracks. A cottonmouth poked its head above the water and slithered in ripples toward the dock like it wanted to tell me something, but I didn't wait to hear what it had to say.

Onion Pie

I tried to throw myself into work, choosing to believe my family was enjoying each other's company and they'd all be home tonight and Kat and I could work this all out. But the itch wouldn't go away. And everywhere I looked I saw a spinning bicycle wheel—in the swirl of coffee or the cauldron of boiled peanuts—and I'd get nauseous and prickly and my chest would close up and I'd have to splash water over my face and sit in the cold room until the air chilled the itch enough for me to leave.

I hid in the office where the faces of my family stared at me like ghosts. Cosmic forces were at work here. My recent sins had caught up with me, and if there was any way to get out of this mess, this sickness, this overwhelming itch, I was going to have to atone for them.

A.J. knocked and came in carrying two pizzas on baking sheets. "Don't be dumb, get you some," he said, and set both baking sheets down on the desk. One of the pizzas was topped with asparagus and the other was a barbeque pizza with caramelized onion and goat cheese. I didn't have an appetite, but I picked up a piece of the asparagus pizza. Gooey and crunchy at the same time, a nice salty tang, not too oily, the crust not too burnt, but crispy.

A.J. smiled. "Everything made in house. Farm-to-table."

I took another bite. The pizza had some sort of shaved cheese on top, no tomato sauce, a combination of inspired flavors. What an idea! Gourmet pizzas made with Hubbs fresh ingredients. How much would it cost to put in a brick oven? Could help tremendously in the wintertime when I had to drastically cut staff and hours. There was no other pizza competition in town, no pizzas like this, only the big chains. A.J. and Ben may have finally hit upon a winning concept.

"Y'all might be on to something. How come Ben never comes in here with his ideas? Always sends you to do his bidding..."

"He's scared of you."

"Why?"

"You can be scary."

"Are you scared of me?"

"I'm scared of all you bosses, boss," A.J. said, and left me with the pizzas.

I took a bite of the barbecue pizza, the sweet onions and sweet sauce blending with the creamy goat cheese into a taste sensation unlike anything Charity had shoved in its grits- and ham-eating maw. This was really good, and it was almost enough to make me forget my troubles. Food could have that effect on people. Why else was the country so damn fat? Everyone liked to sooth their multiple anxieties and daily wounds with sweets and lard and gooey casseroles made with condensed soups.

And that's the way it should be.

I'd been wrong about the dream. When I'd lost my eyes and Valentine flew away, he did not fly off as an eagle. He'd become an angel.

I left the office and called Ben over to help in the kitchen, told him to bring some onions. The store had a small kitchen, a griddle cooktop that we hardly used anymore since I abandoned the idea of Hubbs becoming a breakfast place, a double oven for cobblers, a deep fryer for our famous onions rings, and a soft serve ice cream machine. I got out a chef's knife.

"Don't be scared," I told Ben. "I like your pizza." I asked him to slice some onions and turn the oven to 325.

Whenever somebody died, my father would make an onion pie for the family of the bereaved, a simple gesture of kindness and community and caring. He carried the onion pie to the grieving family, put it with all the other Tupperware dishes crammed with casseroles, and sat with them and told them how much he'd loved their daddy or sister or mama or brother or cousin or aunt or uncle or pawpaw, and how much they would be missed.

"You got any of that bacon left from the other day?" I asked.

Ben nodded and fetched the bacon from the cold room.

I fried it up, then sautéed the onions in a mix of bacon grease and butter. I had Ben mix up some eggs and flour, then sour cream, milk, salt. This was my father's recipe as best I could remember. The measurements were a guess, but I knew the eggs and flour and milk and salt would inspire a delicious custardy middle. I needed a pie crust, so I asked A.J. to go to the store and get one, but Ben said he'd already made a better one from scratch, so he got it from the cooler, and I spread the sautéed onions in the bottom of the homemade pie crust, then poured the batter over the onions and popped it in the oven to bake for about a half hour.

"What's this for?" A.J. asked.

"Grief," I said.

While I waited for the pie to bake I went into my office and got on the computer and Googled Valentine to see what else I could find out about him, to see if he had any kin around.

A search for "Valentine" and "Charity, Georgia," turned up hits for the Hallmark store that had closed, a bunch of porn sites, some non-profits trying to raise money for heart conditions, and a hundred florists, most of them not even in town. I Googled Clarence Hart and got a dentist in Omaha and a New Zealand war hero. Who knew New Zealand was ever at war? Everybody was on the internet at this point, so it was surprising not to find at least a crumb or two on Valentine. Type in Lee Hubbs and you get all sorts of information about the family, Hubbs Fresh Produce, my grandfather and the invention of the Charity Sweet Onion, my father's obit, even the same pie recipe I'd just made. I checked it over to make sure I'd remembered all the steps. Of course I had. I Googled up Mel Blanc and was surprised to see that Valentine had been mostly right. Some radio actor had voiced Elmer Fudd, Mel Blanc providing only the occasional scream or laugh.

Given the shallow results of my search efforts, the plan I was cobbling together felt like a lot to accomplish, but I was determined to give someone an onion pie. Valentine had come to me in a dream and helped me understand why I had been dealt so many unfortunate blows of late. The world, no, the universe, sensed my carelessness and fucked everything up: had Jodi confess to my wife, made Kat leave me, knocked off her muffler, drowned my phone, slapped makeup on my best employee, burned my only son, stole my children, struck me with an itch I couldn't stop scratching, had me seeing a wheel everywhere.

Jodi might've had it right to begin with. I needed to face Valentine's family, look them in the eye, hand them a pie.

I called Marty again. "You got anything else on this thing you're not telling me?"

"I'm sure she's fine, Lee. If she's not home tomorrow, I'll go look for her. Will that work?"

"Not Kat. Valentine."

"I believe you know more than anyone about that."

"You sure he didn't have any kin?"

"I don't call you several times a day and tell you how to sell onions."

"I'd like to offer my condolences."

Marty snorted into the phone. "You're a piece of work. You run over the dude and you want to offer condolences? Seems to me you got some priorities out of whack."

I hoped he hadn't said this loud enough for Todd to hear.

I hung up and called the hospital to see if anyone had asked about Valentine or Clarence Hart. The woman wouldn't answer any questions because I wasn't family. We went around in circles, me claiming I was family and her wondering why I was looking for family if I was the family, and me saying I was looking for more family, and her going back to saying she couldn't answer my questions unless I was family.

"What happened to his body?" I asked.

"Ah-ha!" she said. "If you were family, you would know."

I poked around the internet some more looking for answers without really knowing the right questions. If somebody had claimed Valentine, I wanted to know who that was, but the internet wasn't going to tell me that. What it did tell me was something I hadn't really considered until now. What if nobody claimed him?

I found a Q&A on the Eechacohee County message board, a message board I didn't know existed, run by someone with the initials A.O. Who was this A.O.? What individual was the great and powerful know-it-all of the county? A certain questioner calling himself Curious Citizen asked a question about hitchhikers.

> Q: *What happens to hitchhikers when they die here and have no family? Thanks.*
> *— Curious Citizen*

> A: *Thank you for your question, C.C. Although it is not often the case that a vagabond expires in our county without contacts, it does happen. Last year the county experienced four such unidentified expirations and disposals, all of them paid for out of the county's coffers! Typically the vagabond expires at the hospital, and if there are no family members present, the body is taken to the county morgue—in our county, one of our local funeral homes. (I am not at liberty to say which one.) In Eechacohee County the length of cold storage lasts seven days while officials put in a "good faith effort" to find next of kin. If, after seven days, no next of kin can be located, or, if for various reasons they refuse to have anything to do with the deceased— understandable sometimes, huh?—the body is then either donated to the medical college or cremated at the*

*county's expense. Your tax dollars at
work!*

– A.O.

There were several oddities in this answer. The word
vagabond for one, and calling a dead person *expired* made them
sound like they were a carton of sour cream, nothing more than
a condiment with a short shelf life. And what was so secret about
the name of the funeral home? The information was most likely
public, and if not, the public could probably guess. There were
only so many. A.O. also appeared to have some personal
concerns about his or her tax money and could not refrain from
editorializing. Who would've guessed that unidentified bodies
sat in cold storage for a week waiting to be claimed, like a
refrigerated lost-and-found? And if nobody showed up to get the
body, then it was off to the laboratory or the ash heap,
Frankenstein or fertilizer. Valentine's body going to the medical
college probably wasn't such a bad thing. Maybe they'd use him
to finally discover what caused the quailing, harvest his organs
to save an entire population from genetic malfunction. A life
positively affecting other lives, even in death. Better than
cremation. Cremation didn't sit well with me.

My mother and I fought about this after Daddy died.
She wanted to take him with her. She wasn't planning on
staying in Charity forever, and if she wasn't staying in Charity
forever then she wanted him to be with her wherever she went.
I wanted him in the ground, on the plot with the rest of the
Hubbs family, a headstone I could visit out of a sense of
obligation and let flowers die upon. Cremation felt like total
destruction, erasure, whereas a tombstone bore your name and
your dates and a pithy saying or a bible verse of personal

meaning and significance. I had the perfect epitaph picked out: *The Lord hath given him rest from all his enemies.*

Pierce didn't care one way or the other, so sided with Mama because he couldn't see fit to agree with his brother on anything, so in the end she got what she wanted. Our father's ashes rested in a brassy urn she kept in her room at the nursing home, like she'd won him in a golf tournament.

The funeral home acting as the county morgue had to be either Anderson's or Faber and Moore. These were the largest. I called Anderson's because they were first in the alphabet. The woman at Anderson's was very helpful and expressed regret for my loss in a voice practiced from many past expressions of regret. She told me that, as far as she knew, Faber and Moore still took up this favor. I couldn't see how storing dead bodies was much of a favor if they were getting paid for it. Your tax dollars at work! But the woman's answer was a good answer for me, because I knew Floyd Faber.

A.J. poked his head in the office. "Pie's ready," he said.

The Unwanted

Faber and Moore funeral home was housed in an old mansion supposedly built in the early part of the last century by a man named Judge Coolbaugh, who wasn't a judge but a grocery store proprietor who founded the local grocery store Coolbaugh's, a Charity institution until the chain groceries swept through and put him out of business. The house had thick white columns and twin gnarly oaks out front looking like they might come to life at night when no one was watching. Whenever I'd ride by with my parents when I was little, I wondered what went on in there, how a person could work around dead people every day. Being around the dead so much, more so than the living, was bound to turn a man crazy, or at least spawn some bizarre nocturnal cravings.

Technically Faber and Moore was still owned by Floyd Faber's father and the descendants of Theodore (Teddy) Moore, but Floyd was the day-to-day operator. The Moore kids didn't want anything to do with the place except for keeping the name on the sign so they might feel entitled to some of the cut. I always liked Floyd. He was a few years older, but in some ways we were alike. He was a man who recognized obligation as opportunity. His father had a business, and so to resist going into that business would be to effectively stanch a legacy. And to him that legacy offered an opportunity, an opportunity to man up and make a living and raise a family and commit to a path through life as the proprietor of a business sure to withstand any ebb and flow in the market economy. People will always die, and the living will always need someone to take care of their dead, just like people will always need onions.

I told A.J. to wait in the car.

"Nope," he said, already out of the driver's seat. "This place is spooky as hell."

Floyd met us at the door and shook my hand coldly, then shook A.J.'s hand before leading us inside. I took my cap off out of respect, and tried to resist the urge to scratch. Floyd didn't notice the sore, or if he did, he didn't say anything. Probably well-trained in not pointing out people's flaws during their time of need. He took us through a wide foyer to a round room reminiscent of the Oval Office. One lonely plant sat on a stand where the corner of the room would've been had it possessed any corners. A rug in muted colors covered the floor under his desk, and two chairs wrapped in yellow upholstery sat opposite. Inoffensive pictures hung on the wall: landscapes, a black and white photo of the mansion, a tractor, a stack of barrels. Kat should sell him one of her paintings. It would blend right in. The books on the built-in bookshelf had never been touched, bindings color-coordinated in drab browns and grays to give the place a monkish feel. Maybe this was a design element I needed in my own office, a staged discomfort that would make the space less inviting to intruders.

Floyd always looked like he was made of wax, but I could never tell if this was actually because he was waxy or if it seemed that way because he was a mortician, like the power of suggestion, like Gabby, their occupations determining their appearance. Floyd was never sweating, and his black hair was always slickly combed and never out of place. It was like he ate light.

Did I look like someone who sold onions? What would that look like anyway?

He sat us down across from his well-cleaned desk in the upholstered chairs and asked how he could help.

"This may seem a little odd to you, Floyd, but do you have a man here named Clarence Hart?"

Floyd picked a Post-it note off the base of a desk lamp, his eyes scanning the pencil scribbles. "Did you know him?" he asked, a sparkle of hope in his voice.

"I talked to him a few times," I said.

"Who's Clarence Hart?" A.J. asked.

"We had some business together."

Floyd put the note on the base of the lamp and ran his finger across the top to activate the sticky strip.

"Too bad," he said. "I was hoping you'd come with helpful information. The unwanted are bad for business."

"The unwanted?"

"More trouble than they're worth. A waste of time and resources. Nine times out of ten if nobody shows up on day one then nobody's coming. It's depressing."

"He's talking about a dead guy, right?" A.J. asked.

Floyd sighed. "The unwanted make me confront the worst reality of this job: we all die alone." He shook his head and repeated this bit of doom and gloom. "We all die alone."

Perhaps we'd come to visit Floyd on a bad day. He sounded like the worst mortician in the history of mortuary sciences. An undertaker was probably better off not confronting the reality of man's solitary demise. His job was to assure people that death was the final fiesta: the bigger the party, the bigger the life. The more loved ones and flowers and music, the bigger the headstone, the more extravagant the statue, the more gaudy the mausoleum, the fancier the coffin—

the more proof of a rich life. And the richer someone lived, the richer Floyd Faber became. So maybe Floyd's morose approach on this day had more to do with money than with any sort of existential dread.

"Can you let me know if anybody comes by asking about him or looking for him?"

"Not likely, but I'll let you know."

We all stood up and shook hands again. Then Floyd motioned with a finger in the air like he'd forgotten something. Told us to stay put. He'd be right back. He left through a side door, a curved door molded to fit into the wall, some kind of secret door for quick escapes.

"Who's Clarence Hart?" A.J. asked again.

"You didn't know him."

"Doesn't sound like you did either." A.J. walked over to the plant and rubbed a leaf between his fingers, broke off a piece like he was seeing if it was real, smelled it, and let the broken leaf flutter to the floor. "When I die I want a party, a big party. I don't want nobody to cry either. I want music and stories and jokes. A thousand people. And I want to be cooked up and put in a cake, pieces of me passed out to everybody who loved me. My life a sweet dessert: the end of me, the end of the meal."

"I hope I die before you so I don't have to attend."

Floyd returned through the same secret door, flapping a Polaroid picture in his fingers. He handed it to me. A picture of Valentine, dead, of course, cold, a stony bluish gray. His head was covered, like he was wearing a hood so you couldn't see his plume, and I wondered if this was part of some insulation or space-age polymer the morgue used to zip someone up for increased shelf life. He had a sneaky kind of grin on his face, held in place by a snaggle-toothed incisor in the shape of a guillotine between his cracked lips.

My head itched so I put my cap on. We were on our way out anyway. "What'll you have me do with this, Floyd?"

"Reproduce it," he said. "Put it up at the store in the windows or on some napkins like a missing person flyer, wrap the napkin around every ice cream cone you sell. You get a lot of travelers through your place, Lee. Somebody might know something. Could you do that?"

"Sure," I said. But I had no intention of putting a picture of a dead quail on my ice cream napkins.

"You should be prepared with cost details should anyone want to know." Floyd pointed his taper-candle finger at a stack of brochures held in a glossy black plastic case at the edge of his desk. He slipped one off the top and handed it to A.J. "Cremation is most economical."

"What happens after cremation?" A.J. asked.

"That's up to the bereaved."

"Would it be possible to bake somebody in a—"

"—thanks, Floyd," I said.

"Hope you find something. Come next week he's headed to the medical college, and I'm out of luck."

"He's the one who's out of luck," A.J. said.

Floyd led us out, the double mansion doors creaking closed in front of him as he stood there in the foyer and waved like the butler of some haunted house.

Outside, A.J. grabbed the Polaroid. At first he didn't react, then he twisted up his face and tilted the picture this way and that, angling his head in thought or confusion. "That's the quail always riding that yellow bicycle."

"Used to be."

"What happened to him?"

"He had an accident."

"Can I keep this?"

"What for?"

"I don't know. I've never seen a dead body."

We got in A.J.'s car, the interior smoldering in the morning heat, an intense smell of baked onions and pie crust cooking in the floorboard. A.J. cranked the car and the AC. The air from the vents did nothing to help the smell.

"Know who he looks like?" A.J. asked. "Snoopy's cousin. What's his name?"

"Spike," I said.

"No."

"I'm positive it was Spike."

"I don't think so."

"He lived in the desert," I said. "His name was Spike."

"That ain't right. That's Scooby Doo."

"You're thinking of Scrappy, and he didn't live in the desert. Plus, that dog wasn't Scooby's cousin. He was his nephew."

"I thought Scrappy was Snoopy's cousin."

"Well, you're wrong."

"Look it up on your phone."

"My phone's dead," I said.

"We all die alone."

The Lord Hath Given Him Rest from All His Enemies

My mother's nursing home was across the street and only two blocks down, well within sight of Faber and Moore, ostensibly to give the residents a reason to rage against the dying of the light. Either that or the proximity was intended to ease the efforts of the orderlies as they wheeled the dead down the street. Typically I visited on Sundays after church. I'd try to bring the whole family, but Leo was scared of the place and said it smelled like underwear, and Kat never did care for my mother in the first place, so most of the time it was only me.

My mother was one of the younger ones there, and when she first arrived she fought us on it and said she was fine and wondered why she couldn't keep on living at the house with us because we sure did have enough room. But the thought of taking care of my mother as she battled a slow burn with dementia, while also trying to maintain a household, filled Kat with dread, so it wasn't happening. Kat convinced me that none of us would be able to give her the help and care she needed. The doctors agreed, and off she went.

This past Sunday she'd asked me to bring her a six-pack of canned Yoo-hoos. She kept them in her bedside table and drank them warm from multi-colored bendable straws. She believed she was getting away with something, hiding contraband, but nobody cared if she drank a damn Yoo-hoo. I had A.J. drive me to the closest drugstore so I could buy them; I bought A.J. a bag of Flamin' Hot Cheetos as a reward for toting me around.

Again I asked him to stay in the car because I wouldn't be long, but he refused, saying he'd never been in a nursing home before and was keen on acquiring new experiences.

I was a mama's boy through and through, while Pierce had been closer to my father. I suspect he secretly admired the fact his eldest son pursued a life of gallivanting and womanizing and petty crime, but my father held all his admiration in (just like he did everything else: affection, warmth, intelligence, care) until Pierce got into trouble and it withered into disappointment. I was the soft one growing up, the one who cried too much, the one who sucked his thumb, the one whom Mama protected, the one who hardly got in trouble, the one who toed the family line. She was proud of me for some reason, probably because I kept quiet, and she'd parade me around town dressed in the dumbest little outfits—matched shorts and shirts, my hair slicked down—while Pierce got to be whatever he wanted. He must've already been a lost cause in her eyes. Our family Christmas photos every year had me looking sharp in a Christmas sweater and khakis. Pierce had to wear the same thing, but he'd always manage to make it look sloppy. His pants would be wrinkled or his hair all messed up or he wouldn't be smiling, but there I'd be grinning like a slaphappy elf, holding whatever pet we had at the time, who'd be outfitted with a Santa hat or some other embarrassment. Mama made us stand in front of the tree for our annual Christmas card, and she sent it out every year until we both graduated from high school, and every year I grinned.

My mother would tell me things I didn't need to be told, things about her and my father, how she suspected he loved somebody else more than her, which was never proven. And she'd tell me that she could not possibly love anybody else more than she loved me, an odd thing to hear, because even though I loved my mother, I didn't feel like it was the kind of love she was talking about. I mean, there were times I felt more love for our dogs than I did for her, so how could anyone rightly say they could never love anything more? At night, she'd fall asleep in my bed with me sometimes when I hadn't asked her to. She would read a story, turn out the light, and lie down with me, and we'd both fall asleep. At some point she'd get up, but I never knew when.

If I was scared of the shadows in the middle of the night, or a noise outside startled me awake and I couldn't go to sleep I'd leave my room and walk down to my parents' room, the hallway lit by a single bulb nightlight, and I'd crawl into bed with them. There were times my father would wake up and tell me to go back to my room, assure me I had nothing to be afraid of, reiterating that this was their bed and I had my own bed so I should go get in it, but my mother would always wake up too, and tell him it was okay. She'd say, why's it okay for us to sleep together and for him to sleep all alone? And I'd nestle in the bed and my father would snore so loud that I assumed he was faking to get me to leave, which I never did.

Mama talked a lot. Liked to hear herself talk. Talked to me about people in town, about how their marriages were rotten, about how they were bankrupt, about how they were tight with their money, about how they were hypocrites, about how terrible they were to her in high school and how she was showing them all now. Never one to shy away from revenge or public embarrassment. One time when I got hit by a pitch in little league she came out on the field and started yelling at the pitcher. The pitcher started crying and his mother came out on the field and soon enough the two of them were yelling in each other's faces, and between the two red hot flares of shame on my cheeks I watched my mother pull this other woman's hair and karate chop her right in the throat like she was some kind of ninja. More people stayed away from us after that, and we became a dynamic duo, sitting on the same side of booths together, watching soaps together, doing everything. Together.

The disease hit out of nowhere and took her down fast. Soon after my father died, she got into her car and drove west two hundred miles until somebody found her in Alabama eating at a Waffle House. She knew who she was, where she lived, the year. But she thought she was at the Waffle House in Charity. This caused some alarm around the house, and so Kat started treating her like an infant, following her everywhere, trying to keep her constantly in sight. Mama got paranoid. Said that Katherine was plotting to kill her. So she started sleeping with a dull kitchen knife beside her bed and hoarding things from around the house, not valuables, not memorabilia, but shit: toys and Lego pieces and opened junk mail envelopes and pinecones and popsicle sticks, pieces of tape, pencil erasers. When she disappeared again—this time to Atlanta, where she was found eating sunny-side-up eggs at the Majestic Diner on Ponce de Leon—we knew we had to act. In her mind, the move to the home proved we were trying to kill her. But after a year or so she got used to it.

I was a minor luminary at the nursing home, because usually I'd bring fruit and gift baskets for the nurses to dole out or take home to their families. I'd say hello to all the residents too, ask them how they were doing. It doesn't take much to make an old fart's day. So I'd kneel next to their wheelchairs and say, "Hey, Miss Honey, you're as pretty as ever." And she'd smile and swell with pride. I'd pass old man Gundy—one of the meanest sons-a-bitches ever, principal at the high school before my time, but his reputation earned him a permanent place on the high school baseball field. (Gundy Field, they called it, even though the asshole never coached baseball, swung a bat, or attended a game for all I know. Maybe they all assumed he had by the way he swung his paddle.) Gundy would be creeping the halls in his walker, looking mean as hell, and I'd tell him hello and ask him if he was getting any. He had to act appalled by the question, scowling as if passersby could hear. Then he'd lean close to me and say, "I'm made of snatch!" which never made sense to me, but he always got a kick out of it. And there was Delight, an old quail who loved her coloring books. No idea if Delight was her real name, but that's what everyone called her. Sometimes I'd bring Delight a coloring book. She was always coloring in the TV room, stuck at a round table streaked with Crayola, the crayons piled in a Nike shoebox. She took them out one by one and put them back one by one, and her coloring made no pretense at realism: purple skins and red skies and black trees. Horrifying stuff, seeing Hello Kitty shaded a burnt orange in front of hot pink clouds while riding a blood-red skateboard. Leo would love it.

But this morning I had nothing to give, nothing to offer anyone else but my mother, so I skipped out on playing mayor, and A.J. and I went straight to her room.

She sat in her plush rocker and held a big book of Sudoku puzzles. She had remarkable spells of clarity, the nurses told me, times where she would seem totally herself, where she could work puzzles and remember songs and understand why she was where she was and how she ended up there, where she could remember the names of her elementary school teachers and phone numbers of her friends. This could last anywhere from a few hours to a few days, and they always ended badly, always with Mama trying to escape or hurt herself.

"Hey, Mama," I said, and kissed her on the top of her hair. She smelled like fruity shampoo and drugs. The Sudoku puzzle hadn't been worked at all; she'd simply been coloring in the squares with a pencil, each square perfectly shaded in diagonal strokes of gray. I leaned down and whispered. "Brought you some Yoo-hoo."

She smiled and raised a finger to her lips. "Hush," she said. "They'll hear you."

My mother had never not known who I was. I had never walked in and had her look at me in confusion. I was always her son, always Lee. She'd say the craziest shit about things that had never happened, and even claim sometimes to have had a daughter that she believed was killed because she drank poison and somehow Mama was responsible. These fake daughter episodes were the worst, always getting her too upset to visit. She'd mistake Kat for this daughter sometimes, and it freaked everybody out. They say everything keeps getting smaller, shrinking: your brain, your organs, all of it shriveling up inside the shell that's still the body.

My mother smiled and held out her arms, gesturing to A.J. for a hug. He obliged, even though they'd never met. I opened up a can of Yoo-hoo and stuck a purple straw in and stashed the rest in the cabinet of her bedside table. She'd been right. She was out. Sometimes she'd ask for more when she didn't need them, and I'd bring a six-pack only to find out there was still a six-pack sitting there in the cabinet, and I'd have to leave the extra for the orderlies.

"That boy is very handsome," she said.

"Yes ma'am," A.J. said, and sat down on a bench near the window where he picked up one of those triangle golf tee games you see at the Cracker Barrel, the ones where you've got to leave one hole missing and jump all the tees to reveal your I.Q. It was supposed to keep her mind sharp and occupied. I worried she'd use them to poke her eyes out.

"How's Pierce?" she asked. She was always asking about my brother, even when she couldn't remember his name. How's my boy, she'd say. How's my other one? It was like she harbored a deep guilt for never going to see him, essentially disowning him during his troubles. The way they treated him then was all my father's doing, and as much as my brother was a fool, it bothered me the way they let go of him as if they'd never made any mistakes. I always made up a few lies to tell her about Pierce. He was never coming to see her anyway, and she had no way to fact-check.

"He's good. Won a golf tournament the other day on some amateur circuit. Told me he'd send you the trophy."

She waved her hand across her face like she was swatting flies. "That old witch would steal it like she did my other one. Came right in and snatched it. The thief." Mama sucked her Yoo-hoo through her straw.

A.J. was deep into the golf tee game. He left one tee in the holes and lifted it up to show me. "Genius," he said.

My mother hadn't had any trophies in her room, so I wasn't sure what she was talking about.

"What trophy, Mama?"

"The one your daddy gave me for putting up with his poop." She laughed a laugh that revealed every bit of her as my mother, the one I'd known my whole life: a high, chirpy laugh, almost like she was trying to keep it in, tamp it down, like laughing wasn't ladylike, like a laugh was a sneeze you had to cover up. It made me miss her. It occurred to me then that she was talking about the urn with my father's ashes. It was gone. She knew this to be true even if the facts she gave were dubious, so I didn't want to get her more riled up then she already was by revealing the fact that her husband's ashes were actually what was missing, not some imaginary trophy.

I kissed her again on her head and told her we had to split but that I'd come see her as usual on Sunday. "They'll bring your trophy back," I said. "Somebody'll find it."

"Gone and forgotten," she said.

A.J. stood up from the bench and set the golf tee game down.

"Who's your friend?" she asked, pointing at him like it was the first time she'd seen him.

On the way out I asked one of the nurses what happened to the urn that had been in my mother's room. The nurse I spoke to told me to hold on a second and she called over some other woman I'd spoken to several times in person and on the phone. She was a counselor or physical therapist or Alzheimer's expert who held some special dominion over my mother's particular condition. A tall, thin woman, taller than me, a woman who drew a kind of strength from her height, literally and figuratively towering above everyone. She could almost look A.J. in the eye. She held the urn in her long arms like she was cuddling a baby.

"I tried to call you," the woman said. "We had to remove the urn from your mother's room. We found her dumping it on the floor and scrubbing like she was trying to clean up a stain. I'm sorry."

"My father's in there," I said.

"I know. We're truly sorry. We saved what was left of him." She held out the urn for me.

A.J. could sense my hesitation and took the urn from her. He tapped the brass with his fingers. "Heavy," he said.

I rode with the urn in my lap all the way to the store. I didn't really think I was holding my father, what was left of him. Didn't think about the irony of him holding me as an infant and me holding him now inside a vessel more fit for flowers. Didn't think about the fact that the only person who still cared about this man—my mother, his wife—had tried to dump him out and clean the floor with him, and now wouldn't miss him. Whatever glow the curve of the urn gave off at night assuring her he was still with her was gone, and would stay gone. Because this wasn't him. This wasn't a man. This was dust.

I took the urn inside my office and set it on my desk. A.J. followed me in, carrying the onion pie.

"Can't leave this in my car, boss. It stinks."

I scribbled the words *Don't Eat* on a Post-it, slapped it on the foil, and asked him to put the pie in the cold room.

I stared at my father's urn. It stared back. All judgmental. I grabbed it and went outside, took the lid off the slop bucket of rotten fruit and vegetables we always saved for Mr. Ferris and his hogs, a bed of squashed and rotten tomatoes, bruised and soft peaches, leaky melons, black onions, burnt cobblers.

"The Lord hath given him rest from all his enemies," I said, and dumped him in. Seasoning for a hog feast.

I rinsed the urn out in the dish sink and left it upside down on a drain board to dry.

Buckets of My Brothers

I was eager to head out to the quail park with the pie and see if I could find anyone who knew Valentine, but I was also hungry, so I asked Ben to walk down to Kentucky Fried Chicken for me, but he politely refused. Said he was sorry but he couldn't encourage the consumption of fowl. Apparently turning quail also turned you vegetarian. I told him I understood and appreciated where he was coming from, but since he wasn't the one doing the consuming, why did I have to be a vegetarian today, too?

"They look like buckets of my brothers," he said.

I didn't press the issue, pleased that Ben had found the courage to express himself, even if it was a gruesome defiance of my request. Still, it wasn't going to stop me from eating fried chicken, so I walked down to KFC myself and got a meal deal: a breast, two legs, and a thigh, mashed potatoes and gravy, biscuits I drenched with local honey from my honey bee man over in Hawkinsville. Lucky for me I always kept an emergency bottle of Beam in the desk drawer reserved for files.

I poured some Beam in a coffee mug and ate at my desk while I checked email. Finally. One I wanted.

Lee,

They're fine. And Katherine's fine too.
That's all I'm going to say to you right now.

Memu

Kat was all right. I had no idea if she was with her parents or if she was with the kids or if they'd taken the kids to her, but she was okay, and they were okay. I was no closer to reuniting with my family, but I was thankful that Memu thought enough of me to send an email with an update on their well-being. This meant all was not lost, and besides, if I harbored any intentions of giving somebody a pie today, then it would be a helluva lot easier to service this errand with my kids out of the way.

There was a light tap on my door, so I told whoever it was to come on in.

Jodi. She shut the door and sat in the leather chair. The left side of her head was buzzed while the rest stayed shaggy, like she'd now tried to style what she'd originally done impetuously. At this rate she'd be skinned before she left for the Amazon.

"It smells like farts and whiskey in here," she said.

"My signature."

"You look like doo-doo."

"You look like a boy."

"Boys don't have these," she said, and pushed her tits up until they were almost spilling up and out of the low cut V-neck girly-girl T's I had all my female employees wear. Let me tell you something, if it walks like a duck and talks like a duck, and one night after closing, the duck offers you a back rub, and then that back rub leads to other forms of rubbing, would you be able to resist for what all intents, purposes, and appearances was a fine-looking duck?

"I know where you've been," she said.

"I've been lots of places, sugar."

"I want to help. I'll start a GoFundMe page."

"A what?"

"For Valentine. A.J. told me you went to the funeral home. I'll write something up and ask for donations."

I had a better idea. I couldn't keep asking A.J. for rides, and I'd kept him away from the store too long anyway. Jodi's eagerness to make amends would work to my advantage. "You really want to help?" I asked. "How about you run me by the quail park?"

"What for?"

"Valentine lived out there." I finished off the bourbon in my mug. "And you owe me for ruining my marriage."

Jodi curled a phantom piece of hair over her left ear. "I'll do it for gas," she said.

She had me fill up her tank with dirty gas from Kroger even though I offered to buy her the good stuff from BP.

"They still haven't cleaned up that oil spill," she said.

I tossed her a bag of Fritos, as a bonus.

The Charity Quail Park and Campgrounds was down a service road and tucked in a wooded area near the Eechacohee Creek. If you were being politically incorrect, you called the park a coop, and if you were being generous, you called it a sanctuary, but it was really no more than a trailer park where some quails lived. Originally, the park and others like it across the country were designed as quarantine camps for those who turned quail, penning up the afflicted with the hope of biding time for a cause or a cure. Only problem was, it didn't spread like that, and families were separated across high concertina-wired fences, and grassroots organizations and protest groups started up demanding they be released. Then came what the updated history books refer to as the Great Toledo Terror, where quails in Ohio ripped down the fence with the help of vigilantes. The National Guard was already there and opened fire. It was a massacre. This enlivened the sympathies of even the most anti-quail among us, seeing dead quails lying in piles, gas scorching the eyes of children, men in full combat gear beating the shit out of women like they'd been itching for such an opportunity. It was a gross display of wanton force, and it greatly swayed public opinion on the quail question. The camps were all closed, but some quails reclaimed them as sanctuaries, finding it better to live peacefully among their own kind than in a world that didn't know what to make of them.

A worn dirt path circled the perimeter of the quail park like a racetrack, probably used for such a thing late at night, barefoot kids on tricycles and four-wheelers trying not to break their necks whizzing around the curves. No helmets. Along the path in no detectable shape or pattern sat RV's, pop-up campers, Winnebagos, mobile homes angled with makeshift additions, patios, and green-shingled carports. In the patchy grass out front an old plastic slide sat losing its color next to a brown brick building, likely a community bathroom and shower and rendezvous for gay sex. Two dogs chased each other around trash bins and stacks of recyclables. Unlit Christmas bulbs were roped from utility poles to the eaves of trailers and into the trees. The park probably transformed into a carnival atmosphere at night, with those lights lit up and everybody outside their homes grilling and talking about their multiple failures over cases of cheap beer.

At the front entrance was an office in a trailer, which I knew to be the office because of the peeling mailbox letters on the front door that said *OFFICE*. Jodi pulled in and put her car in park. "I hope nobody sees us together," she said.

"What're you worried about it?" I asked. "You already told the one person who mattered."

"People don't need any more reason to talk about me."

She was feeling sorry for herself. People talked about Jodi no more than they talked about anybody else. "Let me explain something to you, Jodi. People will talk, and they won't know half the shit they talk about when they talk."

"That's brilliant."

"Wait here. And don't eat the pie." I pointed to the tin-foil covered pie in her floorboard.

"What's the pie for?" she asked.

"Grief."

At first I didn't see anyone inside the office as my eyes adjusted to the dark. An AC unit chugged and spit in the window. Two oscillating fans curled the corners on magazines and papers pinned down with coffee mugs.

A woman's voice came from somewhere in the murk. "Can I help you?"

I blinked twice to make her out. She sat behind a desk, almost camouflaged against her yellowed and faded surroundings, the quailiest looking quail I'd ever seen: plump, with great big round glasses and a yellow-brown plume that quivered every time the fans rotated toward her face. She didn't move, and I wondered if she was capable of movement or if she was wedged behind the desk against the wall so tight she'd have to be rescued with the jaws of life so she could go on her lunch break.

The AC whined like a hurt child. "I'm looking for Valentine's place."

"Nobody here by that name." Only her mouth moved, nothing else. Maybe it was too hot for her to move. She was conserving her energy.

"Clarence Hart?" I asked.

"Nope." She still didn't move. She was like some animatronic quail mascot at a bad historical monument to the camps. I wanted to shove her, poke her, pick up the hand grenade paper weight at the edge of her desk and throw it at her.

"Rode a yellow bicycle," I said.

This set her in motion. She leaned forward, and a valve released air from places I couldn't see, an inflatable raft seeping out. She picked up a clipboard. "End of the road."

I thought she was telling me my business here was done, I'd reached the end of the line, but that's not what she meant.

"Lot 29," she explained, and melted into her chair, folding her fingers together over the sunbaked hills in her brown shirt.

I thanked her and started to leave.

"He's dead, you know?"

I hadn't gotten her name, probably a Maggie or a Laverne, a big woman's name. What did Maggie-Laverne think of Valentine? Did she know him enough to be the recipient of this onion pie? Did she care enough to be the one to claim his body and send him off? It was more likely they had no relationship at all. Valentine probably paid her in cash. If he paid her. Never needed to know each other's names. She didn't seem like the type of woman who'd care one way or another what you did in your own home as long as you paid on time. And since Valentine had stopped paying for reasons he could not help, he was out of her mind.

"Sorry to hear it," I said. "I'd like to offer my condolences."

"Keep 'em," she said.

I climbed in with Jodi and told her to drive around. She followed the oval all the way to the rear edge of the park where a rusted blue-and-white sign marked the number, 29. She parked at the edge of the path where the red clay met what was trying to be grass. The home at Lot 29 was a large white Fleetwood travel trailer. Out front, two plastic chairs that were probably white once upon a time sat on either side of a small stool topped with the mouth of an ashtray coughing up cigarette butts. The place looked deserted and sad, like the face of an old dog begging to be shot. A ripped and billowy awning hovered over the door, and a muddy waterline squiggled around the siding like the whole trailer had been buried in a great flood and later exhumed, a shipwrecked yacht salvaged from the deep.

"How long is this going to take?" Jodi asked.

"I'm looking for somebody who knew him. You should be happy about that."

"This place is straight out of a horror movie."

"Well I hope he's not in there waiting to eat our brains."

"He'll starve if he gets you first," she said.

The air was swampy. Bugs wheeled and whizzed in my ears, dive-bombed my nostrils. I heard a baby crying. Someone yelled. "Eat shit!" and then what sounded like "hegemony!" Some rednecks having an intellectual debate. A steady *clank, clank, clank* of metal hitting metal echoed over the campgrounds, someone trying to repair an engine or forge a weapon on an anvil. Other than the two gray chairs and the stool, nothing else was in the front yard. On cinder block steps leading up to the door, a small terracotta pot stood with an oily puddle covering its black soil. A foil wrapper from an ice cream sandwich tumbled across the steps.

Jodi was still in the car eating her Fritos.

I peeked in the window on the front door and couldn't see anything. Just dark. I circled around the outside of the trailer. On the other side, parked underneath the shade of a tree, was a white Monte Carlo with orange mud splattered up its side. The grass got thick and heavy closer to the woods, so I was on the lookout for snakes. Water trickled in the creek, but I couldn't see it. I wondered if a flood really had washed the whole campgrounds out, if that was what had happened to this trailer. Had the great flood of '94 sunk the trailer park, swallowed the small RVs and crawled halfway up the larger ones? Had this poor Fleetwood been here since then?

When I circled back from surveying the property, Jodi was standing there. "You're the world's shittiest detective." She walked up the two steps of the trailer and turned the small metal door knob. The door opened. I could tell she expected it to be locked because she tripped backwards as she pulled.

"The hell?" a woman's voice shouted from the trailer.

Jodi backed down the steps and we both retreated, hoping not to be shot.

A figure emerged from the dark of the trailer into the day, a cavewoman framed in the opening of her home, woken up from hibernation. She had hair more gray than blonde, dirty and sprung in all directions. She was not a quail, as far as I could tell. She wore black sweat pants with the word *Pink* stretching in glitter letters down the side of the leg. She wrestled her arms into a red cardigan like it was chilly outside. Underneath she wore a tank top, no bra, but not because she didn't require one. "Can I help you fuckers?" she asked, without a tinge of welcome. We were lucky she hadn't come out firing.

"Do you know a man named Valentine?" I asked.

The woman ran a hand over her hair, taming it down. "I've been through this," she said. "Unless he left me a million dollars or a boat, I don't care."

"So you know what happened?"

The woman took a seat in one of the gray chairs. She pulled a cigarette from the pocket of her cardigan and lit it up with the flick of a purple disposable lighter. She eyed Jodi suspiciously, as if she didn't trust her, or at least like she didn't appreciate her yanking the door open and waking her up from a snooze. Understandable. "I know he's dead," she said, and offered us both cigarettes.

I said no thanks and took a step closer to her. Jodi didn't move. Her eyebrows told me she was scared.

"I'm sorry," I said. "I'd like to offer my—"

"Why?"

"Pardon?"

"Why? Why are you sorry?"

I wanted to tell her I was sorry because I was the man who ran him over, but was that really why? Or was I sorry because his dying had screwed up my life? I was sorry to be running around searching for somebody to give a pie to. I was sorry that my wife had stolen my truck and left, and that my in-laws had kidnapped my children. I was sorry that I'd shaved my beard and that my whole body itched like a symposium of scabies. We all say we're sorry when somebody dies, but what we really mean is, glad it wasn't me. "We were friends," I said.

She laughed and blew smoke from her nostrils. "That man had friends?"

"I take it you weren't close?"

The woman smiled at Jodi and cocked her head. "She your girlfriend?"

Jodi rolled her eyes and huffed to her car. I worried she was about to take off and leave me like the other night, but she started the engine and stayed put, some dull music murmuring behind the rolled up windows. There was no evidence of the accident on the vehicle, still I questioned the wisdom of us driving the weapon right to this woman's front door.

"A little young, don't you think?" the woman asked.

I put my hand out to introduce myself. This encounter was heading in the wrong direction. And I did not need morality lessons at a quail park. "Lee Hubbs," I said.

The woman grabbed my hand but didn't shake; instead she used my grip to yank herself up from the chair. The move brought her close to me, close enough to smell her: fry grease, cigarettes, and a mixture of motor oil and gasoline, like she'd recently been operating a lawnmower. Heavy rings looped below her eyes, and she had thin red branches on both her cheeks like she'd been aggressively blowing her nose.

"Anne," she said. She patted me on the shoulder. "Want a drink?" She looked down at her arm to a watch that wasn't there. "It's five o'clock in Zaire," she said, and walked up the steps and inside her trailer. I was glad Jodi wasn't there to correct the woman on her ignorance of time zones and countries lost to history.

I followed Anne inside. The door clattered from its hinges and about fell off in my hands. She dropped her cigarette in the open hole of a ginger ale can. The room was dark, a rust-colored dark that matched the mud stains on the exterior, and the place stunk like ashtrays and mold. Anne stood in what passed for a kitchen, plopping ice cubes from a tray into two clear plastic cups next to a whiskey bottle with a brown label and red letters that said *BOURBON* on it like a stage prop. She poured both cups half full of bourbon then reached into a small, square fridge for a ginger ale and filled the cups the rest of the way. She stirred both of them with her finger.

I felt queasy. I twisted the bill of my cap to scratch the itch. Some kind of AC unit sat on the floor dripping and clugging in the corner, barely pumping out damp air. She squeezed by me and went to what would be her bedroom where she plopped down on her bed.

"Make yourself comfortable," she said.

I found a metal folding chair and sat down.

"He was my brother," she said, raising her drink to me in a toast. "I let him crash here because I'm a saint."

This woman looked nothing like Valentine. One obvious difference being she wasn't a quail, but it didn't happen to entire families, nothing genetic. Her place didn't bear any other evidence of cohabitation despite being pretty spacious for a trailer. It was odd that someone who wasn't a quail would choose to live here, but it wasn't unheard of. The park was cheap and secluded, and I took Anne for a woman who valued those two qualities.

I took a swig off my drink and stared into the cup watching the ice melt to tiny oars floating on fizzy currents. The bourbon was terrible, distilled from a mash of rotted wood chips and barbecue sauce.

"Half-brother," she said. "Same mama, different daddies."

I didn't know what to say. I wanted to rush right out and grab the onion pie, hand it to her, offer my condolences, but I couldn't move. My head was floating away like a soap bubble.

"I'll tell you what I told the cop. Our mama's down in Statesboro. Doubt she'll much care, either."

The thought of completely losing track of one of my kids, not caring if they were even alive, settled raw in my gut. What I was hearing didn't make any sense. She'd talked to a cop, but Marty'd said he couldn't find any next of kin, couldn't find anybody who cared. But I guessed I was mistakenly conflating a half-sister with somebody who cared.

"Statesboro." I swallowed the nausea rising up my throat. "Can you be more specific?"

"Why? You looking for money or something?" She gazed up at the ceiling with her cup resting on her stomach. I followed her eyes. A large poster hung on the ceiling, an old, fading poster of what appeared to be a rainbow cornucopia. A waterfall cascaded in the background, and springing from a curved rainbow was an all-star cast of mythical beasts and figures: a unicorn, a cyclops, an ogre, nymphs and fairies, elves, a minotaur, centaurs, and sirens, all of them with happy faces like they were headed to a Renaissance festival. In red Magic Marker, someone had drawn a quail joining the parade.

Anne took a deep breath and shut her eyes like she was praying. "It's rare," she said. "But sometimes we get what we deserve."

I stood up wobbly and knocked my chair over trying to balance. The tiny AC laughed at me. My stomach churned and I ran outside the trailer, tripping over something on the way out. I stumbled down the cinder blocks and skidded on my knees in the dirt and grass. I coughed and threw up my lunch: chunks of fried chicken skin and half-digested biscuit. I caught my breath. My eyes watered and my throat burned. Propped not twenty yards away, next to an ancient Airstream, was Valentine's bicycle wheel, staring at me like a spoked eyeball, yellow rimming its edges.

Jodi came over holding the pie.

The trailer door opened and slapped against the siding, no stop chain.

"A lightweight?" Anne asked.

No more was coming. I spit and shut my eyes tight. Opened them again. The wheel was there, not propped against anything, but standing on its own in a patch of grass.

Jodi hooked her free hand through the crook of my elbow and helped me to my feet. I took the pie from her and held it out to Anne.

"We'd like to offer our condolences."

She was too far away to grab the pie, but she didn't look interested.

"It's an onion pie," I said.

She scrunched up her nose. "Who the hell wants an onion pie?"

Jodi led me and the pie to the car.

"Look over there." I nodded to the Airstream. "Tell me what you see."

"It's a trailer," she said.

"No. In front. Do you see a wheel?"

"A wagon wheel."

She was right. Stuck in the ground was the rusted frame of a wagon wheel, probably used to tie up dogs or wild children.

Jodi opened the passenger side and let me in, pointed the vents in my face. She shut the door and walked over to where I'd thrown up; she kicked dirt over the mess like a kitty cat erasing all evidence of its crap.

Anne sat down in one of the gray chairs and lit a cigarette. Jodi walked over there. Anne didn't stand up, and Jodi didn't take the empty seat. They talked. The way Jodi stood there hovering over Anne made it look like she was reprimanding her, giving her a stern talking to, but if she was it must've been in a way that Anne found amusing, because she smiled the entire length of their conversation, which wasn't long. Anne stood up and went inside the trailer. Jodi turned around, and her eyebrows told me everything was going to be cool. When Anne came back she handed Jodi the Care Bear backpack Dawn had given Valentine, pink with the Care Bear who's got a big red heart on its belly, whichever one that was. Might've been what I'd tripped over on my way out the door.

The two of them waved at each other and then Anne waved to me as Jodi walked away. I held up my hand.

Jodi got in, handed me the backpack, and drove us around the dirt oval.

"What's this?"

"His personal effects."

The backpack smelled faintly of iron.

"What do I want those for?"

"I told her I was taking up donations for Valentine's memorial service."

"So she gave you all his shit?"

"She said she wasn't giving us a dime, but we could sell all his stuff if we wanted."

We drove by the office at the front entrance. The woman had extracted herself from behind her desk and was sitting in a big chair under a wide green-and-white golf umbrella, a newspaper spread in front of her face. As we drove by, she folded a corner, and her plume carefully followed our exit.

Tenderheart Bear

I went through the Care Bear backpack in my office, but not before I Googled up which Care Bear adorned the backpack, wanting to put a name to the sweet-smiling face. His nose was shaped as a heart. Couldn't help but want to give him a squeeze.

Tenderheart Bear.

Inside the pack was a zippered pencil case shaped like a pencil, and inside the zippered pencil case were actual pens and pencils, a pencil sharpener, a small flashlight and some erasers, and fifty-five cents in change, which I figured could go towards Jodi's memorial fund. The backpack itself still bulged to busting, and as I pulled out more and more stuff, its girth didn't seem to diminish. It was the clown car of carryalls. A smushed up roll of toilet paper. Three packs of guitar strings. A pair of tasseled moccasins that looked like they'd never been worn. A foam tomahawk from a Braves game, a paperback copy of *Love Story*, some plastic binoculars, a half-eaten Almond Joy, three bottles of 5-hour Energy (pomegranate flavored), a cassette tape of Neil Young's *After the Gold Rush*, a pack of Marlboro Menthols with two broken cigarettes, a handful of AA batteries, a puka shell necklace, a phone charger, a bag of salted nuts, a small brown notepad with nothing in it but poorly rendered sketches of pigeons, a pair of cutoff jean shorts, a silver travel mug for coffee bearing the letters of a radio station *WRVR – The River! Statesboro's Home for Classic Rock!* And at the very bottom of the backpack, wadded up next to a set of blue Trivial Pursuit cards held together with a rubber band, was that red-and-black western shirt with the badass eagle.

Somebody knocked on the door. "Come on in," I said.

Ben stood there staring at me from underneath our extra soft and comfortable 100% cotton Hubbs hoodie, hiding like he'd done something wrong or was waiting on my permission to speak.

"Why you wearing a hoodie, Ben? It's a thousand degrees outside."

"But it's cold inside."

"What are you doing inside?"

"I'm transitioning."

"Pardon?"

"A.J. said it'd be easier for me to work on our menu inside."

"Your menu, huh? Did you speak to me about this?"

Ben shook his head.

A.J. was over the line. The extra responsibilities I'd given him had gone straight to his fake plume. We'd have to have a talk.

"I need you outside. Stay outside. The girls got the inside covered."

Ben's shoulders slumped and he started to walk away. "Ben," I called. "Didn't you come in here for a reason?"

He turned around. "Oh, yeah. Some kid out there wants a cone for their ice cream."

"And this is news?"

"But she don't want the ice cream on the cone. She wants it in a cup with the cone on top."

"I'm still looking for your point."

"Should I charge the price for a cup of ice cream AND a cone of ice cream? Or is there, like, a separate price for the cone. Feels kinda wrong to charge for both when it's really just getting a cup with a cone on top, you know?"

"Birthday-hat style."

"Sir?"

"Birthday-hat style. That's what it's called. Cone on top."

"I never knew."

I hated being bothered with this. My employees were always coming in to ask me questions they already knew the answer to. If Ben could've reviewed his own words he would've discovered the answer to his own question. But that's the price I pay for being a strong leader.

"What do you think you should do, Ben?"

"Give her the cone?"

"No. We're not in the business of giving anything away."

"We give away slices of peaches."

"That's a sample, to get people committed to buying the whole peach. Everybody knows what an ice cream cone tastes like. There's no variation in the taste of an ice cream cone. Therefore, there's no need for them to sample it or get it for nothing."

"Charge extra for the cone then?"

"There you go."

"What's the price of the cone?"

"Whatever. Fair market value. I don't know. Twenty-five cents."

Ben smiled like he'd received his MBA.

"Now take off that hoodie," I said. "You look like a thug."

I stuffed all Valentine's crap in his Tenderheart backpack and walked it down to Dawn's. The quail with the pink plume was there, but Dawn was gone, which was probably for the best given what had happened after I borrowed her truck. I introduced myself, and she said she knew who I was, but didn't offer her own name in return.

I dumped the Care Bear backpack on the glass countertop and asked her if they'd like to buy any of this stuff. Whatever money I got would go to a memorial fund for Valentine.

"Valentine's dead?" she asked.

I thought everyone who'd known him had already been made aware of this fact, or else had simply assumed he'd disappeared without a trace.

"I'm afraid so."

She shook her head, indicating the rotten luck of it all. "He was funny," she said. "Always in a good mood." She smiled as she poked through the contents of the backpack with a miniature Louisville Slugger baseball bat, perhaps remembering fondly a conversation they had about their similarities, something he'd said that brightened her day, a time they'd shared lunch on a breezy weekday exchanging hopes and dreams. Maybe this woman was the one to receive the pie, right here under my nose the whole time, the one person who gave a shit about Clarence Hart. "Did you know much about him?"

"He cut my grass once," she said.

"That's it?"

"I know Dawn had to lock all the guitars in her office when he was working. I caught him walking out of here with a Telecaster once. He claimed he was taking it out for some air. Told me guitars are like pets and need to be walked and bathed and paid attention to or else they die of loneliness." She never looked up from Valentine's stuff, poking and prodding like it was all tainted with small pox. When she was done, she swept the pile of Valentine's goods into the mouth of the backpack and tamped it all down with her tiny bat. "Nothing in here's worth a damn. But I'll give you five dollars for the backpack."

I told her the backpack wasn't for sale.

Only Love Can Break Your Heart

The afternoon got busy, picking up with weekend traffic. The sheer number of travelers any given weekend during the summer was heartening for a small business proprietor: all these people cruising up and down I-75 in their cars and trucks and SUVs and motor coaches, all headed to and from the Sunshine State, because everybody knows there's not one destination in the southern half of Georgia between Charity and the Florida line. Kids watching movies from the backseat. Dads drinking light beer in the front, promising themselves they'll only have one more. Moms knitting or reading trashy magazines or wondering where they might've gone wrong in their life to be hurtling down the highway in a car they can't afford with kids they can't stand to a state that's no fun. And what do we do here at Hubbs Fresh Produce? We add a little light to these lives. A beacon of blessed fruit in the highway wilderness. Stop in for fresh homemade peach ice cream and some southern hospitality and catch your breath. Peruse the aisles of summer harvest, the colors almost popping your eyes out with intensity. Would you like to try a boiled peanut? A what? A boiled peanut. A goober pea. It's a delicacy. Warm and salty on the tongue. Mmm-mm. How about a painting of an old Coca-Cola sign rusting on the side of a filling station? You like decrepit landscapes? We got that. Floral patterned picnic baskets? Monogrammed beach towels? Scuppernong wine? Come on in! Have a seat out front in one of the white rocking chairs and fan yourself with one of our custom *I'm a Hubbs Fan!* fans while the juice from a slice of fresh watermelon drips down your fingers. You can transport yourself to another time, a simpler time. It's a lot for a produce market to do, but we offer the taste of a memory, living history, a hokey vision of a falsely idealized past. In the fall you should see how high we stack the cotton.

So the day got away from me, and with it my determination to find someone who deserved an onion pie. This is what work is for, when it's good: to keep us from the thoughts that would otherwise break us down, cripple us with self-doubt, self-reflection, self-awareness. We work so we don't have to work on ourselves.

Around seven I slung on Valentine's backpack and asked Jodi for a ride home. Told her she could knock off for the rest of the evening.

"Wow," she said. "A whole hour."

The ride was quiet, so I put Valentine's Neil Young cassette in the tape deck, and Neil sang to us in that rusty-hinged voice of his that somehow was supposed to inspire rebellion. Never a big fan myself, but I'd be a fool if I didn't recognize the significance of his words at that particular moment, like Valentine was sending them to me from the great beyond.

Jodi pulled up in my circular driveway. My family wasn't home. The dark house reeked of loneliness in the falling dusk. I didn't want to get out of the car.

"You want to come in?" I asked. "I don't think there's much in the fridge, but I can probably make us something to eat. Peanut butter sandwiches. I know there's peanut butter."

"I don't think so," she said.

"You know Kat left me, don't you? Stole my truck and left me."

"I'm not telling you I'm sorry."

I reached for the dial and turned down the volume, snuffing out Neil's squeaky voice. "So none of this is your fault? I seem to recall you starting the whole thing."

"You gave me permission."

"Listen, a man will permit a lot of things with a girl's hand down his pants."

Jodi turned to face me, her eyebrows all stern and serious, at odds with her comical hair. "And because you gave me permission, *you* set the rules. And yeah, that was exciting, a new set of rules, thinking there might not even be any rules, and believing you loved me. You, a man, a man with a family, a job, a grown man. Believing I needed to be loved like that."

"Your therapist is worth every penny."

"But I was wrong," she said. "You never loved me. You don't love anybody."

I grabbed the Tenderheart backpack and got out of the car, held the door open. "Let me explain something to you. People don't need to know everything there is to know about everybody else, and it's the withholding of certain bits of information that allows this world to continue on without spiraling into chaos. Too much truth, too much honesty, our lives open on the internet. This is not a bright future, sweetheart. When nobody's got secrets anymore, we all show our true selves, and it ain't pretty. We need protection from that. From the basic truth of humanity, the truth every swinging dick's been running from since the garden: we're all sinners. And that includes you."

She didn't say anything. Her eyebrows crept away from her face toward my front door.

I went on: "Now. Since you've potentially torn apart my family, how about you tell Kat you were lying about me and you? Do that and I'll donate to your Valentine fund. Anonymously, of course."

Jodi turned up the volume. Neil Young whined back to life.

"Let me explain something to *you*," she said, and popped the shifter in drive and squealed away from me, reaching over as she swung around the driveway to pull the door shut, a highly professional driving move.

I walked around the side of the house to go in through the garage. Only strangers and Jehovah's Witnesses come to the front door. Kat's crossover had been towed, along with the muffler, the first positive signs all day, and I remembered I needed to call Wayne Salley and see what the damage was so I could get some wheels again, with the hope I could actually get behind the wheel without having another panic attack.

Inside the house was dark, and I called "hello" out of instinct, but nobody answered or came running to give me a hug. A crunch sounded under my feet as I stepped into the kitchen. Must've dropped some food or spilled the rice when I set my phone in a bag. Another crunch and another crunch, too much to be an accident. When I looked down, the floor was teeming with ladybugs, red and black thumbtacks crawling over each other and flitting into brief flight, so many of them I couldn't see the tile floor underneath. One of them launched into the air and landed on my arm. One in my hair. On my face, my other arm, my fingers, my neck, an angry mob of ladybugs, and even though I know ladybugs can't really hurt me in any way, that's never really allayed my fear, and so I hauled ass right out the door.

This cataclysmic infestation was not the work of my brother, or any human for that matter. There were far, far too many of them. Jill the Ladybug knew I was gone and had called all her friends over for a party. A door or window must've been left open, and the ladybugs had converged on my place like a kind of insect sorority house.

Outside I could see that the windows were filled with them, ladybugs masking the glass like blackout curtains. Supernatural. I picked one from behind my ear, flicked another two off my forearm, swept a dozen or more off the Tenderheart backpack. One crawled up my thigh, like a bead of sweat headed upstream, so I had to take my pants off and shake them out. The sun porch was worse, the windows alive with red and black, like a kaleidoscope. If I tried to go in, there'd be enough of them inside to haul me away, to lift me high in the sky and deposit me somewhere far afield, or worse, eat me like a leaf, tear open holes in my flesh until there was nothing left but bone. Kat and the kids would eventually come home to see my skeleton holding on to the yellow kitchen phone, my desperation captured in ghoulish relief. There was a chance that the upstairs remained ladybug-free. I couldn't really tell from the windows, but there was no way to get in and find out.

What does a man do when his house has been taken over by ladybugs? I was thankful I hadn't been home, asleep on the couch, stuck in the living room in the middle of a swarm. I could call an exterminator and they'd probably come out and set off some kind of poison bomb in the house that would drop their candy-shelled bodies to the ground so that the bug guys could suck them all up with an industrial vacuum. I'd probably have to stay somewhere else for safety. I thought about the number of couches I could sleep on, the number of people who would offer me safe harbor in my time of need, and the number I came up with was one: Marty. A remarkably low number for someone who knew just about everybody in town by sight or by name.

I tightened the straps on the backpack and set off down the highway toward town, hoping some asshole wouldn't run me over.

Steak and Potatoes

"Nice backpack," Cora said when she answered the door. She was dressed in pajama bottoms and an extra-large pink T-shirt with a neon green flamingo on it, a far cry from her usual power pantsuits. Her plume was brown and beautiful. Cora was the president of the Bank of Charity, just about the best name for a bank ever, but I didn't bank there because it was mostly for quails. Some other banks weren't too keen on doing business with quails because they had a reputation for being bad with money. "Like throwing a dollar to a quail," as the saying goes. Cora saw to it that her kind was taken care of, handing out loans and mortgages to the quail community when other's wouldn't. Like most of them—the older ones anyway— she hadn't always been one, but when she turned, she adopted it with grace and pride, like it was just another thing, like getting crow's feet around your eyes.

It had taken me a sweltering, sweat-drenched hour to walk to their house, and I was desperate for a beer and a shower and a bed.

Marty wasn't home yet, she said, but I was welcome, as always. I explained my predicament, about the ladybugs, describing the biblical nature of my ordeal, and Cora told me that ladybugs were a sign of good luck, and she sang me a song I'd never heard before, one she said she used to sing to her own kids. "*Ladybug, ladybug, fly away home. Your house is on fire and your children are gone. All except one and her name is Ann. She hid under the frying pan.*"

As a lullaby this song was no better than "Ring of Fire." Still I considered adding it to my night time routine. If I ever saw my kids again.

Cora cooked supper and drank a glass of red wine. She gave me a beer, and I sat at the table with her two kids, June and Michael, nine and seven, not quails, not yet at least, and we all entertained ourselves with an art project. Paper plates, glitter glue, markers, construction paper, pipe cleaners, stickers, pompoms, and popsicle sticks covered the table, and I couldn't really tell exactly what was going on, but the object of the project seemed to be to make faces on the plates, some kind of mask or animal, or in a couple of cases an unrecognizable monster, and then attach a popsicle stick to the bottom with glue. In the end you could cover your own face and scare somebody, or hold them above the table like a puppet show.

"Does Marty seem...I don't know, blue lately?" Cora asked.

"I guess." I nosed my way through the craft supplies.

"I think he's depressed," she said. "But he won't see anybody about it."

I took a purple marker and colored the outside ridges of one half of the paper plate. "That why you gave him *The Secret?*"

"The what?"

"Some book he's spouting off like it's God's word."

"I never gave him *The Secret*. Wish I knew what the secret was."

"Law enforcement can be stressful."

"Especially if you're not very good at it."

I found some plastic googly eyes. I stuck one of those in the center of my plate and made a cyclops. No other adornments necessary.

When Marty got home he didn't stop to ask what I was doing there, like it was a normal thing for me to be sitting at his table making a paper-plate cyclops with his kids. He went to his bedroom, changed out of his uniform and took a shower, came out smelling of leathery aftershave and hair gel, and proceeded to kiss everybody in the room, including a fake kiss at me that I swatted away.

I wanted to confront him about the quail park. Tell him I'd paid a visit to Valentine's home and lo and behold had found his sister. A small bit of detective work uncovered what he'd neglected to share. I wanted to know why he'd kept this to himself, such a simple thing, but I couldn't figure out the best way to work this in to the natural flow of conversation.

The kids cleaned up the art mess and set the table.

"To what do we owe the pleasure?" Marty asked.

"Ladybugs," Cora said, before I could say so myself. "My house is filled with ladybugs."

"A sign from God," Marty said.

Michael spoke up then as he folded paper napkins and topped them politely with a knife and fork, and said a friend of his told him there was no God.

Marty told him to start kicking the kid's butt and see who he prays to. Cora popped Marty in the shoulder with a serving spoon.

"Kat and the kids left him alone," Cora said, which had me wondering how she knew. Our wives were not all that close, but the sewing circles in Charity were small, so it was not beyond the realm of possibility that the word was already out.

"I don't think they've gone for good," I said.

"Of course not. A cruise has to end." This was more information than I'd given her, but no more than I knew, and still only speculation. How'd she know this? Had I told her and couldn't remember? Was there a runaway wives hotline? Had my wife gone to Cora looking for help and happened to break down in her office wondering what to do about her husband's philandering?

"Why do you think she's on a cruise?" I asked.

"You told me so."

"No, I don't believe I did. I don't really know where they went, to tell the truth."

"You told me at the door. Said your house was filled with ladybugs and the rest of your family had gone on a cruise. We went on a cruise once to the Bahamas. Marty got seasick. Remember, Marty?"

Marty grunted and took a seat in front of his plate of veggie lasagna.

That settled it. I was losing my grip on reality, on what I'd said and hadn't said. It made me want to go home and check if there really had been any ladybugs. Was anything that had happened this week really happening? How the hell do we even know? Maybe there were two versions of myself, one doing what I wished I was doing—carrying on with my normal life— and the other enduring some splintered crazy-ass reality. It was as much a possibility as men on the moon. The other Lee took a different path last Tuesday and never hit Valentine and was now sleeping peacefully under his ladybug-free roof with his wife and kids dreaming about peaches, while this version would be lucky if his friend let him sleep on his couch. Maybe the thing to do was to have those two Lees cross paths again and merge. Or if I could find him, maybe I'd have to kill him and take his place.

"Take your hat off at the supper table," Marty said.

I'd forgotten I was wearing one, and at first I thought he was talking to the kids, but neither of them displayed such a crass violation of table manners. I didn't want anybody to see what was under there, especially the kids, who might latch on to my deformity in that innocently ugly way kids do, so I told him I had been sweating a lot, and that I didn't want to take off my cap and perspire all over the beautiful meal his wife had made and spread my stink about her aromatic kitchen, and so while I apologized for my manners, I told him I'd be thankful if he'd allow me a breach of propriety just this once.

"You let one thing slip like that, Lee, and what's next?" Marty said. "Kids stop saying 'yes ma'am' and 'yes sir.' No Christ in Christmas. No Pledge of Allegiance. Starts with a hat, but where's it end?"

"Leave him be," Cora said. And that ended that.

The kids didn't eat the lasagna, but Cora refused to make them anything else, which was a parenting move both Marty and I approved of. Kat was always making extra waffles or bowls of noodles when they weren't on the menu. Drove me crazy. If we were having steak and potatoes, by God, the kids should be eating steak and potatoes. There are no other choices. My mother would never have stood in the kitchen waiting for me to tell her what I wanted. Daddy bought the groceries and she cooked them and we ate them or we didn't. Both Michael and June ate cubes of cheese Cora'd cut up for them, her only concession since lasagna was already full of cheese. They were going to get cheese one way or the other. She also gave them Ritz crackers. So they were eating cheese and crackers for supper, but still, Cora got to believe she was holding them to the high standards of the Bishop family supper table.

When we were all done I thanked her for the groceries despite not having eaten much.

"My pleasure," she said. "Y'all clear the table," she told the kids, who both eagerly did so. And I could tell by the looks on their beautiful faces that a treat waited at the end of this chore.

And this whole scene of domesticity stuck in my gut and made me miss my own family. I hoped I had not done some irrevocable damage to my domain such that I might never again enjoy another meal around my own supper table with my own kids. I had my kingdom, and while it may not have been perfect, I had created a unit of protection with an assurance of longevity, a clan that would band together to get through the daily plagues of ladybug infestations and car trouble and midnight itches and whatnot, together. And while his wasn't a perfect home either, Marty had his own kingdom too, where he could demand obedience from shameless cap-wearers. And thinking about all this made me more sorry for Valentine, a man who had a sister who didn't care about him, no place to live, nothing more than a bicycle and a Care Bear backpack filled with crap, none of the things we all need to get through the day—other people who give a damn, who by either obligation or want are beholden to us and us beholden to them.

Being alone isn't freedom; it's a type of death.

"Get up," Marty said. "We're going out."

I told him I'd just as soon stay put at his house if he didn't mind. I'd like to take a shower and call it an early night. I wasn't feeling so great and my recent span of days hadn't been excellent, so it might be best if I took it easy. If I didn't move, I couldn't invite trouble.

"What's wrong with you?" he asked.

"I think you know where I'm coming from."

"I know where you're going. Now get up."

I did as he said, knowing he'd never talk to his wife the way he did me.

Marty didn't kiss his family before we walked out the door, but at least he was thoughtful enough to let them know where he was headed.

I asked him to stop at Walmart for some more Benadryl.

"Friend, you don't need Benadryl."

"I'm afraid I do. I've got an itch," I said, and scratched it.

"What's the opposite of an itch? Calm. Stillness. Cool. This will be hard for you, but the more you exude a calm exterior, concentrate on keeping still, keeping cool, that's all you'll need to do. Beer helps."

"That's why I wanted to stay at your place."

"My place ain't cool."

I kept scratching. "Why didn't you tell me about Valentine's sister?" I asked.

"His what?"

"His half-sister. Anne. I went out to the quail park where she lives. Paid her a visit. She said their mama lives in Statesboro."

"He's got a sister?"

"You didn't go see her?"

"Shit, must've been Todd. Only person I talked to was his mama."

"You talked to her? Why didn't you tell me?"

"Tell you what?"

"That you talked to his mama. You said he didn't have any kin."

"I was covering your butt, remember? Didn't know you'd go all Columbo on me. Best to let Valentine be who we thought he was. Nothing. Nobody. A dead quail. You want to know he had a mama that don't give a crap? Want to see his baby pictures and wonder if yours'll turn out like that? Ready to get all depressed? You in need of a midlife crisis? Want to start reading self-help books like me? I know where this all leads, Lee. I've been down this road before. I'm accustomed to police work, you know. You don't have to follow the road too long before you start wondering what your own life is worth. And nobody wants to think about that."

"I'd just appreciate it if you'd be honest with me."

"Fine. Hazel DuPree."

"Who?"

"That's his mama's name. Runs a joint called DuPree Salvage down in Statesboro. Give her a call. See if she gives a hoot." Marty took a deep breath and exhaled slowly. "What did his sister say?"

"Nothing."

"What a surprise. I'll take care of Todd. Now you be cool and stop kicking up dust, all right?"

Marty was right, something I rarely admitted. I stopped scratching. "You're buying," I said.

Let's Dance

Weekends at the bar were to be avoided. The place filled with kids who'd come home from college looking to replicate their campus experiences; couples who secretly hated each other guzzling weekly specials with the hope that alcohol might make their partner more attractive; strangers here for the shitty band; dancers pretending they were professionals, tossing and spinning each other over the worn parquet. The scene was that of a party full of uninvited guests, not your typical after-work crowd that Marty and I preferred, the crowd that bellied up to the bar and moaned about business and how much their knees hurt, then played a few rounds of easy trivia because there was nothing else to do. Regulars vs. amateurs. And weekends at the bar were always filled with amateurs.

The Allman Brothers pinball machine was now adorned with a drape of black vinyl, like it had died alongside Valentine, the two of them connected in some kind of symbiosis. Or perhaps he'd managed to beat his own high score that night after all, and that's what happened to the machine once it had been bested: it put itself to rest like a giant beast. Despite the crowd, Marty and I found two seats together at the bar, ordered some beers and two shots from Dave because Sister Rose hated the weekend crowd as much as we did.

I always wanted to be one of those men who got phone calls at a bar, whose wife called and asked the bartender to tell Lee to bring home some milk. Cell phones had made opportunities like this obsolete—opportunities for a man to identify his individuality by aligning himself with the denizens and bartenders of a specific haunt, opportunities for men to find a home away from home. And here I was with no phone, and no home to go to, or at least one absent of the things that made it home. What the hell would Kat do if she came home and saw all those ladybugs? Probably think I had something to do with it.

"Greetings." A hand slapped my shoulder. Todd stood behind me in his uniform. At least he'd taken his sunglasses off. "May I ask you a question, Mr. Hubbs?"

I checked with Marty. Marty nodded.

"If you have to," I said.

"I believe you were sitting right here the other night when that poor quail met his maker out on the highway. I'm wondering—"

"His name was Valentine."

"That's correct."

"And I wasn't sitting here in this exact spot. I believe I was over there."

Marty held a finger up for Dave, signaling for a beer.

Todd took his hand off my shoulder. "Well, I'm wondering if you can recall anything out of the ordinary. Patrons in the bar you didn't recognize. Something of that nature."

"I remember I told him to shut up."

"Good advice," Marty said. Dave brought the beer and Marty handed it to Todd. "You're off duty. Have a beer."

"I don't see any harm in asking a few questions," Todd said.

"You're not supposed to wear your uniform when you're off duty."

"Then how will anyone know I'm a cop?"

"Nobody likes to drink with cops but other cops," Marty said.

"That's not what she said." Todd tipped the nose of the bottle toward a quail in a pink tank top sweating and gyrating on the dance floor, banging her plume like she was in a hair metal music video. "Quails have big breasts," he said. He took a long swig of his beer and patted me on the shoulder again. "I trust you'll inform my partner if you remember anything," he said, and grooved on out to the dance floor.

"What's that saying?" Marty asked. "Youth is wasted on the youth?"

"Something like that. Let me borrow your phone," I said.

Marty unclipped his phone from his civilian belt, which he kept equipped like anything but a civilian. A knife, hand sanitizer, a cell phone, a small flashlight, his keys, and God only knows what else was strapped to his waist. He thought he was Batman.

I called Kat. It rang and rang then told me the voicemail box was full.

"Send her a text for me."

"Use your own thumbs."

I typed out a text: *Are you on a cruise? Lee's worried sick.* My strategy was if she received a text from Marty and Marty spoke of my worry, that this would be sufficient enough for her to at least text back.

I stared at Marty's phone waiting for those three little dots to appear and indicate she was composing a response, but they never came. Oh, the hope of those dots, the pulse of a life on the other line, an anticipatory glee. Someone else is out there, talking to me, saying something to me. What are they going to say? Get ready for it. Get ready. Get ready.

I sat there getting ready for a good two minutes and didn't see any hopeful dots.

The band played a mix of Motown and other dusty grooves that were easy to dance to. Todd was out there holding on tight to his quail, both of them smiling and having fun and rubbing up and down on each other. She squeezed his biceps, checking their girth. Nearby, a trio of other quail chicks danced together in a covey, until one of the quails walked over to the bar mid-song and ordered three lemon drops. I didn't understand shots like this, shots created with the whole intent of making shots palatable. It was called a shot for a reason, because it was the needle going in quickly, pricking you with a pain followed by the cure. Shots shouldn't taste like candy. When Dave put them on the bar she motioned to the other two chicks and they wiggled over and they all did their shots together, making melodramatic pained contortions with their pretty beaks before wiggling out on the dance floor. One of the chicks, blonde with silver glitter in her plume, looked at me and flicked her plume toward the dance floor. An invitation.

"Let's dance," I told Marty.

"Me and you?"

"It's a group thing," I said, and pointed to the chicks who'd been shooting lemon drops.

"You have no moral fiber," he said.

"I'm just dancing."

"You're never just dancing."

The singer did a sorry Michael Jackson impression, reminding us all not to stop until we got enough.

Todd gave me a fist bump when I got out on the dance floor. Somehow the quail he'd been so eager to dance with had wrestled herself loose, and now it was a free-for-all. Groups of mismatched men and women jumped and rubbed and groped on each other, swapping sweat, breathing booze on necks and ears, the heat cooking their spray-on smells into a sticky soup of desperation. I shuffle-danced into the middle of the chicks, who still smelled of sugar and lemon. They laughed. A short guy with a mustache had joined the group now, one of those ironic mustache guys, heavily curled on the ends with wax. A *hey-look-at-me* mustache, an *aren't-I-funny* mustache. I hated this mustache attitude as much as I hated sweet shots. Some men can get away with a mustache like my father had. I prefer the beard so as not to be mistaken for a pederast, but you either look good with a mustache or you don't. It's not an in-between sort of thing like wearing a light jacket in the fall.

One of the chicks whispered to the one with the glitter plume as she bounced from one sandal to the other. She smiled and her plume beckoned me like a curled finger. So I shuffled closer to her. She hung her arms around my neck, stared me deep in my eyes, and took off my cap. I guess checking to see if I had anything to hide. Hopefully the bar was dark enough she couldn't see my sore, or didn't care one way or another. We were having some sort of connection; an electricity charged from her glittery plume lit up my insides. It was just dancing. We were only dancing. But if Kat walked in right then is that what she'd see? Oh, sure, Lee, go right ahead and press your crotch into that chick's hips and call it something you can get away with.

"Is it true what they say about those plumes?" I asked.

She stopped dancing, her arms fell from my neck. She smoothed her plume with her hand until it lay flat on her head, then let it spring forward like a catapult. Glitter sprayed from its end and splattered all over my face and in my nose and mouth. Tasted peppery. Then my eyes started burning and I had to keep blinking them shut to generate some tears to wash out whatever she'd flung on me. Some kind of quail poison? A plume dipped in pepper spray as a defense against male advances? I blinked and she was back with the rest of the other chicks, but now she was wearing my cap. She covered her mouth, whispered something, and they all busted out cackling. Whatever she'd said they all found it hilarious, and I figured the whole thing was a setup, a trick these dirty birds pulled at roadside bars across the South, lure a vulnerable man out on the dance floor and cut him down for wanting what they were flaunting, take a souvenir as proof. Probably had a hidden camera somewhere recording the hilarity to turn me into the latest viral fuckhead.

My nose flared. Flaming snot-lava dripped from my nostrils. I thought I might pass out. I walked to the bar to pour water on my face.

"You got a text," Marty said, and showed me his phone. *???*

That was it.

Before I could type anything or understand what the hell this all meant, the mustache guy had his hand on my shoulder, and I didn't want any more hands on my shoulders, and my face was on fire, and my wife was nothing but question marks, and my house was infested with ladybugs, and I'd run over a quail on his bike, and somebody needed an onion pie, and I couldn't slap the smile off the chick's face that had glittered me and stolen my cap, and he had that stupid mustache above a smirk that was about to start saying something just as stupid, and I didn't want to hear whatever he had to say, so I punched him right in his mustache and knocked him on his ass.

I'm not a violent man. Do not believe that violence solves much. But I do understand that every man has his breaking point and if pushed too far will snap. And I also know, that when that man reaches that breaking point in front of a room full of witnesses, he might want to run.

Meditating Heathens

The doors to Charity United Methodist Church are always open, but that doesn't mean they won't kick a bum out for stinking up the sanctuary. Pastor Phil poked me with the business end of a putter, trying to rouse me from the place I'd found to rest my head. He stood at the end of the aisle, a half-dozen golf balls at his feet. He wore khaki shorts, a red golf shirt and a white visor, which I was surprised to see atop his head in a place of worship.

I swung my feet down to stand up, tried and failed to catch my balance on the pew in front of me, and plopped my ass on the bench. The Gospels played out around me in swirling stained glass. Jesus raising Lazarus. Feeding the multitudes. Healing the blind. Walking on water. What a guy! I remember coming here to pray, to pray to see my family again and to ask for forgiveness, but there'd been no answer, so I'd fallen asleep, dreaming I'd wake up the next morning and the pews would be filled with the congregation, and in that congregation would be my wife and kids, all of us in our Sunday best, and we would sing hymns loud and clear and then later go home for a big Sunday dinner and some relaxation in the pool.

Nobody was here but Pastor Phil.

"Can you keep this a secret? Between you and me?" I asked.

Pastor Phil pointed to the rafters. "And God," he said.

I tasted pepper on my tongue. "Where is everybody?"

"Who were you expecting?"

"It's Sunday."

"You're a little early. Come back tomorrow."

"It's Saturday?"

"All day."

"Then why are you here?"

"One might ask you the same question." Pastor Phil lined up a golf ball in the middle of his stance, aiming way down the aisle to a small plastic cup turned on its side below the pulpit. His putter swung in a smooth and easy pendulum, and the ball rolled down the carpeted aisle within an inch of the cup. "Perfect place to practice lags," he said. He looked at his watch and sat down next to me in the pew. "Do you have something you'd like to talk about?"

"I've had a rough few days," I said.

Pastor Phil didn't say anything. A man accustomed to listening to people bare their souls knows not to speak until the confession is done.

"I understand that I have not been the most righteous man, but I want to be good. I really do. God is making it real hard to turn the corner, though."

"The Lord gives us no more than we can handle."

"Forgive me for saying so, Pastor Phil, but I believe that's a load of horseshit."

"So you think you've had about all you can handle?"

"And then some."

"You need to trust that God knows what's best for you, and knows you better than you know yourself, so while you may feel at your wits end, in God's eyes, you may be nowhere near."

"That's real comforting."

"Let me be honest with you, Lee. I can tell that you're not truly open, you are not *truly* humbling yourself before God. You are begging because you want things to get better. It's no different than a kid asking for a toy from Santa Claus. God is not Santa Claus."

"I thought your job was to make me feel better."

"My job is to tell the truth."

"How do we know what that is?"

"It's staring us in the face every day."

Pastor Phil was staring me in the face. So Pastor Phil was the truth? Don't think that's what he meant. He probably meant Jesus in the stained glass, or the Bible on the pulpit, or the hymnal in the pew, or the giant cross behind the choir loft, or golf balls, or my own reflection—hell, I didn't know, but he wasn't helping. Why do men of God always have to speak in riddles?

"That's the best you can do?"

"We're all sinners. You know that, right?"

"Sounds like something I've heard before."

Pastor Phil looked at his watch again, patted me on the knee. "I've gotta run," he said. "Stay as long as you want."

"What time is it?"

"Ten to seven. I like to play an early round and spend the afternoon with my family. You play golf?"

"It's been a while."

"We've already got a foursome or else I'd ask you to come along."

"You got time to give me a lift to the store?"

"Happy to help," he said.

Pastor Phil drove a white Crown Victoria that made everybody slow down when they passed him on the highway for fear he may be a cop. We didn't talk on the ride. Afterwards I thanked him and told him he could come by the store after his round and I'd set him up with a free bag of onions. I hoped some complimentary produce might compel him to put in a good word for me.

"Thank you, Lee," he said. "Sometimes we must be broken before we can be repaired."

It wasn't until he'd driven off that I realized Pastor Phil had played me in the same way he probably played hundreds of other parishioners. He didn't have any answers. He never did, and he certainly hadn't wanted to hear me unburden myself on his day off, right before his relaxing round of golf, so he'd started talking in aphorisms to confuse the hell out of me and make me want to shut up.

The back door to the store was unlocked, which it shouldn't have been because we weren't open yet. The smell of chocolate and something else, spicy and sharp, wafted through the interior, like somebody'd been baking a cake. A faint sound of music curled through the dark. Somebody was here or had been here, and for all I knew it might've been me. After punching that mustached guy in the face I might've strolled in here, baked a cake and turned on the radio. I didn't really know how to bake a cake, but then again lack of knowledge hadn't really stopped me from anything before.

The smell led me to the cooktop, where a small sauce pan simmered over an open gas flame set on low. The bottom of the pan was caked black, whatever being simmered having gone past simmer into charcoal. I turned the stove off.

The music was soft and low, mixed with a murmur, and I followed the sound to my office door. I saw no reason to be scared of whoever was in there—a late-night chef who liked to listen to new age music. I had a pretty good idea of who I'd find.

I swung open the door, and the two little shits in the middle of my floor didn't even move, both of them sitting there with their legs crossed like black and white Buddhas. A.J. and Ben. A cone of incense burned on a saucer, and a voice from the music spoke above the woodwinds and whistles and bubbling brook. "Now see if you can bring some kindness to whatever you're feeling right now."

"What the hell's this?"

Neither startled. Neither recoiled in shock at the sight of their boss walking into his own office to find two meditating heathens on the floor. This ritual must've really been working on them to keep them of calm mind and body. They did open their eyes though, and looked at each other before they looked at me.

"Namaste, boss. What're you doing here on Saturday?"

On the weekends I never opened or closed, and usually only came in to put out fires. This made me wonder what all I'd been missing.

"This won't work," I said. "Find some other place for this."

They both stood up. A.J. turned off the meditation and pocketed his phone, the source of the music and gentle instruction.

"It helps us focus, gets us centered in a positive space so we can approach the impending day with clarity," he said.

"So much focus you could've burned the store down. Did you forget something on the stovetop?"

A.J. ran out the door to check on what he would soon discover was a worthless brick of shit.

Ben tried to follow him out, but I put a hand on his chest and stopped him. "Nothing else was going on in here?"

Ben shook his head. "No, sir."

"Some pregame meditation?"

"Yes, sir."

"Don't let it happen again. If I find out y'all were playing grab-ass in here I'll have to let you both go."

"Yes, sir."

"Did you make coffee already?"

"No, sir. Would you like me to?"

"That'd be the best thing for you and me."

I grabbed six ibuprofen out of my desk and went to sit in the cold room for my own bit of morning clarity. Whatever that chick had flung at me with her plume still burned, a radiating sting to remind me of what I'd done. My itch flared up, too, so I shucked an ear of corn and rolled the cold kernels over it for relief. The pie sat on the shelf where I'd left it. *Do Not Eat*, it said on the flag of a yellow Post-it.

Ben came in the cold room with a silver travel mug of coffee, the mug that had been Valentine's. *WRVR—The River! Statesboro's Home for Classic Rock!*

"Where'd you get this?" I asked.

"That cop who's always stealing peaches. He's in your office."

I watched the steam curl from the coffee. Time to face the music. I could run over a quail in the middle of the night, but the law would not allow me to assault a hipster. "What do you see, Ben?"

"Sir?"

"In the steam. You see how it's curling up here out of the coffee and taking shapes. What do you see?"

Ben, God bless him, leaned in to get a closer look, because surely his boss wasn't a crazy man; surely this proprietor of a very successful produce market and onion farm was sane as rain. If he saw things in the steam rising from his coffee cup in the cold, then things were indeed rising from his coffee cup.

"I'm not sure," he said, scratching his chin in a pantomime of deep thought. "But I think I see...a ghost."

A Disciple of Momentum

Marty had the unzipped Tenderheart backpack and tossed it in the leather chair. He was in his uniform, ready to serve and protect Charity in the name of truth and justice for all. "You left this at my house."

"Thanks."

"Why's it smell like a burnt hippie in here?"

"We're rebranding. New age desserts."

"It'd probably be successful, too. Tell me how you keep getting so lucky. How's a man like you, with so much negative energy, end up touched by fate in such mind-boggling lucky ways?"

"You clearly have not spent much time with me lately."

"The mustache isn't pressing charges."

"Dude was lucky I only hit him once."

"But he would like you to call him and apologize."

Marty handed me a business card. *Joshua Felton. Woodcarving and Craft Whiskey.* "Maybe he'll carve me a flute and give me a shot."

"Knowing you, that's right."

"Tell him I don't have a phone."

Marty looked down at the phone sitting on my desk. "Suit yourself. But he may change his mind. And he's got a bunch of witnesses that saw you deck the guy and run away. Two of them cops."

"What about the chick who sprayed me?" I said. "Ask Todd. He saw. He'll be on my side."

"Todd's on Todd's side."

"Why don't you take Todd some peach ice cream?"

"He only likes froyo. Give me the card."

I handed him the business card. He put my phone on speaker and dialed the number. "Tell him you're sorry."

We stared at each other and listened to the ring, each one of us hoping for a different outcome. I was sorry, but not for hitting some mustachioed, whiskey-distilling druid who probably deserved to be hit for any number of reasons. I hoped Mr. Felton was sleeping off the injustice, surrounded by all three of those chicks taking turns fanning him with their plumes. He'd be fine. No need to apologize. His phone kept ringing and we kept staring. "Any word from Kat?" I asked between rings.

Marty shook his head.

Joshua Felton's phone finally went to voicemail. "This is Josh. Tell me what you want me to hear."

After the beep, I obliged. "Your mustache is stupid," I said.

Marty hung up. "I told him where you worked. He said he'd stop by after lunch."

"I'll make sure I'm not here."

"I hate to tell you this," Marty said, "but there will come a day when I won't be there to scoop up your fumble." For a moment I wondered if this was a reference to some experience from our shared past that I'd forgotten, Marty dredging up high school football glory, but Marty'd been second-string, and I never fumbled.

He left the card on the desk and I dropped it in the trash. I checked email. Nothing from my family or my in-laws. What was this hell they were putting me through? Didn't anybody want their daddy? There was an email from Jodi. It appeared to be a solicitation for one Clarence Hart's memorial fund. I clicked on a link that took me to a GoFundMe page.

The daily indignities that quails in our community still endure are widely documented. Despite overwhelming evidence of their humanity, some of us remain committed to intolerance at the expense of decency. Clarence Hart was a local quail with a heart of gold. If you ever needed an errand run or a joke to tell, Mr. Hart was there to help you out or make you smile. Some may remember him riding his cheery yellow bicycle around town, a man so happy to be himself he didn't care how silly he might've looked. Sometimes kids would follow him on their own bikes and they would ride around town in an impromptu parade, all of them joined together in a chorus of "Pure Imagination." He had an excellent singing voice. While Mr. Hart certainly entertained us all with his big smile and warm heart, many of us were blind to the hurt inside. You see, Mr. Hart was homeless, brought to Charity by the winds of fate, no family, not much to his name. Behind the infectious smile was trauma, trauma so deep it finally caught up to him. We never truly know what others might be going through, and when it comes to quails, some of us don't care. Mr. Hart died last week during a tragic hit-and-run accident. Donations will be used for the sole purpose of providing Mr. Hart with the peaceful rest he and so many others like him rightly deserve. With no place to rest his head in life, let us devote ourselves to providing one for him in death.

Jodi made it sound like the Mayor of Happy Town had died. Valentine had never once paraded around town with kids. No parent in their right mind would let their kids be seen with him. What was more surprising, was that the page had already received two hundred and thirty-five dollars in donations. What else might be funded this way? Could I get my brick oven for the new pizza enterprise? Jodi could write the copy. This girl had a future, that much I knew.

She'd also completely excised herself from her involvement in the proceedings that brought this man to the end she now tried to honor. She was pressing on in a way that a man like me, accustomed to pressing on, devoted to not looking back, a disciple of momentum, found himself unable to do. Maybe this had to do with youth, a recognition and acceptance of the capriciousness of life. Virus, disaster, war, terror, quailing. Kids her age had grown up in uncertain times, forced to embrace the here-and-now, not out of choice but out of necessity, which made them believe that cultivating their identity and practicing self-care and curating their own narratives—woodcarving and whiskey—was the path to happiness.

But who told them life was supposed to be happy?

I needed a vehicle, some wheels, some motorized transport to get where I needed to go. I wasn't calling Joshua Felton to tell him I was sorry, and I wasn't waiting around for him to find me so he could give me a hug and tell me how I'd gone wrong in my life, and somebody, dadgummit, somebody deserved a pie.

I called up Wayne Salley over at Wayne Salley Ford to find out about my muffler.

"Morning Wayne, do you have my car?"

"Who is this?"

"Lee Hubbs. My car. You sent somebody to my house to pick it up. The muffler fell off."

"Oh, hey, Lee. You say the muffler fell off, did you?"

"Slap off. Just as I was pulling out the driveway."

"I'll be damned."

"That's what the gal said the other day when I told her."

"Who was it?"

"Hell if I know. The pretty one."

"Let me do some digging, Lee, and I'll give you a call back. But I've got to say I'd probably remember."

"Well the car is not at my house where I left it, and I talked to somebody there who said they'd get on it."

"You drive a truck, don't you?"

"It's Kat's. The one I bought from you too recently to have its damn muffler falling off."

"I gotcha. That's not a car, Lee! That's a crossover."

"Whatever the hell it is, a vital part of it has *fallen off.*"

"Who'd you talk to?"

"I already told you, I don't know."

"How do I know you talked to anybody?"

"Why would I call you and tell you you had my car—"

"—crossover."

"When you didn't have it? What kind of shit would I be trying to pull on you?"

"Easy now. I don't know. Make me think I'm going crazy is all."

"I'm the one going crazy."

"Look, somebody's got to know something. I'll give you a holler when I find out what's going on."

I went into the bathroom and washed my hands and face, trying to clean off the leftover sting, but more than that really. I was trying to wash off days, trying to cleanse myself right out of this impossible dream, hoping I'd look up and see my beard restored, my life restored, my wife outside in the store putting a bow on a nice prepackaged basket of assorted peach-flavored sundries—body lotion, hard candy, salsa, preserves, tea bags, so much peach-flavored crap. I wanted to lift my face out of my palms and feel purified, open my eyes to see Leo and Lisa playing in my office, to see Jodi's full head of hair, to see my truck parked in the space where it had always been, to see Valentine leaning on his bicycle and smoking a cigarette next to the hay bales. I wanted to be reborn into the life I'd left only a few short days ago, baptized into myself again. So maybe all of this explained the amount of water on the floor and my wet shirt wadded up in a puddle and my shoes off and the sink full and the drain plugged with paper towels and the water running and splattering over the bowl and me in my underwear like I was taking a bath in the sink. Water seeped between my toes. My shoes were soaked. My socks, which I'd taken off at some point, saturated like a sponge. Everything I'd had on was wet, and I couldn't remember the steps I'd taken to get to this point, couldn't remember thinking to myself it would be a good idea to take off the shirt because it was burning me, and maybe I should wash the shirt, and while I'm at it, my pants too, and hell, my whole body. Couldn't remember the thought process that might've gone into any of this as I stood there in my underwear staring at my face, new stubble barely peeking through, a flaming red sore on my forehead, the floor of my bathroom covered in water, a flood, a flood, destroy it all in a flood and rebuild. Break it down then repair it. The real question is, why repair it at all, God, if we're such a sorry damn sight for your eyes? You're the one who screwed up anyway! You made us!

I left the bathroom and stood in my store in my underwear, and I told Ben to get his ass in there and clean up my mess. Without asking what I was talking about or why I was so mad about it and why I'd chosen him to bear the brunt of this duty, he said yes sir, and hopped to it. I told A.J. to get me a roll of paper towels and follow me to my office.

It takes a lot of paper towels to dry yourself off after a breakdown. A.J. stood by and peeled off sheets, whirled them around and around his arm before ripping them from the spool and handing them to me. He brought in the first aid kit and I swabbed my forehead with alcohol and wrapped a roll of gauze around my head to cover the sore and to keep myself from indulging the itch.

"You look like you been in a war," A.J. said.

"Good, maybe somebody'll be nice to me."

Once I was dry, I gave him some petty cash and told him to go over to Walmart and get me a pair of jeans, size 38 x 34 or thereabouts, and to load us up on some travel snacks, sunflower seeds, chewy candy, soft drinks, and the like. We were going on a trip.

"Aren't you going to need a shirt?"

I told him no, because I already had the baddest motherfucking shirt in town.

Ole Man Trouble

A.J. came back from Walmart with jeans, two sacks full of snacks, and a red trucker hat askew on his noggin that said *'MERICA* in bold white block letters. Valentine's shirt and moccasins fit like they were made for me. After I dressed, I grabbed the onion pie from the cold room and stuck it in the Tenderheart backpack, filled the WRVR travel mug with coffee, and we got in the Cadillac and headed south.

A.J. told me my shirt smelled funky. He asked me to reach in one of the sacks and find the air freshener he'd gotten at Walmart because he'd known riding with me would stink. It was shaped like a donut covered in white icing and pink sprinkles; it made the interior of his car smell like a fresh bakery, and it immediately made me hungry, so I busted into a package of powdered donuts, ignoring his insult.

I got the impression he wasn't too happy about being my chauffeur, but I was none too happy with the way he'd been using his privileges at the store so liberally, abusing the responsibility I'd given him, so I didn't care about his feelings.

"Don't go into my office anymore when I'm not here," I said.

"Whatever you say, boss."

"And stop calling me 'boss.'"

"Stop calling me 'boy.'"

"I've never called you 'boy.'"

"You ain't got to say it to say it."

A.J.'s phone was plugged into the cigarette lighter, keeping charged for the drive. I grabbed it but couldn't get past the home screen, a picture of himself rendered as a cartoon character.

"I need your code for directions."

He took the phone from me, entered in the digits and handed it back. "Don't tweet anything stupid."

"I don't even know how Twitter works."

"What a surprise."

I Googled up DuPree's Salvage and plugged it into the navigation app. That bit of technology I *was* familiar with. I lifted the mug to him as if I was toasting our destination. "Statesboro," I said. "We need to see Jolly about some melons."

"Business trip?"

"Business trip."

This immediately changed A.J.'s attitude. He bounced in his seat, excited to be included as a sideman on an excursion downstate to purchase product for our store from Jolly Hayes. My faith in him, in the responsibilities I'd given him, was suddenly restored. Fortunately, A.J. had no idea where Jolly Hayes's farm was, so he'd have to take my word.

Outside of Charity the terrain shifted ever so slightly. The trees squeezed closer to the road, and the farmland melted from peaches and pecans to tracts of soybeans and cotton. The billboards ceased advertising big chains and touted more local fare, slaphappy with alliteration: the Perfect Pear, the Frugal Frog. Some signs gave up subtlety all together and commanded travelers to *Get Right With God* or claimed firmly that *Jesus Was NOT a Socialist*. A.J.'s hat was perfect for south Georgia, although he wore it with a sense of irony, like that asshole's mustache from last night. We passed through towns smaller than Charity, towns with flag-waving traffic circles and nothing but a post office, old courthouses with statues of Confederate soldiers, cannons aimed north, elderly men sitting outside a filling station or barber shop drinking cold Coca-Cola from bottles, wiping their foreheads with bandanas and finger waving to everyone who drove by. Including us.

With the landscape changing and the store and Charity behind us, a weight began to lift. The burden evaporated. And surely this was akin to what Kat experienced when she decided to leave me: the chance to be somebody new. You get to a point in your life where that opportunity doesn't exist anymore, where you are too far finished with becoming who you're meant to become that starting over isn't an option, so what's left are pitiful attempts at originality: putting on a pantsuit and running away from your cheating husband, going on a Disney Cruise, heading to the Amazon to live with natives, dying your hair green and wearing an ironic hat.

A.J. dialed up a podcast on his phone as we drove. Some dude was talking in a deep voice about isolation and protectionism being the only way to save late-capitalist America. What was late about it? How did he know? Was there some timeline I wasn't familiar with? The dude sounded like any other fool with a bad idea, so I asked A.J. to put on some music.

He turned up some rap like it would annoy me.

He was right. "You got any Otis Redding?" I asked.

"I've got everything," A.J. said. "It's called a phone." He thumbed the screen without taking his eyes off the road, and soon Otis's voice came yearning through the speakers, pleading from the bottom of his busted, broken, and beautiful heart for Ole Man Trouble to find some other soul to pick on. I got the sense that the song meant something a whole lot different to us both.

Statesboro Blues

Statesboro is on the way to the coast, but not close enough to be appealing in any way: no salt air, no sand, no tourism. As we entered, we passed a white sign that said *Welcome to Statesboro, birthplace of General George Comstock*, a man I'd never heard of but who must've been a huge deal, like Charity's own Dick Haley. Every town's got a local hero. We passed the Frugal Frog, a diner with a healthy advertising budget. A.J. wanted to stop and eat, but I told him he'd have to wait. We were close to where we needed to go.

We followed Main Street through downtown, and just past the bypass, the woman's voice told us we'd arrived. It was a dirt road beneath a sign peppered with buckshot: DuPree's Salvage.

"Take a right," I said.

"Where?"

"Down that dirt road."

"Don't look like a farm to me."

DuPree's Salvage wasn't in the best part of town, or any part of town for that matter. Nothing but abandoned sandy lots, yards piled with smashed metal, smoldering trash fires, pit bulls tied to leashes snapping at fences ready to clamp their jaws on your jugular. Across the dirt yard of a dilapidated house, we passed a group of men sitting around a small table playing dominoes. They laughed and drank from paper bags and watched us, then resumed their game.

Behind a border of skinny pines, the whole DuPree operation was secured by a high chain link fence topped with razor wire. I didn't see any dogs. A small house and several double-wides sat on the other side of the fence. Car parts were assembled in like piles. Pyramids of carburetors, hubcaps, fenders, trunks and hoods, mufflers. Maybe one would fit Kat's vehicle, which, come to think of it, was a good cover story for A.J. as to what we were doing here.

"I need a muffler," I said, "so you can stop driving me all over the state."

We both got out of the car. A.J. stretched his quads, pulling his right foot up to his butt, then his left. Next to the front gate was a yellowed plastic intercom box with a black button worn smooth from repeated pressings. I hit the buzzer and couldn't readily tell if it had done anything, if a corresponding buzz had sounded somewhere within the compound. I turned my attention to the men playing their game, keeping track of their numbers, not wanting any one of them to slip off and come mug us, steal my backpack and my pie, the Cadillac. The men were all accounted for, except now they had an extra.

A.J. stood next to their table, watching them play.

I hit the buzzer three times and got nothing. I was about to give up when an older woman came out on the front porch of the house. She wore a purple track suit and had stark white hair, and she was pulling a large rolling suitcase. She locked the door behind her and banged the suitcase down the front steps and up to the gate where she was startled to see me waiting.

"Can I help you?"

"Are you Hazel DuPree?"

"Most of the time."

"I knew your son," I said. "Clarence Hart."

"I can't do nothing about that," she said. "I was just leaving. Eli will be here in less than a second."

"I was a friend of his."

"Eli's?"

"Clarence."

"Sorry to hear it," she said. "Hope he didn't do that to your head."

An engine rumbled behind me. I turned to see a car driving up the dirt road, a cloud of red dust billowing in its wake. The car stopped at the gate, a silver car with another silver-hair behind the wheel.

Once she saw the car she must've felt safe. Hazel opened the motorized front gate and tried to wheel the suitcase by me, but I stepped in front to stop her. She wore pink glasses and was in great shape for her age, but it could've been the track suit giving off a healthy vibe. The car door opened. I wished A.J. was with me. I had to admit he was a better salesman. Could talk a customer who'd come in for a single peach into leaving with three melons, a sack of onions, six ears of corn, and a T-shirt.

"We've got a plane to catch, sir," she said. "Don't make Eli get rough." She faked to the right before she did a spin move and peeled off me to the left, running to Eli's car. Eli came over and dragged her suitcase to the trunk.

"This man causing trouble?" he asked. He lifted her suitcase into the trunk and shut it. "What's wrong with his head?"

"Something to do with Clay," Hazel said. "Boy's dead and still twisting the knife."

Clay? Had I come to the wrong place? Found some other mother so wracked with spite for her dead son it'd shocked her hair white? Impossible. Valentine. Clarence. Clay.

The man was well-practiced at being different people for different people. "Listen," I said. "I've come a long way, and I'm just trying—"

"How far you come?" Eli asked.

"Charity," I said.

Hazel scoffed. "Come to collect, huh? That boy dug his own grave, so he can pay for his own funeral as far as I'm concerned."

They both stood behind Eli's car. She was taller than him by a good six inches. "Want to know what's a long way away?" she asked. "Prague. Prague's a long way. You ever been to Prague?"

I told her no I hadn't. In fact, I'd never left the country, but I didn't see the need to add that level of detail.

"That's where Eli and I are headed. Looks like a real-life Magic Kingdom."

"Czechoslovakia," I said.

"Not for decades. Keep up."

They separated to their sides of the car. Eli climbed in the driver seat.

"What's your name?" she asked.

"Lee. Lee Hubbs." I stuck out my hand. She didn't accept.

"Hubbs? Charity? You related to the produce people?"

"I am the produce people."

"Don't suppose you brought me any peaches?"

I shook my head. I had a pie, but it was becoming clear she wouldn't want it.

"Doesn't matter. Couldn't take 'em out of the country anyway." She looked at a gold watch hanging loosely on her wrist. "Got time for one story," she said. She peeked in the car at Eli who was checking his phone, his glasses pulled down to the tip of his nose. She resembled Anne, and I wanted to tell her that

I also knew her daughter, could tell her how to get in touch with her, but Hazel was going on a trip, and apparently did not care too much about her family. "You ever heard of Miki Volek?"

"No ma'am."

"Czech King of Rock-n-Roll. Clay toured with him once, all over Europe. Or I guess I should say Clay snorted coke with him all over Europe. Huge star. Buried in Prague with a marker the size of a shoebox. You know what's on that stone?"

"I wish I did."

"A relief portrait of the man wearing sunglasses. He always wore sunglasses. So, now, when people walk by that stone they see something odd, a guy in sunglasses, and they want to know who that man was, and they look him up on Wikipedia to find out what his life was like. And then they realize they can't read Czech."

"I'm not sure I understand what this has to do with Clarence."

"Miki had a tragic life. Drug addict. Once had a million fans, and he ended up on a shoebox decorated with a fool portrait of himself wearing sunglasses." She got in the car and left the door open. "Clay did not have a million fans. Not sure he had one. A tombstone is too good for him. *Dobry den.*"

She shut the door and Eli drove them away.

A.J. was still watching the men at their game. I grabbed the backpack from the car and walked over. All of them turned their heads, their eyes yellowed, some teeth missing in spots, scratchy beards, assorted expressions of menace. A.J. should've been scared of them, but he stood there chewing on a Twizzler. All the men had Twizzlers, either in their mouths or on the table in front of them with their dominoes or behind their ears. The biggest one, the leader of the group apparently, a quail with a stunted plume charred like the end of a frayed rope, offered me a drink from his paper sack, welcoming me to the place they thought I must belong as naturally as they did. And maybe I did, but I wasn't ready to sit down with them and accept their welcome.

"Cool shirt," the man said.

I took the onion pie out of the backpack.

"Y'all hungry?"

"What is it?" the man asked, but he didn't look at me. He looked at A.J., as if he was the only one who could be trusted to offer the truth.

"Onion pie," A.J. said.

At first it was small, his laugh, a chuckle, but soon all three of them were cackling, the quail pausing only to catch his breath to say, "Ain't nobody want an onion pie."

The River

A.J. stopped at a Flying J filling station even though I urged him to drive to the nearest BP. "We're not down here for melons," he said.

"You guessed right."

Truth was, I wanted A.J. along for more than his wheels. He was good company, and bright, and presently one of the few friends I had, and if he hadn't been watching some vagrants play dominoes he might've been able to work his charm and elicit some more information from Hazel DuPree. But that ship had sailed.

It was depressing to think Valentine's own mother wanted nothing to do with him. How do you screw up so much that you alienate your mama? I wasn't going to tell A.J. how much I needed him, and have him get all full of himself. But since he'd grown suspicious, I didn't see any harm in letting him in on the real purpose of our mission, especially since I'd finally found out something worthwhile about the man, at least a curious tidbit of trivia. I confessed to A.J. that I'd lied to him to get him to come down here with the hope of finding Valentine's mother, which we had done.

"The woman in the track suit?"

"The woman in the track suit."

"She didn't want the pie?"

"I never got the chance to ask her, but I'm pretty sure the answer is no."

"That's cold."

"Valentine was a musician. Played guitar with some communists in Europe."

"I ain't driving you to Europe." He got out of the car. "You owe me some gas."

I gave him the coffee mug and asked him to fill it up for me. I pumped dirty gas while he went inside the food mart.

I was stymied. No next move immediately presented itself. I'd seen Valentine's half-sister and his mother, and neither one of them had expressed an ounce of love or hurt or regret or sorrow.

So why the hell did I still care?

A.J. came back with an Arnold Palmer and my coffee.

"Dude inside said he worked at the radio station," A.J. said, handing me the mug.

"What?"

"Valentine. The man this is all about."

"How do you figure?"

"He saw the mug. We had a polite conversation about music. I asked him if he'd ever seen your guitar hero. Showed him this." A.J. reached in his pocket and pulled out the Polaroid picture of Valentine we'd gotten from the funeral home.

The gas pump clicked.

WRVR—The River! Statesboro's Home for Classic Rock! wasn't that far from the Flying J. The freshly painted letters in its mirrored windows matched the letters on the mug I'd been drinking coffee from all day. Why hadn't I thought of this? Massive satellite dishes and towers surrounded the tiny building like it was full of high stakes secrets instead of burnouts spinning Led Zeppelin. To the left of the radio station was an open field full of overgrown grass littered with junk: spools and axels, a refrigerator, an entire El Camino slowly succumbing to rust. To the right of the building was a dollar store, toys and clothes and furniture lining the front sidewalk and spilling over the parking curb.

A.J. handed me the Polaroid. "Hurry up," he said. "I'm hungry."

"You're not coming in?"

"All you."

"Fine. Won't take a sec," I said, and got out of the car.

A.J. whistled from the open window. The Tenderheart backpack dangled from his long arm. "Give 'em the pie," he said.

I snatched the backpack.

The front door opened to the sound effect of an electric guitar playing a popularized riff that sounded familiar but I couldn't immediately recognize. A small box like a walkie talkie hung off the door handle, emitting this classic sound to all who entered the halls of WRVR. Inside was a reception area; a desk without a receptionist; an empty swivel chair in front of a computer; a coffee table surrounded by leather and chrome chairs, the coffee table strewn with music magazines. A bud vase with a small white flower cheered up the scene. Beyond the reception desk stood a single blacked-out glass door leading to where all the magic happened. Signed publicity photos of rockers covered one entire wall of the room. I recognized Alice Cooper with a snake around his neck. On another wall hung two clocks above a white porcelain water fountain. One of the clocks registered the actual time, as noted by the placard below that said Georgia, the other had a similar placard, but the clock face held no hands. The placard read: *Rock-n-Roll.*

Voices chattered from somewhere, and I wondered if anybody'd heard the guitar announcing my arrival. A man laughed. I coughed. After a few more seconds without an appearance I went to the door again and re-opened it to the guitar effect, hoping for recognition.

A woman came out from behind the glass door. She held a manila folder against her hip. One side of her head was shaved, and she had her bleached hair swooped over the other side like a wave, but she was way too old to be wearing her hair like that, somebody who'd obviously visited the salon recently and held up a picture of some twenty-year-old from one of the music mags on the coffee table and told her hairdresser to make her match. She dropped the manila folder next to the keyboard and took a seat in the empty office chair at the receptionist's desk. "You hurt?" she asked. "You need something?"

I set the backpack down on the high counter next to a tit-shaped candy dish full of loose Tic Tacs. The woman eyed the backpack then combed over every part of my shirt, tilting her neck like she was hearing a dog whistle, almost urging me to spin around so she could see the detailed embroidery.

"Anybody work here by the name of Valentine?" I asked.

"Like Bobby Valentine?"

"Could be. He had a lot of names."

"You remember Bobby Valentine? That baseball manager who put on a mustache that one time and tried to sit in the dugout after he'd already been tossed?"

"How about Clarence Hart?" I asked. "That ring a bell? Did a Clarence Hart ever hang around here or work here?"

"Not a baseball fan?"

"Yeah, I like baseball. A friend of mine used to work here. Wondering if you knew him is all."

"What happened to your head?"

"I had an accident."

"Who are you looking for again? Did he do that to you?"

"Clarence. Clarence Hart. Or Clay. Some people knew him as Clay."

"Are you in some band I should've heard of? That's an awfully peculiar shirt."

"He gave it to me. You recognize it?"

"It don't look right on you. You know how sometimes people are wearing things they shouldn't be wearing? Like a bikini on a fat girl. What's this Hart fella look like?"

I thought about mentioning her hair as another example of incongruity, but instead I pulled the Polaroid out of my pocket, the picture already faded. I set it on the counter next to the backpack. Valentine looked worse than I remembered, or maybe the photograph held some kind of magic powers, decaying like he would've decayed had he not been stuck in a funeral home fridge. The minute I dropped the Polaroid on the counter I regretted it. A.J. might've been playing a trick on me, making me walk into some random place flashing around a picture of a dead man. I made a move to snatch the picture, but she'd quickly spun it around with a sharp orange nail. She crinkled her forehead and grabbed some reading glasses from a crocheted case on the desk. She tilted her head at me again. "Is this some kind of joke?"

"You know him?"

"He's dead," she said.

"And I'm sorry for that."

The woman fanned herself with the manila folder and tufted out her white see-through blouse. Her bra was Buccaneers orange, the color of her nails, and I wondered if this woman was always so color-coordinated. Saturdays were orange days. Mondays were blue days. Her closet must look like a candy store, shirts stacked like SweeTarts, skirts hanging like sheets of Fruit Roll-Ups.

She pushed a button on the office phone and yelled into the device. "Stack!"

Soon enough, a man in jeans and a black T-shirt emerged from the darkened door, his long gray hair pulled into a ponytail. He wore a holster on his belt that I thought at first held a gun, but it was a phone, a massive phone. He stuck out his hand for a shake and I introduced myself. His shake was strong and firm, so I squeezed harder to match his effort. Unlike the woman, this man didn't slink behind the walls of the reception desk. She wanted to maintain a barrier of perceived safety. He wanted to destroy the perception of distance. Still, he stood way too close to me. I could smell his breath. Tic Tacs.

"Stack Buckley," he said. "What's the good word?"

"I know a lot of them."

We stared at each other, both misunderstanding.

"Not a Tech man, huh? To hell with Georgia," he said, and then slapped the receptionist's desk to get her attention. "Right, Missy?" Missy rolled her eyes and clicked her fingernails over the keyboard. "Missy went to UGA. Told myself I'd never marry a Bulldog." Stack leaned in closer so he could give me his next line in a stage whisper. "But she's a bulldog in more ways than one."

A bunch of sports lovers here at the River. I didn't tell him I was a Georgia fan myself. Tech fans were self-important pricks with an inferiority complex; his next question would be when I graduated, then I'd either have to lie or tell him I didn't actually matriculate, which would lead to a joke about how the worst kind of Georgia fans are the ones who'd never opened a book on campus, and then this would make me feel stupid and then I'd get pissed off and we'd get nowhere.

"You know a man named Valentine? Clarence Hart?" I asked.

Missy showed Stack the picture.

"He died up in Charity," I said. "I'm trying to find anybody who knew him."

Stack turned the Polaroid over in his stubby fingers. "Do you know Roy Bloom?" he asked. "From Charity. I played football with him."

I told him the name sounded familiar, but I wasn't sure.

Stack shook the photo, trying to bring more color to it, like he'd recently snapped it from the mouth of a Polaroid. "You say you don't know who this is?" He held it up for me to see.

"We weren't best friends or anything."

Stack tossed the picture on top of the backpack so it landed on the Care Bear's head. "Clay Corazón. Best damn guitar player you'd ever met."

"Clay Corazón?"

"I'm surprised you hadn't heard of him." Stack's eyes glistened. "If you'd lived at a very particular time in the late 60s early 70s, and listened to a very particular set of music, and read the liner notes on all your albums while you were smoking doobs in the basement, then you'd certainly know this man."

Stack walked to the wall of photographs and called me over with a yank of his head. He pointed halfway up the wall to a big picture of a family of gypsies, lots of hair and beards and bell bottoms, at least two dozen people crowded in front of a tour bus detailed in colorful psychedelic mushrooms. Some of the group held instruments. Some of them smoked weed. Some of them shot the camera a bird or a peace sign. There was at least one bottle of Jack Daniels.

"See anybody in there you recognize?"

Nothing but generic emblems of classic rock to me. Peace, love, and pubic hair.

Stack stuck a finger on the face of a dude near the back of the bus. His body was shielded by a group of other men and women so that he needed to be pointed out to be noticed, a man with a thin mustache and an afro and a happy-to-be-here smile.

"Clay Corazón," he said. "That's him with the Allman Brothers Band, way before all this quail nonsense, probably the height of his game. He toured with a few other bands, cut one record on his own but it was nothing but guitar solos and grunting. Then the world dissolved into disco and we've all been screwed since."

I stared at the image of the man with the afro, trying to match it up to the dead quail in the Polaroid. They didn't look the same, but they were the same. This certainly would explain Valentine's love of that pinball machine. He was reliving a dream every time that ball shot out across the play field, maybe even hearing a guitar track he'd once laid down echoed back to him, remembering the best time in his life. His one true, simple pleasure.

"When he came in here looking for work I thought I was pretty lucky," Stack said. "Clay Corazón. Right here in the flesh, on my airwaves. I let him deejay in the middle of the night, but he'd hardly play music. I never listened so I didn't know till Missy here told me, but he did nothing except read from some book, while every now and again pausing to play some Cher. I can't stand Cher. What was the name of that book?"

"*Love Story*," Missy said, not looking away from her computer screen.

"*Love Story*. Damn quails lose their minds, you know? Course, long before that, Clay'd left his talent at the bottom of a bottle and the end of a long white line. Didn't care for his God-given gift. Didn't nurture it. Us mortals, Mr. Hubbs, we don't get that many gifts. Shame to waste the ones we got."

People would want to know. One of those magazines would want to run an obit. Music nerds were probably sitting around now challenging each other to name every album where Clay Corazón filled in as a session player. The road had led me to the world where he'd belonged. I'd found the people who'd speak highly of him, attest to his virtues, recall his gloried and storied past in song. I unzipped the zipper to the backpack, reached in for the pie. "I'm sorry for your loss," I said.

"Shit. That asshole stole seventeen hundred dollars' worth of equipment and I never saw him again. Is that the loss you're talking about?"

"He didn't mention that."

"No, I guess he didn't." Stack sniffed the air and scanned the room for the source of what had gotten his nostril's attention. I unveiled the pie. He lifted up a corner of foil.

"What you got here?" he asked.

"I'm trying to find folks who knew him is all. Offer my condolences."

"Smells like onions."

"It's an onion pie."

"Hold up," Stack said. "Hubbs. From Charity. Hubbs Produce?"

I told him, yes, that was my place.

"Next time you drive down here, bring me some peaches instead of a picture of a dead guitarist and a stinking onion pie."

"Who would want an onion pie?" Missy asked, her nose scrunched in the air.

"Ain't enough Tic Tacs in the office to get me to eat an onion pie," Stack said.

I slid the pie in the backpack and zipped her up, thanked them both for their time and walked out the door, escorted by the artificial sound of the guitar.

I recognized it then: the opening riff of "When Doves Cry."

Outside, a cop and some grandma were standing in front of A.J., who was sitting on the hood of his car slumped over and humiliated.

"What's going on?" I asked.

"This boy belong to you?" the cop asked. He held A.J.'s 'MERICA hat in his hands. The name on his uniform said *Mitchell*.

I threw the Care Bear backpack in the car, not wanting to be perceived as some kind of joker in my negotiations with the law. The shirt and shoes and bandaged up head were all ridiculous enough. I told him A.J.'s name and that he worked for me at my store up in Charity.

"Hubbs? I've been to Hubbs. Great peaches. And you sell this Vidalia and peach salsa that's righteous on a fajita. You don't got any with you, do you?"

The reception I was getting down here made me think I should open up a second store. Wasn't there any decent place to buy overpriced produce and jarred goods near Statesboro? "I don't," I said.

"Janice here says the boy stole the hat from the dollar store." The cop held up the hat. Exhibit A. "But he has a different story."

"I didn't steal the hat," A.J. said.

I vouched for him. "He bought that hat with me. I saw him do it."

"You got a receipt?" Officer Mitchell asked.

A.J. shook his head.

"I was with him when he bought the hat, officer. And it wasn't at this place. Are there any other hats like that in there?"

"Good thinking," Officer Mitchell said, and slapped me on the shoulder. The mention of his favorite salsa must've lightened his spirits.

The four of us went inside to see if A.J.'s hat matched any of the other redneck trucker hats in the bargain bin. I figured if it didn't match any of them, it would prove it must not have been part of their inventory, so how could he have stolen it?

This proved to be a misguided line of inquiry on my part. The dollar store was filled with hats that said 'MERICA in one way or another. I tried another angle.

"Officer Mitchell, I saw him buy the hat. I can promise you that, but if my word's no good, then how 'bout I send you some jars of that salsa you like?"

"You can't bribe a police officer with salsa. But I'm afraid it's two words against one, Janice. And I know your word can be specious at times."

"Shut up."

"Janice here once accused a man with no hands of shoplifting a box of cereal flakes."

"It was his dog did it for him. That's why I don't allow them help dogs."

"Well, now, that's illegal, Janice," Officer Mitchell said.

"Don't care."

"Why don't you get back to work," Officer Mitchell told Janice. She shot A.J. a look like she'd be sure to get him next time, although I was pretty sure there was not going to be any next time for either of us at this Statesboro dollar store.

We got in the DeVille, and Officer Mitchell leaned his head inside the driver side window, obviously feeling magnanimous for de-escalating the situation and not allowing himself to get carried away like so many of his comrades. He handed the hat back to A.J. "You remember what that hat stands for, you hear?"

"I reckon I know," A.J. said.

A.J. often complained about getting different treatment because he was black, but I never put much stock in any of it, knowing it was possible, but also knowing that A.J. exaggerated. Besides, here I was giving him a job and responsibility and helping him achieve his goals of learning about a small business and making money so he could buy gas and tool around in his granddaddy's DeVille, so A.J. was in no way representative of unequal opportunity and stacked decks. He was what he was, another awkward teenager with limited basketball skills.

"This was not a race thing," I told him.

"Never is, is it?"

A Brother in Need

After the salvage yard and the radio station I was ready to head home. This quail named Clarence Hart or Valentine or Clay Corazón had died unloved, and just like Marty said it was troubling to discover how easy it was to do so.

A.J. wanted to get something to eat. He was probably humiliated by the encounter with the woman at the dollar store, but I figured some lunch, on me, would brighten him up.

We stopped at the Frugal Frog, nothing more than a diner attached to a Shell filling station whose design aesthetic could best be described as brown. The walls were brown. The floor was brown. Dark brown vinyl booths. And tables an even darker brown, almost black. I'd expected green. This place was more like the Frugal Toad, coloration-wise.

We sat in a booth. A.J. ordered a Coke and a western omelet from a waitress with a long brown braid, a brown apron and a white shirt with brown stripes. She was pretty in that fleeting way of south Georgia rednecks, all eyeliner and ear studs. A few more years of Miller Light and Marlboros and she'd be pining for the time she'd won Carrot Queen. I ordered French toast. The Frugal Frog served breakfast all day, a detail I admire in diners. A man should be able to order a filling, budget-conscious meal at all hours.

A.J. looked at me, his Coke between his hands, his hat pushed high on his head and cocked to the side. "Find what you looking for?" he asked.

"Not really," I said. "He used to play guitar with the Allman Brothers. You believe that? Went by the name Clay Corazón. You never know about people, right?"

"Always more than meets the eye."

The waitress brought our food quickly, like they already had it prepared for us before we ordered. Our odd looks, a tall black boy with a fake green plume and a trucker hat, an injured man in a wild western shirt, gave us away as all-day breakfast types. I sipped my coffee. Tasted like burnt graham crackers. I poured syrup all over my French toast, enough syrup to drown them. We ate without saying much. A.J. devoured his omelet like he hadn't eaten all day, then got up and went to the bathroom.

All the folks at this restaurant, couples and families and solo diners at the counter, all of them were unknowable, with their secret lives of guitar stardom and binge-eating marshmallows and serial masturbation habits. Where were we? Not far from home, but feeling farther, a foreigner in my own state. Did people stop at my store and say the same thing, survey Exit 173 and all its fast food offerings and chain hotels and generic sampling of sameness and wonder to themselves who would live in such a place? *Why* they lived in such a place. Did they thank their lucky stars to be in their car on their way out of town, graced by fate not to have to spend their days in a rural outpost suffering under oppressive heat and gossip, enduring the woe of dying industry, opioid addiction, underwater mortgages, stagnant wages, finding faith in talking heads and preachers and snake oil salesmen who remind you of your once and future greatness, your manifest destiny, your God-given rights, lifting your spirits so that you may feed your face full of country ham and peach preserves, pat your belly, watch college football and sing the Star Spangled Banner with a hand over your clogged and dying heart.

If this is what people thought of us, I didn't want to know them anyway.

The waitress came and took our plates. I asked for more sugar for the coffee.

A.J. followed right behind her. "Listen to this," he said, and plopped down in the booth, suddenly reinvigorated from his breakfast. "Teenager driving too fast loses control and slams his daddy's SUV into the side of a house. Inside the house there's a couple, both of them asleep, and the SUV comes clear through the walls and lands on their bed. Kills the wife. The husband? Not a scratch. An SUV through a wall."

"This on some TV show?"

A.J. pointed to the bathroom. "Front page news. Read it on the wall."

An awful story, sure, but one I failed to immediately find relevant. "Damn shame," I said.

"Why don't you take that man the pie? The husband. I bet he's pretty sad about the whole thing. Or how 'bout you look at the obituaries. Bet there's a funeral today. You can drop that pie off somewhere."

"The dude's lucky," I said. "He probably hated his wife. Probably prayed every night for some sort of cataclysm to take her from him so he wouldn't have to look at her ugly face or eat her terrible food. That SUV was an answered prayer."

"Why'd you lie to me about coming down here for melons?" A.J. asked.

I held up one finger. "I've got to piss," I said.

The front page of *The Statesboro Herald* was framed above the urinal with a color photograph of the accident he was talking about. Impossible. An SUV clear through a bedroom wall. I could've been wrong about what I'd told A.J. Now I felt bad for saying it. The man might've just as easily loved his wife and cherished her company. Why did I always assume the worst in people and poison others with my thoughts?

I washed my hands and unwrapped the gauze from my head. It didn't look any better and it didn't look any worse. The air hit the sore and burned. Don't scratch. Don't scratch. But once it was out in the open I couldn't help it. I dug my nails in and scraped out flecks, clawed like I was trying to reach my skull, then turned the hot water on full blast and cupped my hand under the rushing tap and splashed hot water on the wound until I couldn't stand the temperature. I folded some paper towels into squares and dabbed. Rewrapped the gauze around my head. I saw how absurd I looked, so I took it right back off. Tossed the gauze in the trash.

At the booth where we'd been sitting I found two other people claiming our seats, so I went outside thinking A.J. must've paid the check and gotten in the car, eager to head home.

The DeVille was gone.

I circled the whole building. No car.

I went inside to see if I'd somehow forgotten where we'd sat and had approached the wrong booth, but all the tables and booths were filled with new customers, not one of them A.J., not one piece of evidence of us having eaten there. The waitresses had all changed, too. How long had I been in the bathroom? I wanted to find our waitress, the one with the long braid, ask her if she'd seen A.J., but she was gone, all the waitresses now older and weathered.

A gray-haired waitress carrying a coffee carafe for refills came up to me and handed me the Care Bear backpack. The red 'MERICA hat was snapped to one of its straps.

"Who gave you this?" I asked.

"Some tall boy with green hair." She reached in her apron and handed me our check. Coke and coffee and western omelet and French toast. Proof we'd been here. We'd eaten. But where was A.J.?

"Where'd he go?"

"Didn't say." She topped off the mug of a man eating nothing but a plate of bacon.

"That's it?" I asked.

Her eyes narrowed, and she studied my face like there'd be a quiz later. "Did you know you got a nasty sore on your head?"

I put the 'MERICA hat on and went outside.

Payphones still serve a necessary function. Don't let anyone tell you different. I located one outside, hiding on the side of the building as if it was embarrassed. If I'd known A.J.'s number I would've called him, apologized for everything, begged him to turn around and come get me, but all my numbers were in my phone, and my phone was still sitting in a bag of white rice. What numbers did I know? The nursing home. The store. My house. Kat's cell. Marty's cell. My brother's cell.

I called the store and got A.J.'s number from Ben. I had him repeat it so I could remember. I called A.J., but of course he didn't answer.

My brother was the next best option. He was close by.

I had to call him twelve times in a row, careful not to let his voicemail pick up and lose my change, before he relented to the onslaught and finally picked up.

"What? What the fuck do you want?"

"It's Lee," I said.

"What the hell number is this?"

"I'm at a payphone."

"Are you calling from the 80s?"

"I need you to come get me. I'm in Statesboro."

"A brother in need is a brother indeed," he said, "Where you at?"

"Some place called the Frugal Frog."

My brother hung up without saying if he'd be coming or not, but I knew he would, if only to gloat over the trouble I'd found myself in and that he had to help me out of.

A stool opened up at the counter, so I sucked down a tall glass of water and drank black coffee while I waited. I felt sick to my stomach, and my head itched. As if the universe could get any more particularized to my plight, the man who'd been sitting next to me left the newspaper next to his yellow plate of smeared yolk and orange slice, open to the obits. I read them, and they were all the same. So and so was loved by many, held a steady job, left some folks behind. Here was a clipping of a life, a person reduced to two paragraphs in a newspaper nobody reads, a newspaper plastered above a pisser, but there they are. JoAnne Robichaud, died in her sleep, peacefully, mother of two, survived by her husband, loved cats. And Michael Gliss, a member of the chamber of commerce, ran for mayor once and lost, epic tinkerer. And Wallace Horner, a hundred years old, fought in wars, never married, confirmed bachelor. Whenever I saw an obit of someone younger than me, my heart sank. What was it that made it so I wasn't them?

I imagined my own obit, full of love and memories, a column in the *Charity Register*, but who would cut it out now and keep it in a Ziploc bag full of memorabilia? Who would even write the damn thing? The people in my life were quitting on me left and right. And it seemed so easy to be left, to find yourself alone one day, stuck in Statesboro at a Frugal Frog, wearing another man's shirt and a trucker hat for a once-great country, toting around a Care Bear backpack and counting the mistakes you'd made to get yourself here.

A Happiness Quotient

A repetitive blast of car horn had all the diners and the waitstaff turning their attention to the windows. A black Escalade was parked near the front, its horn honking and its lights flashing like an alarm going off. The checkout girl sprinted out in a tizzy, so I figured it was her car, until she came in shouting my name. "Lee Hubbs. Anybody here named Lee Hubbs? Some jerk is looking for you."

Pierce wore madras-patterned shorts, a white golf shirt, aviator sunglasses, and a Titleist visor. This wasn't his vehicle, because my brother would never own anything this expensive, not only because he couldn't afford it, but because he didn't like to own anything. He smiled a big smile full of white teeth, that smile that got him out of so much trouble. Everybody loved Pierce.

"I don't get out of the car in places like this," he said when I climbed in. "What the hell kind of trouble are you in? And why are you carrying around a goddamn Care Bear backpack? Shit. You're having a midlife crisis." He yanked the wheel and hurried out of the parking lot of the Frugal Frog. "The best way to avoid that," he said, "is to never approach midlife."

My brother was an escape artist when it came to responsibility. Never wanted anything to do with the farm, with onions, with family, with kids, with Charity at all. As the older brother, he was supposed to want it all, to keep it all, and dole out pieces of our paltry empire to me, the second in command, but he didn't. He wanted to play golf all day and spend the summer in Europe and go deep-sea fishing for marlin. All that's fine and good until you leave your wife for your yoga instructor and get so fuck-struck you follow her when she decides to make a drastic career move and go to law school. Would he have followed her if she'd been pursuing an advanced degree in Yoga-nomics? No, but I'm sure in Pierce's mind the math was simple. Here was an opportunity to tie his empty wagon to the earning potential of a future lawyer. His ex-wife had taken care of him, I'll give her that. And, like our father, Pierce needed taking care of. Now he'd traded up for a more ideal future, a woman who made the money while he played golf and planned their vacations.

I asked him if he'd drive me home to Charity. Told him Mama would love to see him.

"Hell, no," he said. "We're having a fiesta tonight."

"You can drop me off and drive back. Won't take that long."

"And here I was thinking you wanted to spend some time with your brother."

Pierce aimed the Escalade toward Savannah. "I've got to get back to work," I said.

"Bitch, you work about as much as I do. I'll take you in the morning. Tonight we fiesta!"

"I'm not really in the mood."

"Well, get in the mood. Unburden yourself. Pour out your soul. Confess what unsavory machinations have brought you so low you had to call your brother for salvation. I will never forget this, you know."

"How about if I pay you to take me home? Toss you a couple hundred bucks?"

"Tomorrow. Carpe diem, bro."

I was a passenger, and as such I didn't have much of a choice. I did not enjoy being a passenger so much lately. But I figured it might help me feel better to talk. So I told Pierce about all my shit-ass luck. Told him how Kat left me (although I didn't bore him with the details of why), told him how our house, the house we grew up in, had been invaded by ladybugs. (He laughed at that. "Your worst nightmare!") I told him how I'd punched a hipster in the mustache with little provocation. How I'd had a breakdown in the bathroom of the store and had A.J. drive me to Statesboro in the hope that I might find somewhere to deliver an onion pie. As for what precipitated all this, I just told him Valentine was a quail who worked for me, and after he'd died nobody knew where to find his kin, so I'd taken the duty upon myself. I told my brother how disturbing it was to know that the man's body was zipped in a bag at a funeral home waiting for somebody to claim him, which nobody would, so pretty soon he'd be sent to the medical college to get mauled by baby doctors high off nitrous oxide.

Pierce listened to all this, chuckling every now and then, nodding. He shared a cigarette with me and then, when I was done with my story, he said: "You need to hit some golf balls."

After about forty-five minutes or so we pulled up to the gates of a country club that looked way too expensive for the likes of my brother. He punched in a code to start the mechanism that opened the front gate, and we parked in a small parking lot. Two young kids came out to the Escalade and took Pierce's bag and slung it on a golf cart. From the parking lot I could see the driving range, and the distance didn't make it necessary to use a golf cart to get there. Pierce pulled a wadded-up nylon rain jacket from his golf bag and handed it to me, told me my shirt might get us in trouble and I needed to look more respectable. Coming from him this was absurd. The jacket was blaze orange, high visibility, like I was going hunting or working on a highway. Pierce stuck a few dollar bills in one of the kid's hands and we hopped in the cart and drove not thirty yards to the driving range. The tee box and range grass were perfect, Crayola green, not sun-parched and starving like so many courses in the heat of Georgia summertime sun.

Beside the range, a putting green stretched out in the shape of a bright green amoeba, three short yellow flag sticks plugged in the surface, sugar-white bunkers lining the edges. The pinestraw surrounding the trees and decorating the flower beds was freshly raked and placed in a uniform alignment. A waitress wearing starched white pants and a white golf shirt with gold piping around the arms and collar came over with a tray and asked if we needed anything.

Pierce ordered a gin and tonic from her, so I said I'd have one too. Then another kid came out carrying two buckets of bright white range balls with gold bands circling their dimpled equators, balls so nice I'd probably have played a round with them and never noticed they were range balls, and here we were about to hack at them like a roadside prison detail. No one else was on the range. The place was untouched, a slice of pristine golf heaven. Maybe it was. We stood next to each other on the tee box unmarked by the divots of previous duffers. Pierce took out a pitching wedge and braced it on his shoulders, twisting and stretching.

"Is this club new?" I asked.

He kept twisting his torso as he spoke. "Nope. Super private. The course is even nicer. Only three holes, but they were designed by Jack Nicklaus."

What kind of country club only had three holes? None of the flag sticks had a logo or a fancy crest that'd tell me what this place was called. When the waitress brought our drinks I noticed her golf shirt didn't have a logo either. "What's this place called?" I asked.

He tipped a bucket over, spilling balls from its mouth. He set up, addressed the ball, and swung, sending a high, lofting, slightly fading shot up, up and down, close to the flag stick that marked a hundred yards. Nicely done. He rolled another ball between his stance with his club face. "It's a partner's house. You believe that shit?"

Pierce swung and hit another perfect shot. Everything I'd been looking at suddenly made sense. The house we'd pulled up to was a private mansion, not a club. This also explained the small parking lot. The security checkpoint was for the estate. This was a man's private playground: a driving range, three holes of golf, a putting green, a waitstaff, all made available to guys like Pierce who was doing nothing more than screwing a summer associate. He could see his future in this place and he loved every minute of it. He hit three more wedges close to the same spot.

"Pretty sweet," I said.

He switched clubs to a 7-iron. Took another perfect swing.

"That's how they get you. Tell you all this could be yours. Show you this man's country-club estate, hold it out for you like a golden carrot on a golden stick."

Another swing.

"Then you say, 'Hell, yeah, I'm on board!' And they work you to the bone, driving you with that same damn stick."

I reminded him he wasn't the one working for anything.

"That's because I'm smart."

Another swing.

"This guy's the founder of the firm," he said. "Nobody else is getting this shit. But still, these kids eat it up. Greedy bitches."

Pierce handed me the 7-iron. I rolled a ball over and took a swing. It felt good. The repetition of the driving range used to always make me feel better, no matter how bad I was smacking the ball. It was the smacking itself that did it; the rhythm and aggression helped relieve so much pent-up stress. I liked to watch the ball rocket off the club face and trace up against the pines and into the blue sky and plop down to a wide-open range spotted with white balls like tufts of cotton. I took several more swings, hard swings.

Pierce lifted a 3-iron from his bag and gripped the second bucket, carrying it in front of me to his own patch of tee grass. I stuck with the 7-iron. It was an easy club for me to hit, and I was doing okay with it.

"I've got this theory," he said. He paused after his announcement to roll a ball towards the front of his stance and rope a 3-iron straight out about 200 yards. I'd never seen him hit a 3-iron in his life. He turned around to me and leaned on the club, right foot crossed over left in classic relaxed golfer stance.

I lined up a 7-iron, looked up at him, and while keeping my eyes locked on his eyes, I swung without re-checking the ball or my alignment, a trick I could usually pull off just so I could tease some shithead who suggested I needed to keep my head down and my eye on the ball. This time the shot wasn't great. I topped it, straight but not far.

"Nice," he said. "You watch TV, right?"

"Most of the time it's something my kids want to watch."

Pierce returned to his bucket of balls and hit another laser 3-iron, then threw his club on the grass and sat down on a bench behind me, facing the range like he was going to analyze my swing. He took heavy gulps from his drink, which had been sitting idle in a cup holder on the arm of the bench. It reminded me to do the same with my drink, which I'd nestled in the grass next to the bucket of balls.

"I've come up with a happiness formula," he said.

I drank down half the drink, picked up the 3-iron, and took a swing. A bad slice that almost landed in this rich man's pond. Scared some swans.

"When you're flipping channels in that recliner that's been in our house since 1983, and you go one cycle through all the channels, how many people do you wish you were, do you wish you could trade places with?"

"You're going to have to explain a little more."

"You're on the couch..." He raised his right arm, the one not holding his drink, and simulated surfing channels with his thumb, a solo thumb wrestling pantomime. "...Click. Click. Click. You go all the way up the channels, circle around to where you started. How many people, during that cycle would you trade places with?"

"Nobody really watches TV like that anymore."

"Whatever. How many? Host of a cooking show? Some baseball player? A news anchor? Some jerk selling blankets, how many?"

I'd never wanted to be anybody else. Honestly. I liked myself and I liked my life and I felt I'd done a pretty good job. Until a few days ago. "Doesn't it all depend on how shitty your day is?"

"Mine used to be forty-nine. Forty-nine! That's sky-high. You divide that number by the number of channels and you get a percentage. A Happiness Quotient. HQ. And, yeah, sure, it's going to change from time to time, but you can still come up with a healthy range. Like cholesterol."

"What's a healthy range?"

"I don't have enough data to say, but probably under twenty-five percent. If you're wishing you were somebody else more than that, you probably ought to seek the advice of a professional."

I imagined my brother sitting at home flipping through channels, longing to be forty-nine different people. Who were they? And if they knew a man was sitting at home wishing to trade places with them, a man who never worked and depended solely on his charm and wit and good looks to get through life, would they not want to trade places with *him*? But maybe forty-nine people wasn't that high after all. A lot of people on TV look like they're having a really damn good time, living a pretty damn good life. But I still couldn't say I'd ever seen some bastard grilling ribs on his Manhattan rooftop and wanted to switch places with him.

I hit one more 3-iron, not much better, then took a seat next to him on the bench.

"Of course, the trouble..." he said. He finished his drink and pushed himself off the bench. "...is you only get to be you."

He walked to his spot on the range, teed up a ball, took out his driver and smashed the ball so far I never saw it come down. "How far'd that go?" I asked.

"Kingdom come," he said.

Slow Dance

Pierce drove us to his apartment and parked on the street outside another palatial coastal mansion, this one much closer to downtown Savannah and the riverfront. The house was two stories with a columned double-decker front porch, all white with dark green shutters and a tall gnarly oak in the front yard tinseled with moss, a picturesque beauty that belied the stench. The smell of marsh and river and mill mixed into a meaningful stink, a proximity to the ocean without actually being on the ocean. Savannah smelled spoiled. Or maybe it was the pie in my backpack.

The house was divided into four apartments, two on the first floor and two on the second. He and his girlfriend lived in one of the upstairs units, the one closest to the moss-draped oak. The inside of the apartment was one open front room with a small galley kitchen hiding off to the side where someone banged pots and pans around making general cook prep noises. Other people dressed all in black scurried around engaged in party preparations. A long hallway led to the bedrooms and bathroom. The space was nice: lots of light, high white ceilings trimmed with crown molding. A woman in a sundress lounged cooly on the couch, one long slender arm draped over the back, a glossy magazine in her lap. "This is Lily," he said, and kissed her on the top of the head.

Lily didn't bother to get up, but extended her hand like she expected it to be kissed or for me to bow before her, neither of which I did. I shook her hand. Lily was gorgeous, sophisticated, which made her look older than I'd imagined but still younger than Pierce, but who was I to judge? She had straight brown hair shampooed to a commercial sheen and cut to blunt edges like she'd jumped right out of the pages of her magazine. Her skin was perfectly and evenly tanned. No makeup, a natural beauty, and I could tell she was the type who took pride in this fact, might even tell you apropos of nothing, "I don't wear makeup."

Seeing this place and this gorgeous woman on this couch right after we'd hit golf balls in some millionaire's fantasy made me feel like I'd entered another world from a different era, an old world of old houses and old money and moss-covered trees and private clubs. There was rich, and then there was wealthy.

A dark-skinned quail wearing a tuxedo, plume like used pipe cleaners and a nose as sharp as a carrot, came out of the kitchen and asked Pierce where he'd like him to set up the bar. I wondered if this was also some kind of perk of Lily's summer employment, another enticement, your very own servant for the summer to greet you when you get home and to set up your bar for you.

"We're having a fiesta tonight, Cal." As if that explained everything. "Put it by the balcony."

Each one of these people, these service people, could've been Valentine, holding secrets and talents, dreams unfulfilled, skulking around the edges of everybody else's story. They all deserved their own story, to be seen, to have someone get to know them. But I was tired.

Pierce handed me a beer from an ice bucket and I followed him to his bedroom.

Their bedroom was slick and modern, I assumed to counteract the plaster whites and formal trimmings of the old house. A Juliet balcony overlooked an overgrown backyard where a swing set rusted in patches of knee high grass. A bicycle leaned up against the frame, both wheels intact. Their bed was so close to the floor my knees were around my ears when I sat on it. It was made up with an almost military vigilance, and knowing my brother I could tell this was Lily's doing. Making up beds or not making up beds says a lot about you. Some people refuse to make them up because they may be getting some more use out of them during the day, may need a nap or some place to hide. This was Pierce. Some people made up their beds on certain days, those days where they more closely examined their house and themselves and figured they needed to get their shit together, so they'd start with a nicely made bed. Look at that. I'm on my way! This was me, or rather me and Kat. There were some days when one or both of us wanted the bed made up, so that when we walked in our bedroom it looked nice, clean, like an adult with adult responsibilities lived inside. Then there are those who make up their beds religiously, with varying degrees of compulsion, the extra blanket folded just right at the foot of the bed, pillows fluffed a requisite number of times. And you might think that these people are the organized ones, the ones who know what they want and go get it, and this may be true occasionally. But more often than not, I think the chronic bed-maker is someone who's so tempted by the allure of an unmade bed, so frightened by the morning, that they make up their bed because it's the only way they can keep themselves from crawling back in. Fear disguised as neatness.

Chaos disguised as order. Be afraid of people who always make up their bed.

Pierce put on a tan suit and a pink tie, and told me I needed to do something about my fashion. I told him I didn't have a way to do anything about my fashion and I couldn't fit into any of his clothes because I was bigger than he was, so he went into his closet and gave me a hat, a gray Rat Pack hat with a black band and a tiny orange feather the size of a guitar pick. I traded one hat for another.

"Look at you, you dirty hipster," he said, then sprayed me down with some kind of cologne that reeked like a teenager's hopes and dreams. I was ready to join a boy band and dance synchronically to ballads about girls who won't return my text messages.

More caterers had arrived. Cal set up his bar next to the French doors that opened to the balcony, a full bar with every bottle imaginable. Along another wall of the front room ran a table set up for hors d'oeuvres where another man dressed in a white dinner jacket set out silverware and napkins on small decorative plates, not plastic. Opposite the bar stood a deejay of indeterminate ethnicity. He wore a straw cowboy hat and was talking to Lily, who'd accented her jaunty sundress with a white gardenia pinned to one side of her hair. All of the furniture I'd seen when I came in, including the couch, had been pushed to the edges of the room and arranged in quaint sitting vignettes to make room for spacious dance maneuvers without inhibiting the partygoers' ability to sit down, talk, or make out. Lily saw me come out of the bedroom and rushed over, laced her slender arm through my arm and dragged me outside on the front balcony. "Stay put," she said.

I leaned on the rail and smelled the air, musty and industrial, but now with something sweet riding the evening breeze, coating the stink with sugar. I looked down at my shirt, Valentine's shirt. What the hell was I doing here? The store would be closing soon, and A.J.'d probably made it back, and they'd all gotten through the day without me. The store could go on without me, and tomorrow it'd be even easier and the next day even easier.

Lily came outside with two champagne glasses. We toasted and drank.

"What was Pierce like as a kid?" she asked.

A hard question to answer. In most ways he was the same as now, a selfish clown who hated work and responsibility and lived his life like he was constantly running out of time. But if she was here with Pierce then she probably knew all that, was probably here with Pierce *because* of all that. "You love him?" I asked.

She shrugged and sipped her champagne. "He's fun. And funny. It fits my personality. I can be...," and here she dropped her voice a couple of octaves like an impression of some ghoulish headmaster, "very serious."

"Good-Time-Pierce," I said.

"I don't get those people who marry somebody just like them. There's got to be some yin and yang, you know? You can't fit identical puzzle pieces together."

This had always been my argument against gay marriage, but I think she meant it in a different way. "Y'all getting married?" I asked.

She laughed with her whole mouth, her whole face. Perfect laugh. Perfect teeth. "Oh, God, no. I'm not an idiot."

I finished the rest of my champagne and set the glass on the railing. Lily wrapped her long fingers around the stem of the champagne glass, saving it from the rail and the potential drop to the yard below. "You're married," she said, like she was reminding me.

"I am. Although she's not too happy with me right now."

"What'd you do?"

I scratched a paint fleck off the railing to keep from scratching my forehead. "Being myself for too long, I guess." I needed more champagne.

"You have kids, right?" she asked.

"Two."

"I don't want kids. Having kids is selfish. There are enough people on Earth as it is. I mean, what kind of future do they have to look forward to anyway? I don't have one ounce of mothering instinct in my body, no ticking clock, nothing. I don't see fat rolls on baby's thighs and think I need to nuzzle them. Imagining a parasite growing inside me freaks me out, and then, to imagine pushing that same parasite out my vagina and having it latch on to my boobs to eat. It's horrifying!"

The way she put it made having kids sound like a monster movie. Sometimes it could be like that. "Kids are tough," I said.

"Pierce says he wants kids. I told him he'd have to find another host to impregnate. I've got shit to do."

News to me. I'd never known Pierce to want anything that would interfere with his lifestyle, and a kid would do that. Maybe getting older had made him wonder about his mortality and want to leave something behind, a legacy that wasn't filled with hurt and mistakes. Maybe he saw in kids a second chance, a way to make amends for his failures. These would all be terrible reasons to have children.

"I'm sure he'd make a great father."

Lily laughed out loud again. "You're a terrible liar."

We went inside to join the party. By now about twenty or so people milled about the room accepting hors d'ouvres off trays, all of them dressed up and smelling fine, lots of small black dresses, skirts, heels, men in summer suits, ties colored like Skittles, a couple of older dudes in jeans and golf shirts who must've been footing the bill, but everyone else was young, so young, high off their own entitlement. I had a conversation with this quail chick who had a coil-shaped plume and freckles spotting her cute, round face. She lectured me on what she called multiverse theory, wondering if I was aware that at this very moment there were potentially other universes where she and I were having a totally different conversation, or perhaps doing something else. She grabbed and squeezed my wrist when she said, "something else."

"Like what?" I asked.

"Like anything! We could be spinning basketballs on our heads. We could be riding jet packs. We could be made of light. We could have clown noses. We could be sucking whipped cream through straws that are our fingers. When every eventuality is possible, there are no limits!" She twisted her plume around her finger and let it spring from her head. "I mean, did you ever think you'd live in a universe where people turned into quails?"

Her future was in marketing. I told her that I'd considered this idea before, even though I didn't know what to call it, and that I'd recently had an experience that made me believe I might've switched places with another version of myself and ended up in the wrong universe.

"Hmm," she said. "I don't think it works like that."

This ended our conversation.

I went off and got myself another drink. Cal handed me a champagne flute. I chugged it. The flutes were too small, so I walked around behind the bar and grabbed the open bottle of champagne out of its ice bath. I put a hand on Cal's shoulder and whispered, "Thank you for being here."

Soon I became a bit of a novelty at the party. A middle-aged man in a Rat Pack hat and a kick-ass shirt with an eagle embroidered on the back, toting around and pulling from a bottle of Moet. People wanted to talk to me, and when they did I discovered all they really wanted to do was talk about themselves or their dumb ideas, like that multiverse quail. Nobody asked me about myself except for Lily. The only one. Each one of these kids went on some tangent about the show they were binge watching, the professor they hated, the way their parents bought them whatever they wanted and so of course they'd turned out spoiled. So it wasn't their fault that they were the way they were. Not one person said, hey, cool shirt, where'd you get it? Why are you here? What's your point?

Lily spurred people out to the dance floor where lots of bodies moved together and laughed loudly and held animated breathless conversations about how high they were. I had another conversation with a girl whose bangs were cut at a sharp angle across her right eye, like some kind of pirate of the avant garde. She kept pushing the hair out her eyes while she talked about her dad, who was a judge, a hanging one by her own admission, a man whose judicial philosophy she despised, but everything else about him she loved, which made her, in her own words, "totally conflicted." Thinking of Jodi, I asked this girl if she cut her own hair. She left me to get herself another drink.

At some point Pierce sought me out. My Moet bottle had gotten lighter. He'd been playing gracious host all night, toting around an oversized martini glass he kept refilled and stocked with a pyramid of olives. He cornered me and stood close as he talked, yelling even though the music at the time wasn't all that loud. Most of the dancing had turned to slow and close, so I was jealous of all the couples with willing partners.

"Enjoying yourself?" he yelled, his breath briny and gin-tinged.

By way of an answer I pulled from the bottle.

He poked me in the chest. "So what are you *really* doing down here?"

"Drinking champagne. Why do you suddenly give a shit?"

"I'm your big brother. I don't give a shit. I just like to call you stupid."

"I tried to get you to take me home."

"You keep telling yourself that." Pierce surveyed the festivities, the drunken slits of his eyes gleaming with pride and reverie. He clinked his martini glass to the neck of my Moet. "Good party, huh?"

"It's all right."

"What do you think of Lily? She's great isn't she?"

"She's all right."

"How's Mama?"

"All right. About the same. Still drinking the hell out of some Yoo-hoos. It would be nice if you'd come see her."

"Is there anything in this world worth more to you than an 'all right'?"

I shrugged.

Pierce sloshed his martini glass at the party. "Contrary to your assessment, this fiesta is better than 'all right', it's fucking fire, so—"

"No man your age should use the word 'fire' unless he's in flames."

"If you're not having a good time, it's your own fault."

"That's the point? Having a good time?"

"I have yet to be convinced of another way." Pierce pulled the hat down over my eyes and left me in the corner.

Fine. I'd try to have fun.

I got drunk and started showing everybody the Polaroid of Valentine. "Want to see a dead guy?" Great party trick. "His name was Valentine." I told everyone. "Valentine. This is Valentine. Clay Corazón. Played with the Allman Brothers. Meet Valentine." One girl grabbed the Polaroid from my hand in a way that made me think she recognized him, but when she handed the Polaroid back she said, "Died of a broken heart!"

The party didn't peter out till well after midnight. By then I'd eaten my way through the dessert table—personal cheesecakes, individual brownies, mini-cupcakes, bite-sized cookies—and was halfway through another bottle of Moet. The hat was itching my head, and I wondered if my brother had intentionally made me wear a hat full of lice as a joke. I needed a bed, but didn't know where they wanted me to crash. Some other sad sack had already blacked out on the sofa, the fly of his seersucker pants wide open to his red underwear, his arm dangling from the side, knuckles dragging the hardwood. He looked as dead as Valentine. If I could find some pillows and blankets I could make myself comfortable on the floor somewhere. Pierce was on the front balcony engaged in a boisterous conversation about legal matters with two other guys and a girl I hadn't met. They'd all taken off their sport coats and shrouded themselves in cigarette smoke and ill-informed opinions. I didn't want to interrupt or get involved. I found Lily alone drinking a bottled water in the kitchen.

"I'm ready for bed," I said.

"There's an air mattress," she said. "I'll get it in a sec." She grabbed my hand and pulled me out of the kitchen and over to the laptop computer the deejay'd been using. He'd left long ago, but the music was still playing. She spun the laptop around to face us and clicked, stopping a wavy and cavernous song that sounded like it was being played inside a conch shell. She scrolled down a song list until she found what she was looking for and clicked again. This time a more traditional song, real instruments played by human beings. A woman sang slowly and sensually, sexy, maybe in French. I don't know French. Could've been Portuguese. Lily hugged me tight, leaning her head on my chest, and we danced.

I love a slow dance. It's intimacy without trouble. You don't have to be in love; you don't have to want sex; you don't particularly need to like the person, but what you do want, for the length of a song, is to be close to another body, to hold them tight and press them against you and sway so slowly it's like the spin of the earth is what's tilting you to and fro, and you know it's all finite, you know the song's coming to an end, and you don't want it to, and you count the verse and the chorus and the verse and the chorus and the bridge and you know when you get to the bridge the time is coming for you to let go, and so you squeeze a little tighter or you whisper something stupid in their ear, like, *I wish we could stay like this forever*, but you can't, and you know you can't, but for three and a half minutes the slow dance makes the world a wonderful place.

We swayed in a miniscule circle, our feet barely rotating. Lily'd taken off her shoes at some point, revealing long slender toes, clear nails, no polish. Her cold ear pressed on my skin, on my chest, like she was listening for my heartbeat as proof of life. She fingered the embroidery on my shirt, tracing the thread. Pierce yelled so loud out on the balcony I could hear him inside.

"This is a weird shirt," Lily said.

I told her thank you.

"Are you a good brother?" she asked.

I wouldn't know what it meant to be one even if I had been one, so I said no.

"Pierce says you are. He doesn't really talk about the rest of your family, but he loves you. He can't say it himself, so I'm telling you."

This came as a big surprise to me, Pierce loving me in any way that would show to another person. I assumed that anyone in his life had no idea that he had a family. This confession of love was all simply because I'd been the only one to go see him in prison. I was certain of it. Once a month. That's all it took to be a good brother? Go visit your older bro in prison once a month? Impossibly simple, yet every time the day rolled around to see him I had to convince myself to go. It never came easy. I'd picture him waiting in his cell, knowing a visitor was coming, and think about how that visit marked time for him, and how if I didn't show up then time would dissolve under his feet. The outside world and his connection to it eroded to nothing, and picturing him like this always got me headed out the door. And standing there in the middle of this old house, swimming in champagne, slow dancing with a beautiful woman, I cried. This fool was the one who would miss me. My brother would miss me. I would be missed. If I died my brother would accept an onion pie and be grateful for it. I could say that I protected myself against the inevitability of dying alone by marrying and having a family, building a business where people depended on me, but that was all a house of cards. Lily telling me my brother loved me, now that seemed to matter, because there was nothing I could do to change it, no behavior I could engage in to make him love me less or more, and so I cried, a brother undeserving of brotherly love.

Lily might've been able to tell I was crying. Maybe my skin got warm or a tear dropped on the top of her hair, because she tilted her head to look up at me. My head was itching, so I scratched until my hat fell off. Fine. I was tired of looking like a fool. I kicked the hat across the floor. She put her head back on my chest, swaying again. "You know who you remind me of?"

"No telling," I said.

"That big cartoon bird with the sweet drawl. Foghorn Leghorn. You know who I'm talking about?"

"I'm familiar with him."

"What'd he do again? Like, what was his *raison d'etre*?"

"He was a rooster."

"No, I mean, every other cartoon character has a thing. Scooby solved mysteries. Yogi got into trouble at Yellowstone. The Coyote chased Road Runner. What did Foghorn Leghorn do?"

"Yogi was at Jellystone, not Yellowstone."

The song was over. We stopped dancing.

"I guess he was supposed to be your standard southern cock," she said.

"That was the joke."

Lily pushed away. She lifted her hand and ran two fingers lightly over my forehead. I felt a tug in my navel. "That welt's no joke," she said.

I touched where she had touched. The sore had changed, swollen into a much larger bump now, like somebody'd clonked me on the head with a hammer. It didn't hurt, but it was sensitive, at least when she touched it. Pierce's damn hat must've made it worse.

Lily pulled me by the arm into their bedroom where she shut the door and sat me down on their too-low bed. She dragged the air mattress out of the closet and plugged in its self-inflating engine. We both sat on the bed and stared at it as it inflated noisily, the pitch ascending until it sounded like it might pop. Lily pushed on the mattress to test its firmness, unplugged the engine, covered the mattress with a fitted sheet, and brought out a blanket and pillow from the closet.

"Goodnight," she said. "Let's go get some donuts in the morning." And she left me there in the room so she could rejoin what was left of the party.

Somehow I was able to fall asleep, total exhaustion finally setting in, until Pierce and Lily busted in the room laughing and taking each other's clothes off, stumbling into bed. The air mattress was only a few inches below their bed, and I was scared they might roll over on top of me or ask me to join in. *When I told you your brother loved you I meant he loved you.* I got off the mattress. They were still laughing, and in the half-dark and shadow they transmogrified into a monster made of wet sucking noises and hair emitting a musky funk of alcohol and cigarettes, a fiesta monster. They didn't notice I'd gotten up until I started dragging the air mattress toward the door.

"Doesn't he remind you of Foghorn Leghorn?" Lily asked.

"Who?"

"Your brother."

I wondered if she even knew my name.

Pierce didn't bother with her question, but instead tickled her mercilessly while she punched him in the chest between attempts to take his pants off.

I turned the air mattress on its side to push it through the door, slid it through, and shut the door behind me. I slid the air mattress down the hallway and into the wide front room where I flopped it on what had been the cleared dance space. The room smelled like moldy bread and ashtrays, and a streetlight outside sprinkled everything with orange sparks that twinkled off all the party detritus, the glasses and bottles and general fiesta mess. The boy in the seersucker was still passed out in the same spot on the couch and may have choked on his own vomit. If so, I would find his parents and give them the onion pie.

Peach Preserves

The whole apartment sparkled, like a cleaning crew had come in and scrubbed everything around me to a high gloss sheen. The floors smelled like pine. The countertops shined with the scent of mint. I was the only evidence that there'd been a party the night before, a man waking from his nest on an air mattress to find everyone gone. Even the boy in seersucker had left, his blanket folded neatly and placed over the arm of the sofa. How had I slept through all this?

I got up and went into their bedroom, making no attempts to be quiet, hoping to startle Lily enough that she'd leap out of bed and I'd catch a glimpse of her naked body before she covered up with a forearm or a sheet. Or maybe Lily was the type of woman who didn't cover up at all, nothing to be ashamed of. The curtains were wide open, letting in the brutal light of Sunday morning, and the bed was made, tucked as tight as it had been before they fumbled into it last night. Neither one of them was anywhere to be found. Had they gone to church? Not likely.

I splashed water on my face and found some ibuprofen in the bathroom. My head hurt. The bump hadn't grown or spread but it was soft now with crusty edges, like an open boll of cotton. I thought about bandaging it up again, but it felt good to let it breathe.

In the now-spotless kitchen I searched for coffee. Made one cup in one of those machines with the coffee pods. Dumbest machine ever. Was this invented for lonely people? What'd they do when they had company? Oh, hold on, let me stand here and make cup after cup after cup until I've got enough to fill a carafe. Still I was thankful for it, until I saw that what was coming out of the machine, pouring into my cup in a laser stream, was green, a sickly green, and when I smelled it I knew it was tea. Green tea. I blew on the top and took a sip. Tasted like fish guts and burnt nuts. I searched for some other flavored pods, but couldn't find any. I tossed the tea in the sink.

I looked for a phone in the kitchen, in their bedroom, in their bathroom like at fancy hotels, but this was a couple without a landline. In the fridge I found some bread, and in a cabinet where they kept what minimal food they had—some quinoa, a bag of tortilla chips, three cans of Spaghettio's, and a bunch of other crap in bags or cans—I found a small jar of peanut butter, natural peanut butter, the kind that tastes like paste, but the refrigerator did reveal a jar of peach preserves from Hubbs, and I was thankful he still had a bit of family pride.

I made myself a peanut butter and peach preserves sandwich, sat down on the couch, and turned on the TV. I noticed the channel I was on, thinking about Pierce's personality test, or whatever it was, the HQ he'd called it, about the number of people I might trade places with on the TV. The first person was a news anchor; I could only judge him on his bright white teeth, and that didn't make me want to be him. This was on Channel 13. Next there were two people in a studio kitchen making meatballs, a man and a woman, and the way they rolled the meat around in their hands was almost sexual, and I wondered if it wasn't a cooking show at all, but porn, and so maybe I did want to be this guy. Absolutely, let's trade places right now and I'll get my fingers full of ground beef before we throw away all safe food handling guidelines and screw on the countertop. But it was just about making meatballs. I flipped again. A commercial for a car where a dog stared at the Grand Canyon. I don't know. The Grand Canyon might be good, but who wants to be a dog? Next I saw sports anchors talking about sports in that annoying way they talk about sports, all pop culture references and catchphrases and adolescent silliness. No, thank you. A couple searching for a house. No. A lion eating a gazelle. The lion maybe. An open heart surgery. No. A preacher. No. Another preacher. No. Preacher, preacher, preacher. No, no, no. Cartoon princess. No. Another princess. And another, this one speaking Spanish. Nothing but preachers and princesses. A Sunday morning news show with a bunch of eggheads debating quail culture and assimilation. Lord help me, no. And this went on, the channels never seemed to stop, the numbers climbing higher and higher and never circling around again to the beginning. It was exhausting work determining who I might trade places with, and I was proud that I found no worthy candidates. I assumed, given my recent setbacks, that I'd wish to be anyone but me, but my self-confidence was intact. What worried me was the fact that the channels never stopped, and I imagined there might be somebody else out there, in some other universe, doing the same thing, flipping through their channels and ending up on me, a man on a couch eating a peanut butter and peach preserves sandwich while flipping the channels. There were homeowners ripping up floors. More animals, more anchors, more sports, more Spanish. Every channel filled with crawls and images and extra text, cramming whatever I was supposed to be watching into a smaller and smaller box. Who wants to read so much on their damn TV? I was well into the 400s with no end in sight. What the hell was Lily's cable bill? I landed on some group fitness, a triangle of women in tights. They were on the floor, stretching. I joined them in a few stretches, not wanting to be them but wanting to be with them, but that got old. Princess, screamer, pundit. Man building a house. Woman cooking. Woman crying. Women sitting around a table talking about cooking and crying. Man shooting someone. Man drawing a gun. Nazis. Golf. Each stop blurred with the next stop, none of them distinguishable despite the fact that each would tell you they were a living breathing individual full of themselves. I didn't want to be any of these sons of bitches. The channels never started over, and I was tired of searching for the beginning. I found a piece of paper and wrote Pierce a note. I put it on top of the onion pie and left the pie in the refrigerator. The note said:

My HQ is o.
Love,
your brother

Jokeville, GA

The bicycle in the back yard leaning against the rusted swing set wasn't locked down, and it didn't look like anybody'd been riding it recently, so I figured it wouldn't be missed. It was nothing like Valentine's, more of a trail bike with a thick frame and thick tires. Tires that were supposed to be thick if they hadn't been flat. I grabbed the handlebars, cutting through invisible spider webs, and pushed the bike around the side of the house and down the sidewalk. As the wheels turned they didn't look like Valentine's wheels, they didn't suddenly transform into that yellow-wall that was missing. They were the wheels to this bike, attached to this frame, flat and useless, and I started to wonder if things weren't looking up, if I wasn't starting to feel better given that popular remedy for common ills: time.

At an Exxon filling station I pumped the tires full of air, and with the backpack on I pedaled through the warm morning light like an eager student, careful to ride on any sidewalks that I could find as to stay out of the street and not meet the same fate as Valentine. It's 170 miles from Savannah to Charity, not a distance one might tackle easily on a bicycle. I rode for a solid two hours, more time than I'd ever been on a bike, my ass hurting and my thighs chafing and my whole body soaked to the bone with sweat. I got a reprieve in Eden. Some cloud cover rolled through, and a gentle mist of rain began, but I wouldn't make it all the way home without some help. Every scene I passed on my ride struck me as straight out of one of Kat's paintings, and it didn't make me miss her any more than I already did, but it did make me hate the paintings for being clichés. If I could encounter a man fishing off a bridge on any random Sunday morning in the South, then why did she feel the need to paint it? Images of her unoriginality populated my ride, cotton fields and silos and kudzu-covered barns, farm houses gone to seed, and filling stations so old they bore no relationship to major oil companies, still in possession of their proprietor's names: Harold's, Beckman's, June's, and that's where I stopped to cool down.

A hound dog lay in a patch of the building's shade. Two men sat in rocking chairs under a tin awning and drank Coca-Colas from glass bottles. Did they wipe their sweaty foreheads with bandanas and say *How can I help you?* through the tobacco stained teeth they had remaining? Yes, sir. I told them I was headed to Charity and needed a break. Take a load off for a bit. I'd been riding for two hours and didn't feel like I was getting very far.

"Depends on your target," one man said.

"Pete is a philosopher-king," the man who wasn't Pete said to me.

Of course. The two men would sit in rocking chairs outside the filling station and surprise everyone with their knowledge of renaissance art, their deep and abiding love of some arcane poet who died in obscurity. I wanted to ride my bicycle somewhere less predictable.

I knew where I was, not the exact spot of the filling station, but the town I was in, Smetna, where Jolly Hayes lived, the man I'd lied to A.J. about coming to see. If I found his farm

I could ask him if he wouldn't drive me up to Charity in exchange for me finally agreeing to purchase some of his melons, more melons than I could possibly need. "You know Jolly Hayes?" I asked Pete.

Pete scratched the gray hairs on his chin. "Not too long ago, fella like yourself come riding through here on his way to Charity."

"Maybe he's come again," the other man said, whose name I hadn't gotten yet. "You do know that time is circular, not linear?"

Pete whirled his finger in the air. "Round and round we go. Where we stop, nobody knows."

"And that's why most people never get where they're going!" the other man said, lifting his bottle to Pete's to clink.

I didn't want to ask them what this man looked like or if he'd been riding a yellow bicycle, because I didn't want the answer to be what I knew the answer was, and I didn't want to imagine that these men had seen Valentine alive and had even shared their philosophy with him over a cold Coca-Cola, and I didn't want to think that Valentine was the type of man who could do what I could not, which was pedal his way halfway across the state. I'd tried and I was tired. The onion pie was delivered, not to someone who needed it, but at least to someone who enjoyed a good onion pie. I'd given it a solid try.

"Mr. Hayes's probably at the church house," Pete said.

"Which church?"

"Not much for religion myself," Pete said. "If you need to be scared of a man in the clouds to do good by your neighbor, I don't want to be your neighbor."

The other man said to keep pedaling down the road, straight through town until I came to a small cemetery. The church was right there. Couldn't miss it.

Pete chuckled and dug his bandana into his ear. "Godspeed," he said.

I bought a water and sucked down a package of salted peanuts. As I pedaled away, they resumed their rocking under the tin awning. The hound dog sighed in the red dirt.

I passed through the few boarded up stores that signified town and found the small cemetery. Headstones were swallowed by kudzu, some knocked over or vandalized with spray paint. Those assholes must've been playing some sick trick on me because there was no church here. There'd likely been a church here once, a long time ago if the dates on the headstones were any indication, but there was no structure left, nothing but an old brick sign under an oak, presumably there to post warnings to sinners and announcements for prayer breakfasts and funerals. The glass was all broken out of it, a few letters left offering cryptic guidance.

LL O E R ST D U L URN

Nothing else suggested there'd been a church around here. No busted pews in rotting piles. No mildewed pages from bibles flittering across the dirt. No crosses rising resilient from an ash heap. No congregation.

I rode on until I found a man out cutting his grass on a riding lawnmower. I thought about knocking him right off, stealing it out from under his crotch, riding it all the way home, but I thought better of it. I waved my hands and made some extreme gesticulations to finally get him to notice me and cut the engine. I asked after Jolly Hayes.

He said he didn't know the man. I told him he was a watermelon farmer, and that he dabbled in figs. He said that he must be the man who lives on the watermelon farm then.

"Where's the watermelon farm?"

"Yonder." The man pointed ahead and fired up his engine, puttered off to cut smooth lines in his ugly grass.

But he was right. Not too far ahead was a watermelon farm and a beautiful farmhouse set way back off the road, and there was Jolly Hayes playing wiffle ball in his massive front yard with a trio of kids. He wore dress pants and a white T-shirt, and hurled wicked curveballs and sliders at kids who swung so hard they came out of their braids. He had a beautiful property: the farmland stretched forever behind him, and it wasn't all watermelons. Jolly was diversified. A man who could look out over his fortune in the morning and night, a man who never had to leave his livelihood, always present, his fertile fields. These kids were his grandkids, obviously, or so I hoped. Jolly'd been grey-headed and bearded the whole time he'd been bugging me to buy his damn melons.

The kids were the first to see me, pushing my bike up their long driveway like some kind of apparition manifested from the withering heat. One of the boys pointed, and Jolly turned around and shielded the sun from his eyes with a visored hand before he started to walk toward me, briskly, like I might present some kind of danger.

"Can I help you?" he asked, before we were close enough to see each other's faces.

"Hey, Jolly."

"Do I know you?"

Seeing me down in his parts must've been out of context. "Lee Hubbs."

We kept walking toward each other, me pushing the bike, him quickening his pace to keep me from getting too close to his grandkids, I guessed, until we were within arm's length of one another, and he tilted his head and eyed me like I was some kind of alien.

"Hubbs Produce," I said.

"I've heard of the place," he said.

"It's me. I'm Lee. Lee Hubbs. You've been trying to get me to buy your melons for five years."

Jolly turned to his grandkids, clearly concerned about protecting them from me. I could tell by the way he quickened his stride, the way he kept looking over his shoulder as if the mere sight of me might turn his precious progeny to dust.

"That is something I do," he said.

"I need your help, man. I'm stuck down here with nothing but a bicycle and a backpack, and I was hoping we might work out some sort of deal, so I wouldn't have to pedal my ass all the way to Charity."

"Charity? I know folks up that way."

"What the hell's wrong with you? You know me!"

Jolly held out his big hands and pumped them up and down slowly like he was gently fluffing a pillow, urging me to calm myself down. "Maybe I do. Maybe I don't."

"I'll buy a truckload of your watermelons if you run me up to Charity. If you'd find it in the kindness of your heart to take me home."

"I'd like you to wait right here a minute. Right here under the tree. Have a seat. I'll bring you a cold drink. Would you like some iced tea?"

"Is it sweet?"

"How'd you like it?"

"Ain't but one way to drink it as far as I'm concerned."

Jolly walked back to his group of grandkids and rounded them into a huddle like he was drawing up a play. They broke the huddle and kept on hurling the wiffle ball and taking aggressive hacks while Jolly took the stairs up to his house and went inside. I sat under the tree as ordered. Maybe Jolly was playing a joke on me too. I'd ridden my bike right into Jokeville, GA, all its residents committed to startling acts of satire. He behaved this way because of all my refusals, doling out his own revenge, payback for non-negotiation, which I was well within my right to do. I couldn't buy produce from every swinging dick that drove a truck. But Jolly must've seen me coming up his drive and couldn't get the grin off his face. *Well, well, well, here comes that old Lee Hubbs, the man who refuses to buy my melons! How might I repay his refusal with a refusal of my own?* He knew me, and I knew he knew me, so there was no reason for him to stand in his yard and deny that he knew me. And the more I thought about it the more pissed off I got, until I was standing up and walking to the grandkids and grabbing the wiffle ball bat from the surprisingly strong grip of a little boy with an afro, and I was walking right up the steps of his house with a yellow plastic bat in my hands, and he must've had eyes looking out because the screen door opened before I could get halfway up the steps, and out came Jolly pointing a pistol. "Get off my property," he said calmly, like he'd had to face this reality before.

"C'mon, man. I'll pay you double." I slammed the barrel of the bat on the front porch planks.

"You remove yourself from my property before I shoot you."

"You wouldn't do it."

"I'm standing my ground. You see me standing my ground."

"That only works for white folks."

"I don't know who you are, but I know you best drop the bat and pedal on home before you get hurt."

"How about that iced tea?" I asked.

Jolly shook his head.

I walked down the stairs, passed the gaping mouths and sneering eyes of his grandkids. The littlest one ran up to me and said, "Don't mess with Pappy!" So I smacked him on his ass with the wiffle ball bat and ran to the bike before Jolly could mete out any more justice.

Be Kind to Your Own Kind

I rode some and walked some under a sun so hot and relentless it rendered everything in wriggles, the whole world all shimmering vapor. I poked my thumb out every time a car or truck whizzed by in a wave of heat. Nobody stopped, and I couldn't blame them, imagining what they saw, a man slowly pedaling up the tight shoulder of a two-lane blacktop in the middle of God's scorched land.

Finally, after another hour or so, I came to a filling station, a BP, praise the Lord, a green-and-yellow oasis in the oily haze and heat. I went inside and stood in front of an open cooler door and drank a liter of water, letting the refrigerated air cool me down. I bought another liter of water and a banana popsicle and sat in a tiny booth reserved for people to eat their hot dogs or scratch off their lottery tickets.

An older woman passed by me headed for the freezer full of ice: a quail, her gray plume thick as a flashlight. She held a six-pack of canned Diet Dr. Pepper under her arm like a football.

"I need some ice," she said to no one.

"I need a ride."

She opened the freezer door and pulled out a bag of ice. "Are you asking or telling?"

"Whatever appeals to your sense of grace."

"Bless your heart," she said. "I'll talk to Chuck."

She paid for her six-pack and her ice and I watched her out the window as she made her way to a truck with a beat-up white liquid tanker sitting on a trailer hitched to the rear. A man hopped out of the driver side carrying a small cooler that he set on the pavement. Chuck, I presumed. She pointed at me while they talked. Chuck nodded, spit on a patch of dirt near an air hose, and took off his baseball cap to scratch his head. Also a quail. His plume a vibrant and majestic purple. I couldn't figure out where I'd seen these two birds, but they were familiar. Must be getting close to home. The woman put several Diet Dr. Pepper's in the cooler and poured ice over them before she held the ice bag up and spun it around to twist the neck shut. Chuck put his cap on and came inside, bought something at the counter and walked over to me. Some flavored cigarillos and a package of peanut M&Ms poked from his front shirt pocket.

"Where you going?" he asked.

"Charity," I said, "but if you get me close I can do the rest."

"What's with that crazy shirt? Some kinda uniform?"

"Tell you all about it if you give me a ride."

"Be kind to your own kind," he said.

I threw the bike in the truck bed and climbed into the cab. They let me ride in between them like I was their son. The woman's name was Barb, short for Barbara. Chuck was "short for Charles," he said "but everybody knows that." I told them my name and that I was riding my bike from the coast to raise money for Alzheimer's research with a group of other like-minded philanthropists—the shirt being part of our team's uniform—and I'd gotten separated from them because I was so much faster than they were, but my speed had somehow sent me off in the wrong direction, and I got lost.

Barb kept the cooler in the floorboard and they each drank from their own can of Diet Dr. Pepper. Barb took out a box cutter and split open one of the cigarillos, cognac-flavored, and proceeded to fill it with some stinky weed from a Ziploc bag before she rerolled it and handed it to Chuck. I'd never seen this done before, but it made a lot of sense, especially if you were going to drive around in public. Chuck lit up with a Zippo. The smoke stayed inside the cab, the stinky weed swirling with some other stink like onion rings, and I surveyed the interior for indicators of leftovers but didn't see any. The smell was a constant force, thick and present. It all made sense after Chuck told me what he was hauling in the tanker. "Grease," he said. "Old fry grease. Liquid gold. Got an outfit in Atlanta that renders it. When Barb and I empty out, we'll press on to Chattanooga, fill up, turn around and come right back and do it again. A cycle of riches."

"We're doing our part to eliminate waste," Barb said, and took a hit. She offered it to me, but I refused. I was getting enough secondhand. The smoke hung above the dash like a low fog. "It's called a blunt," she said, and passed it across my face to Chuck. "What line of work are you in, Lee?"

"I sell onions," I said. "And peaches."

Chuck exhaled. "Charity? You know that place...what's the name of that place we always stop?"

"Hubbs."

"Hubbs! You know that place? Best peach ice cream ever."

"That's my place."

"How much grease you got?" Barb asked.

"Some. We sell onion rings."

"And they are good," Chuck said. "How'd you get into that line of work?"

"Family," I said. "How about you?"

"We play to our strengths," Chuck said. "I can drive a truck. Barb here has tried to open four different restaurants that all failed." He passed the blunt to Barb.

"Five."

"Well, the last one is still open even though they kicked you out. I'd hardly call that a total failure."

"Don't draw a paycheck, do I?"

"All right. Five. We know food and we know trucking. Voila."

Barb took a long hit and blew it out the side of her mouth, trying politely not to get it in my face, like it mattered with the windows rolled up. "People only steal what's worth stealing," she said.

I coughed. "You steal grease from folks?"

"Nobody realizes the potential profits in grease."

"If you get me to Charity y'all can have all the grease you want." Technically, by way of a spoken agreement, my grease belonged to Mr. Ferris. But that old fart hadn't kept up his end of the deal. The look on his face would be priceless when he showed up at Hubbs and found out I'd given my grease to somebody else. You've been getting something for nothing for too long, hog farmer! Where's my damn bacon?

"God's plan is a funny one," Barb said. She passed the blunt to Chuck who finally cracked his window. The smoke got sucked out like somebody'd yanked it on a cord. Barb pulled out a magazine from a side pocket in the door. She licked her index finger and flipped through the magazine until she found what she was looking for and folded the front page so she could hold the magazine in one hand.

"Here's a quiz I like to give all our hitchers."

"Barb and I feel it's part of our responsibility as pilgrims to help our fellow quails, help them put their best foot forward."

"I appreciate that, but I'm not a quail."

"There is no shame in knowing who you are," Barb said. "Now. Would you rather eat a bowl full of hair once or be forced to eat nothing but your favorite food for the rest of your life?"

"I've played this game before," I said.

"Oh, it's not a game. This is science."

"And theology," Chuck said. "Dr. James Philbert came up with this. He's got a whole book about it. *Lifting Your Gift.* The testimonials will change your life."

"What's your favorite food?"

"Pizza, I guess."

"Pizza or hair?"

"How big's the bowl?"

"Standard. Your average cereal bowl full of hair."

"I don't think I'd like to eat pizza every meal forever."

"Hair then?"

"Whose hair?"

"Does it matter?"

"Some people's hair might taste better than others."

"I'm putting you down for hair."

Barb took out a small pew pencil from her plume and jotted down my answer next to the question. I could see hundreds of squiggle marks and tallies next to the worn-out quiz.

"Good answer," Chuck said. "The key to that question is they don't tell you how to prepare the hair. You can always cover it in olive oil, pepper, and parmesan, or top it with some chocolate syrup."

"Don't help him, Charles. Okay. Number two: Would you rather have one wild eyebrow over your left eye that you could never groom, or a belly button in the middle of your forehead?"

Is that what was growing on my head? I touched it to see. Still a bump, still soft, but now a patch of something bristly poked from the sore, and I could get a pinch and pull it like a patch of weeds, and when I did my whole head tingled and for a second, a real brief second, it was like I didn't know who I was or how I'd gotten here.

Then Barb snapped me out of it. "Which is it?" she asked.

"These are some weird questions," I said.

"But they get to the truth. Eyebrow or belly button?"

"Remember that eyebrows affect your balance," Chuck said.

"Would you hush?"

Eyebrows made me think of Jodi. It felt like it'd been weeks since I'd seen her. "Belly button," I said. "I could always wear a headband or a hat, I guess."

"I don't need your reasons," Barb said, and scribbled my answer to number two.

The questions proceeded to get weirder and weirder, and all of them had to do with bodily functions or deformities or public humiliation, which I could only assume was due to the fact this was a quiz for quails only. The questions were hard to answer because all the options were shitty. Thankfully, there weren't that many questions.

"Last but not least," Barb said. "Would you rather live for 235 years or die of emphysema at the age of 63?"

"What do the numbers mean?"

"They're just numbers."

"Why emphysema?"

"You ever seen anyone die of emphysema?"

"My dad was a smoker."

"That's not what I asked you."

"I don't think I've ever seen anyone die from emphysema."

"You'd know."

"Sixty-three," I said.

Chuck laughed. "No one ever says 'live.'" He finished smoking and tossed the blunt out the window.

Barb worked her pencil over the markings and came up with a composite score. She sucked in her breath and shook her head, going over the marks again. "It can't be," she said.

"What's his gift?" Chuck asked.

"Did I win something?"

"Your spiritual gift. All God's creatures have been endowed with special gifts from the Creator. I didn't come up with that myself."

"No one said you did, Charles," Barb said, still poring over my answers to the quiz, now for the third time.

"I just don't want Mr. Hubbs here thinking I plagiarized Dr. Philbert's theology and tried to pass it off as my own." Chuck put the end of the yellow M&M bag between his teeth and squeezed a peanut M&M into his mouth. "Barb's gift is teaching. Mine is exhortation."

"What's mine?" I asked Barb, now curious.

"Nothing," she said.

"Nothing?"

"Nothing. You have no score. You are spiritually bereft."

"Impossible," Chuck said. "Tally up the score again."

"I've done tallied it four times!"

"Maybe you missed a question."

"I can take it again," I said, strangely concerned that I'd registered as a zero on some meaningless quiz from some meaningless quail magazine claiming to be science.

"Did you lie?" Barb asked.

"I don't think so."

"Then do with this information what you will," she said, and stuffed the magazine in the side of the door.

Chuck offered me an M&M, but seeing how he'd stuck the bag in his mouth as a method of retrieval I refused.

I tried to sleep, but I could feel Barb checking me out, staring me up and down, wondering if they'd somehow picked up the devil himself.

About thirty miles outside of Charity, Chuck stopped at a place called The Katfish Keg. While I approved of lost punctuation in certain retail establishments, I could not abide a purposeful misspelling. He pulled behind the restaurant where he met a scraggly-haired boy in a red-and-white apron out by the dumpsters. Barb went inside to look for the restroom. I climbed out to stretch and watched as Chuck and the boy hooked a long hose from the tanker to a barrel-sized grease container. I never gave my own grease much of a thought. We didn't generate a lot, and what we did generate was just enough for Mr. Ferris to douse on his hog-slop like salad dressing. These two must have had some behind-the-scenes calculating, some side ventures they'd chosen not to disclose to me, some profits from elsewhere, because stealing grease for money was like squeezing people's dish sponges for bottled water.

I was hungry, so I went inside to see exactly how much a keg of catfish might run me. Was it real catfish? Or did the K indicate some kind of synthetic alchemy of guts and bones and byproducts assembled in cheap imitation?

A girl in a Katfish Keg visor askew atop her oily forehead stood behind the counter with an unparalleled look of meanness.

"How much for a keg?" I asked.

She refused to answer, and instead bent below the register and pulled out a folded paper menu that she then handed to me, even though I could plainly see the menu lit up behind her head. All the items continued their brave misspelling. I figured I might need to pay back some of Chuck and Barb's generosity by buying them a meal of overpriced fried food.

"Y'all got any vegetarian options?"

"Fries. Hush puppies. Slaw."

"That all comes with the Kaptain Jack platter?"

"If you want."

"How much fish?"

"Huh?"

"Is it two pieces, three pieces, four?"

She sighed. "I don't know. It's done by weight."

"A pound? Two pounds?"

"I don't know, okay! I just work the register. They won't let me weigh the fish."

This girl would last at my place for about two seconds with that attitude. A picture of the manager's smiling face and bald head was framed above the napkin and cutlery dispensers. Ed Babitch. Poor Ed had to deal with all these hormonal grease-faced monsters popping off at his customers who only wanted a decent amount of catfish in their baskets. Working produce is much better for a teenager's complexion and general well-being.

"Two Kaptain Jacks. One with fish. One vegetarian. Extra fries, hush puppies, and slaw," I said. "You take BP cards?"

She didn't laugh. "Cash only."

I wasn't sure I had enough cash on me, but I searched in my billfold, past some singles and a twenty hiding among their ranks, and found a fifty-dollar bill, the fifty I'd given

Valentine and had taken back from him when he didn't need it anymore. I'd forgotten my promise to put it in the offering plate and had been carrying it around ever since that night. Before he'd left the bar and fluttered down the highway he'd been carrying it around too, and holding it in my hand, it was like I'd found the key to life's great mystery, or at least the seed of my particular suffering. The bill was cursed. When Valentine had it, he'd gotten run over in the road. When I had it, my life had fallen apart. It made as much sense as any other explanation.

God wasn't fucking with me. It was Grant.

I didn't want to hand the bill to her and have its mojo target some other poor, unsuspecting soul. It had to be taken out of circulation. I pulled out the twenty, a bill I assumed hailed from less auspicious origins. But a twenty would not cover two Kaptain Jacks plus tax. I told her to cancel the vegetarian option. I could share some of my sides.

When I came out carrying my Kaptain Jack, a patch of grease in the shape of a horse's head was spilled in the parking lot, and Chuck and Barb's truck was gone, along with my bicycle. The boy was still there, locking up the top of the grease container with a padlock and a chain.

"The block is hot," he said.

A state patrol car pulled through the drive-thru. The boy waved. I waved too, but the patrol man didn't see us.

They'd left me without so much as a goodbye or a good luck, and here I was planning to share my slaw. I was positive it was because I failed Barb's spirituality test. I wanted to track them down, retake the test, prove to her and whatever publication put out that crap, that I was full up on spiritual gifts, probably in possession of several. Look, I saved the world from the menace of a voodoo fifty-dollar bill!

I was close enough to home that maybe Marty would be willing to come pick me up. As long as a man has one friend who will fetch him from a Katfish Keg in south Georgia, he's not totally alone. But I needed a phone. The surly girl at the register refused to change the dollar she'd given me as part of my change because she couldn't open the register without a purchase.

"I just bought a Kaptain Jack." I showed her my sack of fish.

The girl picked up a clear plastic collection box full of change next to the register. A picture of some starving kid on a piece of cardboard urged donors to cough up their loose coins. He was sure to feel America's largesse from the pennies leftover after their kegs of fried food. She took the top off the box and handed me four quarters.

"How about we make this honest?" I said.

I put the dollar in the box.

"It takes a village," she said, and smirked at me before slapping the top on the collection box.

I went outside assuming I'd find a payphone nearby, but no such luck this time. I stood by the door and gave every customer who came in a sob story about how I'd lost my phone and how I'd been hitchhiking and was almost home, but I was tired, and I needed to catch a break, so could I borrow their phone to call my friend to give me a ride? I would be glad to pay them. Every single person said no, if they even stuck around long enough to hear me out. The only variation in their denial was the degree of their visible disgust at my appearance.

I went inside and watched how everybody stayed tethered to their phones, keeping them on the table constantly within arm's reach, or buried deep in their ass pocket so they had to sit lopsided, or held in front of their face, reflecting cold and blue in their glazed pupils as they stuffed their mouths full of krinkle-cut fries.

The boy who'd been in on the grease deal came out of the kitchen, filled up a large cup with ice and Coca-Cola from the fountain machine, and sat down at a booth to scroll through his phone. I joined him.

"Your boss, Ed, know what you're up to?" I asked.

He sipped his drink through a straw. Wouldn't look at me. "I'm on break."

"About the grease."

"I don't know what you're talking about."

"I'm a friend of Ed's, and he'd probably really like to know his employees are stealing grease right from under his nose and selling it to some geriatric pirates."

"It's just grease."

"It's not yours to sell."

"Nobody has a right to own anything."

"Then I'm sure you wouldn't mind if I borrowed your phone for a second."

He stopped and looked up, clearly not expecting the cool logic of my rejoinder.

"If you'd be so kind," I said. "I pledge not to tell Ed about your side hustle."

"What's wrong with your face?"

"What's wrong with yours?"

I gave him Marty's number and he dialed. He put it on speaker in the middle of the table, but wouldn't take his hand off the phone, probably figuring if he slid it over to me I'd bolt out the door and go pawn it for opioids.

Marty answered.

"I need some help, buddy," I said. "I need you to come get me."

"Who is this?"

"What the hell? It's Lee."

"And Tim," the boy said.

"Who's Tim?"

"Some young anarchist kind enough to let me borrow his phone."

"You sound different," Marty said. "You in trouble?"

"I'm on speaker. I don't know where the hell I am. I need a ride."

"Well, where are you?"

"I told you I don't know."

"How do you expect me to come get you if I don't know where you are?"

I asked Tim. "Where are we?"

"The Katfish Keg," he said, and slurped his Coca-Cola.

I asked the rest of the restaurant. "Where are we?"

The girl at the register said Hell. Some joker coming out of the bathroom said The Twilight Zone. And a woman wiping cocktail sauce off her shirt said Hope.

Time's Up

I waited a long time for Marty, who probably had to take a shower and run some errands. Never did have a real sense of urgency. I bided my time with my catfish basket and the first few chapters of *Love Story*. It was terrible, yet the depth of that terrible made it hard to put down. *I ambled over to the reserve desk to get one of the tomes that would bail me out on the morrow. There were two girls working there. One a tall tennis-anyone type, the other a bespectacled mouse type. I opted for Minnie Four-Eyes.* Who the hell talks like that? Nobody in my real life. I wondered if Valentine carried it around as a joke.

The book was so bad it was good, so I read more than I'd planned on, couldn't put it down, started actually to get into the trash, which made me question my taste and the kind of person I was becoming. When Marty finally walked in, I was so happy to see him I gave him a hug. He bit into a piece of what was left of my Kaptain Jack platter and immediately spit it out. "Something's off," he said.

I took a bite from the same piece of catfish Marty'd bitten. No problems at all. Tasted like fried catfish. "Tastes fine to me."

"What's wrong with your head?" he asked.

I felt my forehead. What was sprouting from it had grown. I hadn't actually seen it in the mirror and I didn't want to, afraid of what I might find. "What's it look like?" I asked.

"A mess," he said. "Do I even want to know what you've gotten into?"

I said I'd tell him on the way home, so I did. Told him how A.J. had left me stranded after almost getting arrested for stealing a hat, or not stealing a hat, as it were. Told him Pierce had picked me up and let me witness his carefree lifestyle, which I did not care for, so I took his bike. Told him Jolly Hayes almost killed me by invoking his right to stand his ground. That two grease tycoons were kind and gracious enough to give me a ride, and that the woman, Barb, administered a quail quiz that tested my spiritual gifts, of which, apparently, I had none. I told him that the book *Love Story* was trash, but I was strangely attracted to it. And lastly I told him that Valentine had been in The Allman Brothers Band.

"Who?"

"Valentine. Clay Corazón. Clarence Hart. Remember?" I tugged on my shirt to remind him.

Marty nodded. "You can't every truly know a person."

The sun was setting when we got home. Storm clouds heavy with rain beat up the sky in purple and blue bruises. I hoped that somehow the little time I'd been away might've changed everything or restored the natural balance of my universe, that I'd see Kat's car and my truck in the garage and my wife inside cooking supper and my kids playing or watching TV, and I'd walk in and they'd welcome me with hugs and cries of "Daddy!" and the ladybugs would be nothing but an idea, a memory, an image forgotten in a dream. I would say I was sorry, and sit down and listen to their grievances, let them tell me about all my problems, and I could promise to really be a better man, promise to do right by all of them. Follow through. I would do right.

I got out of the car and thanked Marty for the ride.

He hung an arm over his open window and stared at me. "You look like him now, you know?"

I could see how standing in my driveway in the twilight, wearing Valentine's signature shirt, with one strap of his Care Bear backpack flung over my shoulder, I might be mistaken for him. But that was all we had in common.

"You ever get rid of his bike?" he asked.

"It's all locked up," I said.

"You might want to do more than that," he said. "You know that quail works with Dawn? Pink plume?"

"I've met her," I said.

"She comes walking in the station with a bicycle wheel the other morning. Says it ended up outside the pawn shop like it'd rolled there on its own. Knew right away who it belonged to, and she thought we might need it, if there was an ongoing investigation. She thought it sure was weird how that wheel ended up there. Started reading it as a sign from God. What do you think, Lee? Was it a sign from God?"

If God created this mess, then *everything* was a sign from God. Or a sign He'd turned His back on us, so disappointed in what we'd become. I couldn't blame Him. "I guess that means you'll be needing a lot more peaches," I said.

"Todd's got the wheel," he said. "I don't know how much more I can help you. I'm sorry."

"You've done enough."

"I feel like something's ending, Lee. Been feeling that way for a while. Like time's up for men like you and me. Nothing left but queers and quails."

"So what should I do about the bike?"

Marty smiled. "What bike?" he said, and drove away.

My front porch swing hung by one chain as if a fat man had been trying to swing in it while pounding a couple of Kaptain Jack platters. I hoped I hadn't been robbed or vandalized. A ladybug landed on my forearm, and another on my finger. I stood still on the porch. Katydids and crickets sawed in the trees, their song rising to a crescendo that burned my ears. I rang the doorbell to my own house like a stranger. If they'd come home they would have dealt with the ladybugs. No answer. I could've put my key in the lock and turned it and gone upstairs and gotten in my bed, but my house wasn't the same house anymore. I'd lived there all my life, but the place was strange to me now.

I walked around the side of the house to my open garage, but none of my vehicles were inside. Down by the pool the water was dark as mud, and leaves and yard trash floated in rotten islands. Not an inviting place to take off my clothes and let the chlorine bleach my skin and the water clean me up and wash off the layer of sweat and grime. Beyond the pool I could see the woods, thick and overgrown, and I knew what needed to be done.

In the toolshed I grabbed a flashlight and a shovel, picked up Valentine's bike, and looped my right arm through an opening in the mangled frame, hauling it on my shoulder out of the shed and through the backyard into the woods.

The woods behind my house used to be a playground for me and Pierce. Our father had built a fort out there for us a long time ago—still standing, albeit barely. We called it Fort Humpter. My kids weren't allowed to use it, as the fort was in a serious state of disrepair and neglect. I promised Leo I'd build him a new one but hadn't gotten around to it yet. Part of the tin roof had blown off, and when I shined my flashlight at the opening where the front door used to hang, a raccoon scurried out. At one time my brother and I could sleep out here, protected from any varmints, wrapped up in our sleeping bags telling dumbass stories to flashlights and looking at pages of dirty magazines my brother had bought with his fake IDs. The whole fort leaned to the right, the walls like two slashes. Rain pinged what was left of the tin roof.

I ducked under the low frame of the door and splashed the light around inside. The old furniture was still there: a warped, round table; a recliner with most of the stuffing picked clean; and amazingly, a tacked up spread of a naked Miss May from a long time ago, caught in a state of eternal seduction. The paper was all faded and spotted and curled up, but I could still read it. She'd listed her favorite century as the nineteenth, *when women wore hoop skirts and...* The rest was torn off. Of the turnoffs that I could still read, *obsessive bodybuilders* and *disloyal friends* made the list. The fort smelled like an asshole. I thought I might be sick.

I carried the bike through the opening in the back of the fort where another door had once been. Behind the fort was our family's pet cemetery. Different sized rocks and other makeshift monuments marked thirty-plus years of me and my brother's pets. Mr. Limpet the goldfish. Max the guinea pig. Hogan the black lab. Odum the next black lab. Sweet-sweet, the meanest goddamn cat who ever lived. And Axel the third black lab, the best and brightest, the dog that swore me off all other dogs. There would never be another Axel. Mama told us that after we buried a pet we had to be on the lookout for signs they were doing all right in the afterlife, like a cardinal alighting on a porch railing, or the shape of a dog in the clouds. She said God would send us signs that our pets were resting in peace. We watched for signs everywhere. But I never saw any signs of

Axel: not a cloud, not a bird, not a stick, nothing. It was no coincidence he was the last dog we ever had.

I dropped the bike and set the flashlight on a stump and found a spot not too far away from what I thought was Mr. Limpet's arrangement of rocks. Who the hell could tell anymore? The shovel sunk into the moistening earth and I dug. The ground was soft and the digging easy, and even though the rain had picked up, the trees provided some shelter. Scattered drops filtered through to cool me off and help stem my climbing fever. The rain and woods sunk into a percussive rhythm, a rhythm that kept me going, deeper and deeper, probably deeper than I needed to go, the noises swirling into a melody that sounded designed, a soundtrack to a man digging a hole, at night, in the woods behind his house. I didn't stop digging until I was soaked with rain and so dizzy I buckled to my knees next to the hole to rest.

I stared into the pit, its blackness like the surface of a wide, deep pond with no reflection. Usually we stood out there next to a hole like this and placed our faithful, beloved family pets in, and my father would say a few words, wishing the pet eternal peace in pet heaven. I dragged the bike over and pushed it into the hole. The catfish roiled in my gut. I pulled out the fifty-dollar bill and dropped it in too. Thunder rumbled. Worms slid from the earth. I tossed in the Tenderheart backpack, along with all its contents. I wished I had some Allman Brothers to play. Thunder rumbled again, the stomach of a hungry God, and the rain thrummed through the trees, and I knew that this was not enough, that the heavens growled for more.

I threw up in the pit, and with the return of my Kaptain Jack platter came clarity, the kind of clarity that typically accompanies a weekend bender, when the hangover settles in as dreamy as dew but carries an insight gained from breaking free, if only for two days of blotto bliss, from the fetters of both body and mind.

The floor of my kitchen was still littered with ladybugs. Their red and black candy shells crunched under my feet, but none of them were airborne, none of them took wing, none of them moved. The place was carpeted in them, a layer so thick I almost couldn't see the hardwood I'd paid ten dollars a square foot for during our remodel. The bag of rice with my cellphone was on the counter. I opened it up and took out my phone, turned it on. The screen flashed bright with hope for a second and died. I grabbed a broom and swept all the dead ladybugs into a pile in the middle of my kitchen, a pyramid of dead shells, like art almost, like I'd gotten thousands of ladybugs to stay still for a picture, smile and say cheese, a much better subject for one of Kat's paintings. Then I went on to the rest of the rooms, sweeping the infestation into neat piles. It took me an hour to rid the house of the ladybugs, all of them collected into pyramids and then swept into a black lawn and leaf garbage bag that bulged with their mass yet still felt weightless. I carried the bag outside and tossed it in the hole. *Ladybug, ladybug fly away home.* I threw up again, but this time I couldn't stop, a constant stream of sick. Things I had swallowed and never swallowed, or swallowed without knowing, flew from my mouth and into the pit. The bag of rice with my phone. The blue lounge floaty from my pool. Ice cubes from my ice maker, then the ice maker itself. A Mexican lollipop. A golf tee game from Cracker Barrel. All of Kat's paintings hanging on the walls. A pint of figs. Yellow watermelons. The flow only stopped long enough to allow me to catch my breath. I lay on my stomach at the edge of the hole, my arms dangling into the deep. It started up again from my groin and spewed from my face like a firehose. The front porch swing. My muffler. A playpen. A turtle nightlight that projected the stars. The kitchen drawer full of junk. The yellow house phone. My father's boat. Rotten onions. A rabbit-fur coat that belonged to my mother. The artificial Christmas tree from the attic. Wet and moldy boxes of baby clothes and wooden toys. But it wasn't enough. My spine unzipped, flayed me open and peeled me like a cheap bottle coozy, and I gushed forth multitudes begging to be buried. A toolbox full of bones. A Georgia state flag. A card catalog of screws. An original Gettysburg Address. A stuffed coyote that wouldn't stop whistling Dixie. Balls of writhing cottonmouths. Silly Putty pressed with *Peanuts* comics. Fireplace implements bearing the faces of Tom and Jerry. A stack of Mad Libs filled out by Mel Blanc. A handle of Jim Beam. That ugly Rat Pack hat. My beard, held together with twist ties, bounced around the pit like a shih tzu. I vomited up halos and pitchforks, boiled peanuts, peach baskets, purple fishing lures, Yoo-hoos, a pair of mirrored sunglasses, a snow globe of the Atlanta skyline, Jodi's eyebrows, and that hipster's mustache. And then I took off Valentine's shirt and his moccasins and my Walmart jeans and my underwear and dumped them all in, and I stood before the hole naked as the day I was born, and I let the rain pelt my face and sluice down my arms, and I pinched the lump on my forehead, felt the prickle between my fingers, and so I pulled on what was growing there, and as it emerged it was like I was running a wire through my brain and down into my sinuses, like nasal floss, and I pulled until what was lodged inside of me popped free, and in my fingers I held a small red feather. I tossed it in. The rain cooled me and cleaned me and baptized me there in front of the hole, and when a yellow bolt of lightning struck and shattered the sky like a pie plate I knew it was a sign, no doubt about it this time, God was talking to me, and what he was saying was to fill in that hole and all would be okay and back to normal, live and learn, forgive and forget. His promise with fire. And so I took the shovel and buried it all away.

I lay naked on the recliner under the shelter of the fort and listened to the water pound the tin and gush off the corners into puddles. I was dizzy with exhaustion and catfish poisoning, but liberated. Another leftover pinup was stuck to the ceiling. I'd forgotten we'd put them there. Each one of us, Pierce and I, had a poster of a model above where we slept in our sleeping bags. I thought about Valentine's half-sister Anne lying in her bed, staring at that mythological fairyland poster above her face. Before she fell asleep, or whenever she woke up, she saw a pageant of fairies and beasts pouring from a rainbow and a waterfall. The poster had to remind her of someone or something, a person or idea she wanted to have in her mind before she slipped off to pleasant dreams. Like us as boys, she wanted to force the content of her dreams, to slip off into some enchanted forest of love and acceptance, just as we thought these posters would bring us dreams of these girls giving us hand jobs before their runway shows or them slipping out of those bikinis, the oil on their shoulders and thighs too slick to hold the straps. I remember the fine blond hairs on her arms, wet and glistening. These were the women of our dreams, and now only a set of blue eyes peered down on me from the torn poster. I loved her once, but now I couldn't remember her name. And I had to close my eyes to keep her from staring at me in judgment. Forgive me, Russian model, I know not what I've done.

Delight

I woke up in my bed. The sun hadn't come up yet, but the sky was glowing at its edges, hinting at a new day with promise. I took an uncharacteristically long shower and dressed in my normal work-a-day attire: khakis and a Hubbs Fresh Produce shirt, black. The inflammation on my head had scabbed over, but still felt prickly, like what I'd pulled out might be threatening a comeback. I made breakfast: a sliced apple, some microwave sausage that doesn't turn out too limp and soggy, an English muffin topped with Hubbs peach preserves, and some scrambled eggs. I ate alone at the table. The house was quiet, free of ladybugs, and my family.

The yellow house phone rang. It never rang. I hoped it was Kat, ready to come home.

"Mr. Hubbs?"

"Speaking."

"This is Lindsay over at the nursing home. Don't worry. Everything's fine. I'm not calling to tell you your mama's dead or nothing. They don't give me that job. But she missed you yesterday, and this morning she's...well, you probably ought to come see her today if you can."

Shit. I'd missed my weekly visit. She sometimes couldn't remember what she'd had for breakfast, but she'd sure as hell remember when her son hadn't come to see her. "On my way," I said.

Kat's vehicle was in the garage, which seemed like a miracle. Nevertheless, there it was with a note slid under the wiper written on a yellow piece of paper with Wayne Salley's name and tagline. "Ten Minutes from Anywhere!" The words were written in a nice loopy cursive in blue ink. *No charge*, it said. *Enjoy your Crossover!*

If I'd known all I had to do to get Kat's car fixed was dig a hole, bury a bike, toss in fifty bucks, a backpack, and some vomit, and cleanse myself with rain, I'd have done so sooner. I got down on a knee and peeked under the rear. A brand new muffler. Must've been some kind of mix-up on his end that turned out in my favor. When he couldn't find my vehicle the other day he felt bad and was now bestowing kindness upon me with this *gratis* muffler. Good old Wayne Salley. Ten minutes from anywhere! Wayne apparently hadn't seen fit to have them detail the inside or give it the free wash that was due me as a loyal customer. The car seats were in the back, and the whole interior smelled like spoiled milk. Food crumbs all over the seats, a squirt of dried up applesauce on the ceiling, oily finger prints and smudges down both windows. All a welcome sight, but the signs of my kids having been here did not make up for them not being here.

I hardly went to the nursing home in the mornings, so everything was different. I didn't recognize the nurse at the front desk. I told her I'd gotten a call from someone named Lindsay who said I needed to come see my mother.

"Who's your mother?" the nurse asked.

"Faith Hubbs."

"Such a sweet lady," the nurse said. She gave me a visitor tag, a protocol I hadn't been subjected to before, and walked me to the cafeteria. "You're just in time for breakfast," she said.

My mother sat at a table with Delight and some other woman I didn't recognize. All their bowls were identical. Oatmeal with slices of banana. None of them had eaten.

I hadn't known that she and Delight were friends, and to tell the truth, Delight had something wrong with her, one of those quails not quite right in the head, a case to prove the popular theories regarding their mental deficiency. I regretted I hadn't brought her a coloring book. I was sure she'd notice. I pulled up a chair.

"You should eat," Mama said.

"You should," I said, and nudged the bowl of oatmeal closer to her.

She looked great this morning. Wouldn't know there was anything wrong with her at all. That's the worst part about dementia. The shell of the person is the same, but the person inside is gone, and what you're staring at should be your mama or your daddy or your granddaddy, but instead it's some monster who's using their body as a host, eating their brains from the inside while leaving their bodies intact, forcing you to imagine, every time you see them, that there's hope, that they've returned to normal, only to be denied when they open their mouth.

"Sorry I missed you on Sunday," I said. "I went down to see Pierce."

She studied my visitor tag with clear blue eyes. Those eyes that would get wide enough to stop us from trying to kill each other. She never had to say anything. She'd look at us with those saucer eyes and we knew to stop pulling all the cereal boxes from the grocery store aisles or slinging dog poop at each other. But that wasn't the look she gave me now. This morning it was confusion, a jitter of wonder behind the eyeball, the tic of something not being right in her world.

"He's dead," she said.

I was never sure the best way to handle her outright fabrications. I'd never read the books that Kat had bought me as a gesture of goodwill, trying to get me to think she was sympathetic to my mother while at the same time trying to educate me on what was going to happen to her. So what was the right thing to do? Play along? Deny the fact? Change the subject? If a person believes so firmly in what it is they say, they're hardly ever going to change their mind, even without dementia. So to a person whose entire world has been upended, denying them what they know to be true must be pure hell. They're trying to hold on to a crumbling reality. If Pierce was dead in the universe of her mind right now, then Pierce was dead. So I nodded and asked her if she'd like some honey for her oatmeal. Delight scowled and spooned up her oatmeal, pissed off at it.

The other woman said, "Now, now, Faith. Don't let yourself get worked up."

"You killed him," my mother said, jabbing the end of her spoon at me. "You killed your brother."

I was fine to pretend that my brother was dead, but to be accused of causing it was a different story. Probably the best thing to do was not to react, to take it as she saw it, to get the hell out of there and come again next Sunday, the normal time, the expected time, the routine time, when I wasn't interrupting her breakfast with her friends. The unpredictability of my visit had thrown her for a loop. So I stood up and told her I'd come see her again at a better time.

"That would be a good idea," the other woman said, the peacekeeper whose name I didn't know.

"Save yourself the trip, devil!" Mama said, then she started crying. "Why'd you do it? Why? Your own brother!"

By this point two of the staff had been alerted to a potential problem here at the table and had come over to help out. My mother sunk her head into her chest, and I had to tell myself that next time she'd be herself again, she'd be my mother. I hoped.

A nurse stood behind her petting her head. She helped her out of her seat. Mama was smaller than when I last saw her. She'd always been a tall woman, carried herself with erect posture and tried to instill the same in us, a beautiful woman with a long neck and high chin, proud as a peacock, and here she was getting helped away from her oatmeal, her spine hunched, her feet shuffling, weeping for a dead son who was very much alive and still very much doing whatever he damn well pleased.

"Pierce's fine," I said. "I just saw him."

I didn't get a response from her or from the nurses, but Delight fixed me with a cold stare. "You can go to grass," she said. "You can go straight to grass!"

We Reached Our Goal!

Hubbs Fresh Produce had opened by the time I got there, the front already filled with piles of fresh fruit and vegetables, a colorful summer bonanza of peaches and blueberries and tomatoes and corn and watermelon, watermelon, watermelon. Onions too, of course. We were never at a loss for onions; although the season of the Charity Sweet was rather short, we harvested so many of them that we'd have a supply at least through mid-August. My employees all said good morning to me and I went straight to my office.

The smell of incense was still in the air. A.J. and Ben had likely kept up their meditation practice in my absence despite my strict instructions otherwise. Sometimes it was like A.J. was trying to get fired, like when you make somebody else break up with you because you're too chickenshit to do it yourself. A.J. seemed to be pushing me to the edge, maybe so he could file a lawsuit claiming racist hiring practices. But I wasn't about to fire him. He was the best I had. Instead of firing him, I would tell him how much I needed him and valued his dedication and enthusiasm for new ideas. Next time I saw him, I'd do just that.

I sat down at my desk and checked email. One from Pierce: *You stole my bike! Hope it got you where you needed to go. Time for a new one anyway, shithead. Good to see you!*

My brother never emailed me, and certainly never ended any of our remote correspondence with any such pleasantries or extension of love or gratitude. After my visit with Mama, I was happy to hear he was alive.

Another email was from Kat.

It was a long one, and it took me some time to read and read again, but the gist of it was this: she'd taken the kids and gone on a Disney cruise with Memu and G-Pop. *I needed a break,* she wrote. *From everything.* At first she didn't think it was all that good of an idea, leaving with the kids, but her mother urged her to teach me a lesson, and that lesson was to stop taking my family for granted. *I saw you that day before we left. That day you came by my parents' house looking for me. And I knew you were coming and I was so ready to open the door and let you in and hear you say you were sorry, but when I looked out you'd shaved your beard and I didn't recognize you at all. You looked lost. It was like you were somebody else.* She went on to say she wasn't sure how we were going to move on from this. She said the kids had a great time without me. *This week has made the possibility of you not being with us and us not being with you a reality. You need to change, and I need to change, and we can't keep on going through the motions like we've been doing. It's a bad example to set for Leo and Lisa. We get one life.* She had carefully edited the whole thing, and I could see her working it over, moving words around, toning down the anger, pumping it up when necessary, moving a word here and a word there, searching for a way to say exactly the right thing, like that was ever a possibility. The great caretaker. I was happy to hear from her, to know everyone was back home, in Charity, where they belonged.

Another email was from Jodi. *We reached our goal!* it said. And as I was reading it she knocked on my door and came in carrying my father's urn, and immediately, my wife's words were lost in the lush thicket of Jodi's eyebrows.

She set the urn on my desk and leaned in over my pens and paper and Post-it notes, the V-neck collar of her shirt drooping open, inviting me to peek, but I steadied my focus on her still messed-up hair. "Did you read your email?" she asked.

"I get a lot of email."

"I found this urn!" she said. "Urns are expensive. It was like it appeared just so I could use it, like it was sent from *God* or something."

It dawned on me, that not only had Jodi met her goal of funding Valentine's memorial, she'd gone ahead and spent that money, spent that money on returning him to dust.

"I took Anne with me," she said. "Some next of kin had to okay the whole thing."

"How's Anne?"

"Mean as hell." Jodi tapped the urn with a low metallic thud. "But I was thinking about this, and I started wondering how you ever really know they give you your person. I mean, these could be the ashes of some dead dog for all I know." Her eyebrows lifted. "But we take some solace in belief, right? Faith. We believe it's him, so it's him."

I stared at the urn on my desk, the urn that had once held my father, or so I'd always assumed. Whatever makes us who we are, surely it's all gone once we're incinerated and poured in a vase.

"That's him?"

"You can keep him here somewhere. Put him on one of the shelves. Or in your office."

"Why don't you take him to the rainforest with you? The tribe can worship him like a god."

"You're the worst," she said. "Do whatever you want. You always do." She turned to leave.

"Jodi," I called.

She stopped and side-eyed me like I was creeping up on her from behind.

"You're a good girl," I said.

"You're welcome," she said, and shut the door on her way out.

The thing to do was to spread him somewhere, to empty that urn of its contents over the ocean or in a field or under a favorite tree or behind my house, beyond Fort Humpter in the pit with his bike, his backpack, and his favorite shirt. Or walk around town with holes in my pockets sifting bits of him down my pants and out my ankles as I strolled, leaving a little sniff of him here and there and everywhere, all over Charity.

But what would Valentine have wanted? As my recent journey had proven, nobody knew, but worse, nobody cared.

I left him on my desk and went to work.

The day was as typical as it could be. A surprisingly steady stream of customers for what most of the time was the least busy day of the week. It was hot and the whole place sizzled. A.J. never came in. I expected him to be working the afternoon shift, but he didn't show. Ben was there and I asked him where A.J. was, and he told me that he was off today, despite what the schedule said, as if I couldn't read the schedule that I'd made myself.

"He's on the schedule," I said.

Ben shrugged and handed me a tiny quiche.

As usual, it was delicious. "Can you do me a favor? Call him and ask him to meet you here later."

"What for?"

"I don't know. Make something up. Tell him you need him to make a quiche or some other bullshit."

"What about you?"

"What about me?"

"You could call him."

"Let me explain something to you, Ben. A.J. isn't here today because he wants nothing to do with me. I'd like to talk to him. Talk to him and remedy that. So do you think if he wants nothing to do with me, he's going to answer the phone when he sees me calling?"

"I'll text him," Ben said. "But I don't know if he'll show up."

"That's all I'm asking you to do."

The day carried on, and I thought I might hear from Kat again or from her parents, but I didn't hear a thing, and for the first time in a long time I stayed at the store through closing, right through eight o'clock, and my employees didn't like it one bit. It was clear they had some kind of system worked out for knocking off early, locking a few doors, packing up produce for the cold room to scare off those late arriving customers. I got into a conversation with a woman on her way home to Kentucky, worried this might be the last stop for fresh Georgia peaches, and she was so relieved we were still open. It was well past eight when she left, not only with peaches, but with a cantaloupe and six ears of corn, and these young employees of mine would've shut the door to this potential income, eager to continue their sexting. When I finally did close, none of them told me goodbye.

Ben didn't leave. He was inside, hunched under that hoodie again, tearing the ribs out of a bunch of collard greens for some reason. I went over and pulled his hood down, let his plume pop out in all its weirdness, white and curled and delicate, more like a flower than a feather. I asked him if he'd talked to A.J. He pointed to my office.

And there was A.J., holding the top of the urn and peeking inside.

"Is that him?" he asked, when I walked in to join him.

"As far as I can tell."

He put the lid on top. "You wanted to see me."

I sat down behind my desk. "Why didn't you show up today?"

"Figured I was fired."

"Did anybody fire you?"

"No, sir."

"Good. Because you're the best employee I got. And I want you here. I need you here, and whatever happened on the road the other day, let's just call it my bad and move on. How 'bout that?"

"Who says I want to keep working here?"

"Everybody likes to do something they're good at."

"Nobody likes to be disrespected."

This was what I expected him to say, so I was prepared. "I got a way to change that," I said. "How about soul food?"

"Soul food?"

"Yeah, soul food. We have all the vegetables already. We'll have a daily special, and when it's gone it's gone, and we'll create some demand that way. People always want what they think other people are getting, right? So you get on your Twitter or your Instagram and you tell everybody, 'Hey, today at Hubbs we got fried chicken, collard greens, and mashed potatoes, for $9.99! Hashtag #getyousome!'"

A.J. tilted his head, jiggling his still-green dreads. "Fried chicken?"

"It doesn't have to be chicken."

"There's a KFC right down the street."

"It doesn't matter. The point is you get to cook what you want. That's what I'm telling you." I didn't really want to turn Hubbs into a meat-and-veggie place, all cafeteria trays and Rotary Club meetings, but I did want A.J. back, and I thought this might be a good opportunity to show him how much I needed him and respected him. "Just come back," I said.

A.J. kept his eye on the urn. "I want you to try harder," he said. "But not like this." He rubbed his hand over the round cheek of the urn and closed his eyes.

"What are you doing?" I asked.

"Making a wish," he said.

Ramblin' Man

Ben and A.J. were still cooking in the kitchen when I was ready to go, which I took as a good sign. I asked them if they needed me to stick around for any reason.

"We'll be alright without you," A.J. said.

I drove to the bar with the urn snug in Lisa's car seat, determined not to pursue some mad search for someone who'd want him. If nobody wanted a pie, nobody'd want his ashes.

I sat at the bar and put Valentine's urn on the stool beside me. Sister Rose wasn't working tonight, which was weird because she pretty much worked every weeknight. Instead it was the mustached hipster I'd punched in the face. Joshua Felton. He wore one of those balancing necklaces favored by professional athletes, and he had a tattoo of some Asian calligraphy on his right forearm. I ordered two shots of Old Crow, one for me, one for Valentine. He didn't act like he knew me, or wonder why I ordered a shot for an urn. He filled the shots methodically and carefully, not spilling a drop on the bar, unlike Sister Rose, who took pride in lining up shot glasses and spilling whiskey over rims in a sign of sloppy generosity. Maybe this was the reason he'd gotten the job.

There weren't many people in the bar, and none of them I knew. The whole atmosphere smelled cleaner, like fresh bread instead of stale beer. My feet didn't stick to the floor on my walk in.

"Where's Sister Rose?" I asked.

"She's dead."

He must've immediately registered my concern, or shock, or flash of disbelief because he started laughing and snapped a bar towel at me like he probably did to all his gym bros when they were playing naked grab-ass in the communal shower. "JK, man. She's on vacay. Bermuda!" and then he shimmied his hips in a hula, a dunce of geography. Then he stopped and took a good look at me. "Do I know you? I'm Josh."

"We've met," I said. "Lee Hubbs."

He squinted his eyes until it dawned on him. "That's right, that's right. Those nasty chicks the other night. What'd you hit me for?"

"I lost my temper. I apologize."

"Happens to the best of us," he said. "I was just trying to tell you to smear some butter or some half-and-half all over your face to help with the burn."

"I wish I'd listened."

"Live and learn," he said, and twirled his mustache.

I drank my shot and left Valentine's alone, like he might somehow walk through the door or spring forth in a twisting cloud of pixie dust like a genie, high on the afterlife but missing his booze and cracking some joke. *You know the only problem with heaven? No whiskey.*

"I'll have another," I said.

"Who's that one for? Elijah?" Josh cracked himself up and poured another shot up to the rim without spilling a drop. "Caw, caw," he said, flapping his right elbow like a bent wing.

The pinball machine sprung to life.

I hadn't heard it before that moment and hadn't even looked to see if its vinyl tarp had been removed and the machine plugged in. "Ramblin' Man" came on like Valentine was over there slapping flippers and racking up points. But nobody was playing. I took three one-dollar bills out of my billfold and shoved them across the bar. "Can I get some quarters for pinball?"

Josh made change from the register. Then he raised his arm like he was about to shoot an invisible basketball and balanced the stack of quarters on the back of his elbow, readying to perform a trick of great quickness and barroom skill by snatching them all into his palm with one swipe. "Can I do it?" he asked no one in particular, so no one answered. "If I do it, I keep your three dollars."

I didn't agree to this, but he spiked his elbow down before I could say anything. Most of my three dollars ended up in his palm. One or two strays spun and clattered around behind the bar. He dropped the quarters into my hand. "You're a winner," he said. "I'll bring you the rest."

"I'll take it now," I said.

He bent down on all fours in a search for the lost quarters. He sniffed the ground like a hound dog before he gave up and opened the register again and pulled out two quarters that he slapped on the bar.

Like any other game, a man could read too much into pinball, could see in its movements and rules a vision of the cosmos that provided symbolic resonance to one's own meandering through the void. Out there on the board a silver ball careens and dashes, and your job is to keep it moving, keep it hitting the bumpers, getting eaten between the legs of groupies, bouncing off drums and shooting through stacks of amps, and the more points you accumulate the longer you get to play, the more balls you get, and you flip and you flip and you flip, sending the ball out, and with deft movements of your quick fingers, you save it from diving down the out hole, from descending into dark nothing, disappearing forever. But if you get enough points you get to stay alive, you get to keep playing the game, get to keep striving for that high score.

I played the Allman Brothers pinball machine for a while, getting into it, getting better at it, timing my flippers just right, learning to aim for chutes and targets, sometimes hitting what I aimed at, most often not, getting by with some good luck and some bad luck, until I was all out of quarters and the board flashed up the high scores along with my score to illustrate how inadequate I was at this game. On top, in red letters indicating the high achiever were the letters *VAL*, evidence of the man's presence, like an engraving on a headstone, etched there forever, or at least until some other pinball badass came along.

This was where Valentine belonged.

Since Sister Rose was not there to ask, I'd have to mention it on my next visit, or never at all if she didn't notice, and who was going to look anyway? I took his shot off the bar and his ashes off the stool and carried them both back to the machine. I set the urn on the floor and slid it underneath, all the way to the wall near the plug. I took his shot and raised it to the heavens, thinking I'd drink it myself, before remembering it was his, so I set it in front of him. Each time I'd come back to the bar the whiskey level would be a little lower and a little lower, floating with fruit flies and maybe a hornet, until it evaporated into nothing but air.

Acknowledgments

Big thanks to Jerry Brennan for riding his bike to my house during a pandemic and asking me what I was working on, then waiting two years for the answer. You are a gift to indie lit and to the Chicago literary community. Speaking of the Chicago literary community, thanks for being so welcoming and supportive and for treating me like I grew up in one of your seventy-seven (according to the City of Chicago website) neighborhoods. Speaking of where I grew up, I'd like to thank everybody who has ever picked a peach and had it get under their skin, all those who can thump a melon and tell if it's ripe, and anyone whose soul is nourished by the warmth of boiled peanuts in paper bags.

Thanks to all the friends who have spent precious time enduring multiple drafts of this book. Ankur, Emily, Jason, Jed, Langley, Schuyler: this wouldn't exist without y'all. To Dan, Juan, Lindsay, Man, Rachel, thank you for taking the time to offer such kind words. And to Super B, thanks again for giving my book an identity. I love that we get to do this together.

Thank you, Sheryl, for your tireless support of all your authors. What a joy it is to work with you.

More thanks and expressions of deep respect for all my creative writing colleagues and students at The Chicago High School for the Arts who endure epic commutes and ungodly long school days in order to express themselves freely and courageously on the page. Every day you remind me why writing matters. Don't forget it can also be fun!

A few other unsung heroes deserving of praise: freshly roasted coffee, early mornings, high intensity cardio, high proof bourbon, Blackwing Palomino pencils, bass players, Thinking Putty, the Notes app, silver maples, Rectify, sunflower seeds, anchovies, Wile E. Coyote, public school teachers, poets, Perrydise, record shopping, Lee St. beach, programs, situations, deep snow, coozies, and pelicans.

Life-affirming love and bended-knee gratitude to all my family in Georgia, but most of all to Shira and Sam: my blue sky, my sunny day.

About the Author

Jeremy T. Wilson grew up in the South but now lives near a great lake. He is a former winner of the *Chicago Tribune's* Nelson Algren Award for short fiction and the Hessman Trophy, presented by legendary principal Durward U. Hessman to the fifth grade student who could eat the most corn. He is the author of the short story collection *Adult Teeth*; his work has appeared in *The Carolina Quarterly*, *The Florida Review*, *Jet Fuel Review*, *The Masters Review*, *Sonora Review*, *Third Coast*, *The Best Small Fictions 2020*, and other publications. He prefers pie over cake, bourbon over scotch, and R.E.M. over U2.

About Tortoise Books

Slow and steady wins in the end, even in publishing. Tortoise Books is dedicated to finding and promoting quality authors who haven't yet found a niche in the marketplace—writers producing memorable and engaging works that will stand the test of time.

Learn more at www.tortoisebooks.com or follow us on the website formerly known as Twitter: @TortoiseBooks.

Printed in the USA
CPSIA information can be obtained
at www.ICGtesting.com
JSHW021223300923
49423JS00002B/5